THE
BEE BALM
MURDERS

A MARTHA'S VINEYARD MYSTERY

CYNTHIA RIGGS

MINOTAUR BOOKS

A THOMAS DUNNE BOOK

NEW YORK

A THOMAS DUNNE BOOK FOR MINOTAUR BOOKS.
An imprint of St. Martin's Publishing Group.

THE BEE BALM MURDERS. Copyright © 2011 by Cynthia Riggs. All rights reserved. Printed in the United States of America. For information, address St. Martin's Press, 175 Fifth Avenue, New York, N.Y. 10010.

www.thomasdunnebooks.com
www.minotaurbooks.com

Library of Congress Cataloging-in-Publication Data

Riggs, Cynthia.
    The bee balm murders : a Martha's Vineyard mystery / Cynthia Riggs.—1st ed.
        p. cm.
    "A Thomas Dunne book."
    ISBN 978-0-312-58179-4
    1. Trumbull, Victoria (Fictitious character)—Fiction.   2. Women detectives—Fiction.   3. Martha's Vineyard (Mass.)—Fiction.   I. Title.
    PS3618.I394B44   2011
    813'.6—dc22

                                                                      2011001269

First Edition: May 2011

10   9   8   7   6   5   4   3   2   1

FOR
DIONIS COFFIN RIGGS
POET
1898–1997

ACKNOWLEDGMENTS

Many thanks to Andrew Nanaa, engineer, equestrian, dreamer, and friend, who introduced me to the Ditch Witch drill and who fed me outrageous ideas for every chapter. Thanks to Neil Flynn, beekeeper and owner of Katama Apiaries, for setting up seven hives in my west pasture and telling me bee stories. Special thanks to Angie McNeill, brand manager, and Randy Richardson, corporate risk manager of The Charles Machine Works, Inc. At my request for a technical review, Angie must have wondered why on earth a mystery writer would pick on Ditch Witch (a registered trademark of The Charles Machine Works, Inc. of Perry, Oklahoma, I hasten to add) for a character in a mystery, yet she obligingly turned my manuscript over to Randy, an engineer responsible for trademark usage who helped me with the technical workings of that magical machine and even gave me suggested wording in tricky places.

Thanks to all the members of my two writers groups, all published (or about to be published): Lisa Belcastro, Mike Ditchfield, Catherine Finch, Elissa Lash, Paul Magid, Shirley W. Mayhew, Carolyn O'Daly, Amy Reese, Sarah Smith, Valerie Sonnenthal, and Susanna Sturgis.

Thanks to Alvida and Ralph Jones, my patient sister and brother-in-law, who willingly read and reread my manuscripts and aren't afraid to be honest when the writing's not that great.

The wonderful troopers at the Massachusetts State Police Barracks in Oak Bluffs helped me with technical details and, in addition, told me a couple of comical Island facts I hadn't known. One being that the Steamship Authority, our ferry service, requires that a passenger ticket be purchased for a corpse going off Island for autopsy.

Ruth Cavin, my longtime editor at St. Martin's, died at ninety-two as this book was going to press. I grieve at her loss. Like Victoria, Ruth will remain ninety-two forever. . . . My condolences to Toni Plummer, who's taken over Ruth's heavy workload. This past year I also lost my friend Nancy Love, my agent from the beginning. Many, many thanks to Christine Witthohn, my new agent, who's filling Nancy's very large (even though they were only size three) shoes.

Most especially, thank you, my readers, who catch my mistakes, cheer me on, scold me when I use naughty words, and tell me you like my books. Keep reading!

CYNTHIA RIGGS

THE
BEE BALM
MURDERS

———

CHAPTER 1

The bee balm, in full ragged bloom in Victoria Trumbull's garden, was taller than she'd ever seen it, probably because of the heavy June rains. Victoria, at ninety-two, had known seasons when the minty-smelling plants never bloomed. This year they formed a dense fire-engine-red blanket that she could see from the west window. True to its name, the bee balm resonated with the buzz of honeybees, dozens and dozens in this patch of brilliance.

Sean McBride, the beekeeper, had set up seven hives in Victoria's west pasture. Each hive had twenty thousand bees. Each of the twenty thousand bees had a specific job to perform for the hive. During its short life, each of the nectar-gathering bees produced an eighth of a teaspoon of honey. And each lived only two weeks, its wings worn out from forays in search of nectar-bearing blossoms.

Sean visited the seven hives weekly to minister to the bees' needs. When Victoria saw his red truck pull off New Lane into the pasture this early July morning, she hurried out to watch him work, careful to stay a safe distance from the cloud of bees hovering around each of the hives.

"Morning, Mrs. Trumbull. Don't get too close. They're acting unusually ornery for some reason."

Victoria moved back to the bench near the fenced-in vegetable garden. The next half-hour of Sean's ministry to the bees would be theater, and Victoria loved theater.

Sean retrieved what looked like an old-fashioned oil can from the back of his truck, stuffed it with torn fabric, lit the fabric with his Cricket lighter, and pumped the handle. The oil can let out a puff of smoke. Next he unfolded a surgically white suit and pulled it over his normal working jeans and plaid shirt, topped it with a sort of Hazmat hood with a clear faceplate, and tugged on protective gauntlets with cuffs that reached to his elbows.

Sean usually went about his business silently. This morning, however, he was talkative.

"You rent rooms, Mrs. Trumbull." His voice was deadened by the hood. Victoria wasn't sure what he expected of her.

"Occasionally," she said.

"Guy stopped by the Farmer's Market on Saturday, looking for a place here in West Tisbury."

"Oh?" Victoria watched him squeeze the handle of the smoker, releasing a puff of smoke. The cloud of bees funneled back into the hive.

"Name's Orion Nanopoulos." Sean's voice was muffled. "Seems like a nice enough guy."

Victoria had the disembodied feeling of trying to communicate with a robot. She couldn't see Sean's face.

"What did you say?"

The faceless head turned. "Orion Nanopoulos."

Smoke drifted toward Victoria's nose and she sneezed. "How long does this man intend to stay on the Vineyard?"

"Couple of years, I expect."

Victoria welcomed occasional weekend guests, but was not enthusiastic about long-term tenants. "Has he checked some of the lovely places in town that take in guests?"

"Nope. I told him about this place, and he said he'd be over this morning to give you a check."

"Why is he staying for such a long time?"

Sean removed the top of the nearest hive and lifted out a frame that looked as though it was coated with black fur. Hundreds of bees. Or maybe thousands of bees.

"He's installing a fiber-optic system on the Island."

"I beg your pardon?" She wasn't sure she'd heard him correctly.

Tenderly, Sean set the frame upright in a box so the bees wouldn't be crushed. "Fiber optics. Glass. Wave of the future. Data travels at the speed of light instead of poking along on copper wires."

"Data." Victoria was not sure she liked the way this conversation was going.

"Emergency response. Cell phone reception. Your television programs . . ."

"I don't have television or a cell phone."

"If you have a heart attack . . ."

"Unlikely," said Victoria.

Sean lifted out another frame. "I told him to stop by. You don't have to put him up if you don't want." He turned his shiny non-face to her. She could see her reflection, and the reflection looked unconvinced. "He'll pay whatever you ask. Double your price. Triple it."

Victoria sighed.

Sean turned back to the bees and she had only the back of his white hood to look at. His voice was muffled. "Winter'll be here before you know it. Heating bills."

Victoria, having viewed Sean McBride's costuming and the opening of the hives, had seen what she'd come for. She levered herself off the hard wooden bench and headed to the house to confront Orion Nanopoulos when he called.

She would let Mr. Nanopoulos know that she had no desire to have a long-term tenant. Occasional guests were fine. She could put up with tiresome visitors for two or three days. But how did one get rid of a long-term guest who didn't fit in? She would discourage him. Her house was not a Captain So-and-So house with polished brass and mahogany. She'd tell him the floors creaked, the doors wouldn't close, that her granddaughter Elizabeth lived with her and could be difficult. Elizabeth, a serene presence, would forgive her. Victoria would let him know the bathrooms were shared and that the toilet in the upstairs bathroom often stopped up. He wouldn't be able to watch the Red Sox games, she'd say, because she had no television. Red Sox games, she understood, were a must for ninety percent of New England's population. That would discourage him, right there.

She was typing her weekly column for the *Island Enquirer* later that morning when a large station wagon pulled up in her drive, a twenty-year-old Chevrolet that looked almost new. Victoria liked cars and felt she understood them.

She watched as a white-haired, mustached, deeply tanned man climbed out. In his fifties, perhaps, but she wasn't good at ages. The man gave the side of his car a pat, as though it was a horse that had delivered him safely to her door. His trim body and mustache gave him the appearance of a cavalry officer, at least from the front. When he turned, his long white ponytail altered the effect. He was wearing jeans, an open-necked short-sleeved blue shirt, and worn, highly polished engineer's boots.

She pushed her typewriter to one side and waited for the man to approach. He climbed the steps, his boots making a sturdy sound, and knocked on the open kitchen door. "Anybody home?"

A pleasant voice, low and mellow. A fine large nose, not as large as hers, of course. Dark eyes.

"Come in," said Victoria, going to the door.

"Mrs. Trumbull? My name is Orion Nanopoulos." He waited in the doorway and offered her his hand. He was shorter than she. Victoria was almost six feet tall.

His hand was as callused as her own. "How do you do?" she said. "My beekeeper said you might be coming by."

"He told me about your house. I'd like to rent one of your rooms."

"I don't rent rooms long term," said Victoria.

"Perhaps we can discuss renting one of your rooms short term, then," said Orion Nanopoulos.

Victoria uncrossed her arms. "Come in."

He stepped into the kitchen. "Thank you."

Victoria moved a stack of newspapers from the captain's chair and dropped them on the table, then turned to look at this man.

Orion Nanopoulos had two deep creases running from his high cheekbones to his strong chin, giving him an extremely pleasant expression. "Sean McBride has a high opinion of you, Mrs. Trumbull. He suggested . . ."

"I know what he told you." Victoria sat on one of the gray-painted kitchen chairs and indicated that he might sit on the cleared-off captain's chair. Then she explained to Orion Nanopoulos that the floors creaked, the doors didn't shut . . . and so forth.

Orion listened attentively, his head cocked at an angle, the deep creases on either side of his mouth expressing both intense interest and delight at hearing whatever she had to say.

Victoria's voice strengthened on her last item. "With no television, you won't be able to watch the Red Sox . . ."

Orion held up his hand to stop her flow of words. "That won't bother me at all, Mrs. Trumbull." His pleasant expression deepened. "I'm a Yankees fan."

Despite her intention to send him packing, she found herself warming to this man with his soft voice and lack of Red Sox boosterism. Still, she tried to hold her ground.

"My granddaughter lives with me and she can be . . ." Somehow, Victoria couldn't slander her granddaughter, even in the interests of ridding herself of a would-be tenant, so she didn't finish her sentence. Studying Orion, with his warm, dark eyes, she was beginning to think it might be nice to have a man around the house, a man who drove a twenty-year-old car that he treated like a fine stallion, a man who could listen to her the way this man did . . .

She tried once more to convince herself and him that he should look elsewhere. "The only room available is a small attic room with no insulation. It's hot in summer, frigid in winter. It's right over the kitchen where you'll hear pots and pans rattling early in the morning, smell cooking during the day, and hear the dishwasher running late at night. You can't stand upright except in the center of the room because of the roof slope, and there's a hornet's nest above the window."

The creases on either side of Orion's face deepened with pleasure. "May I see the room?" he asked.

CHAPTER 2

Victoria charged Orion Nanopoulos double the rent she felt was reasonable. Orion paid two months in advance without protest and settled in.

She and Elizabeth saw little of him the first week. He was gone before they were up in the morning. On Monday, the only evidence of his having been there was an empty wasp-spray can next to the recycling bin, and a mug, rinsed and set upside down on a paper towel on the counter. At night he returned after Victoria and Elizabeth were in bed.

The Sunday morning of his second week in residence, Orion was in the kitchen brewing himself a cup of green tea when Victoria came downstairs.

A northeaster had set in during the night and rain slashed against the windows facing the fishpond.

"We'll have at least three days of wet weather," Victoria predicted, looking out the window at the downpour. "A good time for you to take a break."

"Not a very long break, I'm afraid." Orion spooned the tea bag out of his mug and dropped it into the compost bucket. "I have to work today."

She turned from the window. "Sunday? In this rain?"

"I have a schedule to meet."

McCavity, Victoria's marmalade cat, had entwined himself around Orion's legs and was purring like a locomotive working up a head of steam. Orion leaned down and stroked him.

"I hope you're not allergic to cats," said Victoria.

"Not cats," said Orion. "Just bees."

"Will Sean's bees be a problem for you?"

Orion gave her his pleasant look. "I try not to smell or appear like a flower, Mrs. Trumbull, and I wear shoes when I walk through clover."

"How serious a reaction do you have?"

"Serious. My throat and tongue swell and my heart rate goes way up. I carry an EpiPen with me in the field."

"An EpiPen?"

"A sophisticated hypodermic needle that contains epinephrine, an antidote to insect stings. I can inject myself if I get stung."

"Perhaps I should ask Sean to remove the hives."

"Don't do that, Mrs. Trumbull. The bees were here before I was. I'll avoid them and they'll avoid me."

Victoria opened a can of tuna. McCavity untangled himself from Orion's legs and stretched.

"Morning, Gram. Morning, Orion." Victoria's granddaughter entered the kitchen looking dewy and rested. Her sun-bleached hair curled around her ears. She was as tall as Victoria, and looked exactly like her grandfather, Victoria's dead husband.

"First things first." Elizabeth poured herself coffee. Her mug had once read POOLE'S FISH MARKET but washings had faded it to a simple FISH.

Victoria took eggs out of the refrigerator. "Would you like to join us for breakfast, Orion?"

"Love to. Thanks."

Elizabeth baked a batch of muffins, Victoria whipped up an omelet, Orion set the table, and the three sat down.

"Gram says you're involved with fiber optics," said Elizabeth as they were eating. "They carry phone calls really, really fast, right?"

"Much faster than copper wire," said Orion. "A single fiber, smaller in diameter than a human hair, can carry more data faster than a fat electrical cable." He paused briefly to dig into his omelet. After he'd devoured the first bite, he made a thumbs-up sign and then continued. "Since it's glass, it's immune to corrosion and electrical interference." He stopped again and turned to Victoria. "Enough about my business." He gestured at the omelet on his plate. "This is wonderful."

"Will you install the cable underground?" asked Elizabeth.

"Underground throughout the Island. We've already started in Tisbury."

"How many miles of trenches will you have to dig?" asked Elizabeth.

"Too many." Orion set down his fork. "We won't dig trenches, though. One of my investors is buying a machine that can drill horizontally and pull the cable back through the hole without disturbing the surface."

"Is your investor an Island man?" asked Victoria.

"Woman, actually," Orion replied. "Her name is Dorothy Roche and she lives in Edgartown. I've had several discussions with her and am quite impressed."

Victoria said, "Hummmph," and frowned.

Orion looked mystified.

Elizabeth laughed. "Gram doesn't much care for Dorothy Roche. She thinks she's an egotistical, self-satisfied, nouveau-riche-bitch social climber who'll stamp on the fingers of anyone on the ladder below her. Right, Gram?"

Victoria had just taken a sip of coffee. She coughed and dabbed her mouth with her napkin. "I wouldn't put it that strongly." She gave her granddaughter a look. "I really don't know her well."

"She moved to the Vineyard only a couple of months ago," put in Elizabeth. "Go on, Orion. You were telling us about the drilling machine."

"It's amazing. A radio beacon and receiver track the drill head. It can be steered around rocks, go around corners, go any direction." He stopped long enough to eat. He put his fork down and dabbed at his mustache with his napkin. "If a trench is excavated for some purpose, for a sewer or electric line for instance, we'll use that trench. Otherwise, we'll use the drill." He helped himself to another muffin, broke it open, and buttered it. "Tisbury's Department of Public Works is opening up a trench in the ball field for a drainage line. We'll be laying optical cable in the trench alongside it today."

"I'd love to see that," said Elizabeth.

"If you don't mind mud, come down and watch." He abruptly sat sideways in his chair, reached into his pocket, brought out a cell phone, opened it, and looked at the display. "Excuse me, Mrs. Trumbull. I've got to take this call." He left the cookroom and returned a few minutes later, frowning.

"Trouble?" Victoria asked.

"I'm afraid so." He tossed down the napkin he'd been holding and took the back stairs two at a time to his room. Seconds later, he returned, carrying yellow oilskins. His face was pale and a muscle twitched in his jaw. "A worker on the early shift climbed down into the trench for some reason and found a body."

Victoria laid down her fork. "How awful." She set her napkin on the table and got to her feet. "Who is it?"

"They didn't say."

Elizabeth, too, stood. "What do you have to do?"

Orion shook his head as though to clear it. "I've got to get to the site and see for myself what's going on."

"How deep is the trench?"

"Six feet. The ditching machine was filling in the trench right behind the worker who found the body. Ten minutes later, the trench would have been filled in. The body would never have been found."

Orion slipped his oilskin trousers over his jeans and shrugged into the hooded jacket. "Sorry to leave like this."

"Don't even think about it," said Elizabeth.

"If it turns out not to have been an accident and you need help, Orion," Victoria said, "let me know."

He glanced at her.

"I'm a deputy police officer," she added.

"Ah," said Orion, clearly not knowing exactly what to make of that. "I'll be sure to keep you informed."

He pulled the hood up on his jacket and headed out, his oilskin trouser legs swishing as he walked.

He clumped down the stone steps, patted the side of his wagon, got in, and sped out of Victoria's drive.

Orion drove into Vineyard Haven, quiet this rainy Sunday morning, turned right at Five Corners, right again down an obscure side road across from the Tisbury Printer, and parked. Rain fell steadily.

The muddy playing field was full of flashing red, white, and blue lights. It seemed as though every emergency vehicle on the Island had responded. State police. Tisbury police and ambulance. Marine conservation police. A Harley-Davidson with flashing blue lights. A hearse. A yellow pickup with a magnetic sign on the side that read TWO BRAVES CONSTRUCTION with the profile of an Indian chief in feather headdress.

Orion located Dan'l Pease, head of the town's Public Works Department, near the parking area. He was covered with mud and was leaning on a shovel. Rain washed down the mud on his oilskins in brown streams. Through the steady rain, Orion made out a blur of yellow-clad people milling around the far end of the trench. He turned back to Dan'l. "What's the story?"

"Hell. That damned son of mine," replied Dan'l, stabbing his shovel into the muck. "Danny, clumsy as usual, dropped a wrench into the excavation. Jumped down to get it, yelled, 'There's a body down here!' We fished him back out and called nine-one-one." He gestured at the swarm of vehicles.

"Who's in charge of the investigation?" asked Orion.

"State police. They're trying to get everyone out of the way so they can do their thing."

Orion tugged his hood farther down to shield his face. "How did Danny expect to get out of the trench?"

"You're asking me?" Dan'l shrugged. "My kid doesn't have the sense he was born with."

"Any idea who it is? Male or female?" asked Orion.

"It's a man, but we can't tell much about him. Facedown in about a foot of water. Clearly dead. We left him for the cops to worry about."

"Let's take a look," said Orion.

The trench had been excavated about a third of the way across the playing field. They slogged over to the far end where the body was.

Sergeant Smalley of the state police stood by the trench. "Morning, Dan'l."

"Morning, John. You know Orion Nanopoulos? He's laying the fiber-optics cable."

"How're you doing?" said Smalley. "I don't know what evidence we'll find in this mess, but keep clear anyway."

"Yeah, sure," said Dan'l. He and Orion peered down into the trench from where they stood. At the foot of a ladder that had been lowered into the trench, a bulky figure in motorcycle leathers knelt in foot-deep water. The figure concealed whatever it was leaning over.

"Who's that?" asked Orion.

"Doc Jeffers. Medical examiner," said Smalley.

"I don't envy Doc his job today," said Dan'l. Mud had oozed up over the toes of his boots. He lifted first one foot, then the other with a sucking sound.

"Groundwater's seeping into the trench fast," said Orion. "The doc had better get out of there soon."

At that, Doc Jeffers rose to his feet. When he stood, his goggled eyes were level with the ground. "I'm done. Lift him out." He passed up his black bag to Dan'l then climbed the ladder out of the trench. He was well over six feet tall. His leather outfit was wet and filthy. He bent down and scraped off as much mud as he could.

"Were you able to identify him?" asked Smalley.

"No idea. Never saw him before. He doesn't have a wallet on him. No ID that I could find." Doc Jeffers lifted his goggles to his forehead. His bright blue eyes and white eyebrows were a pale mask in his muddy face. He took out his handkerchief, wiped his face, then looked at the mud on his handkerchief. "What a mess."

"Cause of death?" asked Smalley.

"Gunshot to the back of the head." Doc Jeffers bared his teeth, white against his mud mask. "Any other questions will have to wait for the autopsy." At the sound of squelching footsteps, he looked up. Two oilskin-clad figures were carrying a stretcher toward them.

"Can't wheel it through this muck," said Doc Jeffers. "It's all yours, Smalley. I've got to get cleaned up."

"They do the autopsy here on the Island?" asked Orion.

"Hell, no. Toby takes the remains off Island to Boston in his hearse." He grinned again. "The Steamship Authority makes him buy a passenger ticket for the deceased. Go figure." He turned to the two stretcher bearers, one tall, one short, both Tisbury cops. "I'm done." Doc Jeffers trudged off to his Harley.

"Tisbury's sent a couple of men to give us a hand," Smalley said to Dan'l. He turned to the two bearers. "Thanks for helping out. Appreciate it."

"No problem, Sergeant," said the shorter one.

Between them, they hoisted the body out of the trench and laid it on the stretcher.

"Heavy son of a bitch," said the shorter cop.

"We need another couple of guys to help carry," said the taller. "Can't wheel it in this."

"I'll give you a hand," said Orion.

"Me, too," said Dan'l.

"We'll be right back," said the taller cop. "Getting a tarp to cover him."

The limp body lay on its back, faceup to the rain, which was washing away much of the mud. Orion took a quick look. A man in his sixties. Heavy jowls. Heavy bags under sightless gray eyes. Fleshy lips, parted to expose expensive dental work.

Angelo Vulpone. Orion stood and straightened his back. Head of Vulpone Construction, Brooklyn. One of his potential investors. A potentially *big* investor. What in hell had he been doing here?

Dan'l watched him. "You know the guy?" He wiped the back of his hand across his forehead.

Orion stared down at the corpse. Rain trickled down his back and his forehead. Rivulets streamed into the creases of his cheeks. He smoothed his dripping mustache and absently wiped his hand on his wet jacket.

Who'd killed Angelo? Why? And why here?

CHAPTER 3

The cops returned with a large blue tarp, and tucked it around the corpse.

Orion, Dan'l, and the two Tisbury cops labored across the muddy field with the considerable weight of Angelo Vulpone. Twice they'd had to set the stretcher down to ease their muscles and switch sides.

"You knew the guy, right?" said Dan'l on the first rest stop. Rain rattled on the blue tarp.

"Can't hear you," said Orion, pushing his hood away from his ears.

"You knew him," Dan'l said.

Orion shrugged.

"He came around last night looking for you."

"Is that right?" said Orion.

"Got out of a black Lincoln over there." Dan'l jerked his head in the direction of the parking area.

"Alone?" asked Orion.

"Let's go," called out the lead cop. "Only a short distance now."

Orion switched to the left rear, Dan'l to the right.

"Okay, lift!" called out the cop.

Orion bent his knees and straightened his back. He had to be careful. How much had Vulpone weighed, anyway, three hundred?

Dan'l echoed his thoughts. Grunting, he lifted. "Weighs a goddamned ton."

They struggled over the next hundred feet of muck and set the stretcher down again.

"Did he leave his name when you saw him last night?" Orion asked.

"Nope. Got back in his fancy car and drove off."

"Was he alone?" Orion asked again.

"Couldn't tell. Tinted windows. But he got in the passenger side."

"I don't suppose he said what he wanted of me?" Orion wiped his palm across his forehead.

"Nope."

A gust of wind flattened Orion's hood against the side of his face and sent a trickle of chilly water down his sweaty back. He shivered.

"Exactly what did the guy say?" Orion asked.

"You seem real curious about him," said Dan'l.

"Yeah. Well . . ." said Orion.

"Came by right after you left, eight-fifteen, eight-thirty." Dan'l wiped his face with his wet red bandanna. "Wasn't real dark yet. He asked if the boss was around. I said I'm the boss here. He said, the big boss, Orion Nanopoulos." Dan'l stretched his arms out to his side, then raised them over his head. "So, you're the big boss?" He straightened his legs, bent down, and touched his toes. "This is shit work."

"Yeah," said Orion. "Then what?"

"I told him he just missed you. He wanted to know where you went. You probably went to get supper at the Ocean View, I said. I asked if he knew where it's at." Dan'l shrugged. "The guy said, 'I can find it.' "

"That was it?"

"Yup." Dan'l, eyes half-shut, a sort of smile on his face, looked at Orion.

"Okay," said the lead cop. "This should do it. One . . . two . . . three . . . lift!"

They trudged through the last hundred feet of mud to the parking area, where Toby, the undertaker, waited in the hearse, warm and dry, engine running, listening to the generic rock on WMVY radio. The lead cop opened the back doors of the hearse and they slid in the stretcher. Toby, in the driver's seat, watched them in the rearview mirror. He lifted a hand from the wheel in acknowledgment.

"Guess that's supposed to be a thank you," said the lead cop. The two got back into their cruiser and took off, a rooster tail of muddy water settling in their wake.

Orion's back ached. He eased into the driver's seat of his twenty-year-old Chevy wagon and leaned back. Should have known better than to lift one quarter of Angelo Vulpone one-handed, he told himself. Damned fool. He reached carefully into the glove compartment, found the aspirin bottle, chewed up and swallowed three without water, and leaned back again, eyes closed, waiting for the aspirin to take effect.

A knock on his window. He opened his eyes. The guy from the Two Braves Construction pickup truck. He rolled down his window.

"Can I help you?"

"You the boss?"

"I'm the fiber-optic boss," Orion said.

"The town guy said you're the one I should talk to." The man at Orion's window was wearing the ubiquitous yellow oilskins. Raindrops trickled down his mahogany face.

"Want to get out of the rain?" Orion indicated the side door, not wanting to bend that far unless he had to.

"What'dya say we get a cup of coffee at Humphrey's, and dry out."

"Sounds good to me," said Orion. "I'll meet you there. What did you say your name was?"

"I didn't." He pointed a wet finger at his wet chest. "You're looking at Donald Minnowfish, antiquities officer for the tribe."

"Nice to meet you." Orion rolled up the window and started the car. The inside of the windshield had fogged up during his conversation with Minnowfish, so he turned on the heater, the air conditioner, and the fan and waited until he could see out.

Humphrey's was less than a mile from the ball field. The Two Braves truck was already there as Orion pulled up.

Minnowfish was seated at a small table by the window when Orion entered, a fat briefcase next to his chair. "You buying?" he asked.

"Why not," said Orion. "How do you take it?"

"Double cream, double sugar. And, say," he said as Orion turned to go to the counter, "get me a jelly donut, will you?"

"Right," said Orion over his shoulder.

They went through the ritual of small talk, a necessary prelude to whatever Minnowfish really intended to say. The body at the bottom of the trench, of course. The weather. The mud. They stirred their respective coffees and discussed where Orion was from, what Two Braves Construction did. Minnowfish started in on the Red Sox and how they were going to demolish the Yankees this season. Orion assumed his pleasant look and stirred his coffee some more. Minnowfish took a couple of bites of his donut and then they got down to business.

Minnowfish wiped powdered sugar from his mouth and reached down for the briefcase. He had intense gray-green eyes and close-cropped, light brown, tightly curled hair. "You know, don't you, that you need permits from the tribe before excavating?"

"I'm not excavating," said Orion. "The town is. I'm simply laying cable in their trench."

"Still, you need a permit." He opened the briefcase and took out a thick sheaf of forms.

"What for?" said Orion, who'd researched every possible requirement for permits. He'd applied for them all, even ones he didn't think were needed. He'd done that even though he had no intention of excavating anything.

"Wampanoag antiquities," said Minnowfish. "Artifacts. Fire rings. Campsites."

"But the ball field is new land," said Orion. "They filled in a marsh to create it in the 1970s, before the Wetlands Act. There couldn't have been campsites."

Minnowfish shrugged. "Doesn't matter. You need a permit from the land manager, according to the 1906 Antiquities Act." He pointed to his chest with his thumb. "That's me."

"It's town land, isn't it? Not tribal land."

"You excavate that field without a permit and you'll find out whose land it is." Minnowfish's dark face had become a shade darker.

Orion could see this talk turning into a confrontation, and he'd lose if that happened. "Tell you what," he said. "Why don't you send a tribal rep to work alongside us and watch out for artifacts. We'll give you GPS coordinates, documenting exactly where the artifact shows up, and your rep can turn everything we find over to the tribe along with where we found it. Would that work for you? That way, we don't have to go through all that paperwork nonsense." He realized immediately that he shouldn't have used the word "nonsense."

Minnowfish finished his donut, wiped his fingers on a paper napkin, wadded up the napkin, took another, wiped his mouth, wadded that one up, tossed it onto the table.

Orion waited. He hadn't touched his donut.

"You said you're not digging?"

"That's right. Whatever the guy from the town said, they're doing the excavating, not us."

Minnowfish stood. "I'll have someone from the tribe bird-dog you."

"Good plan," said Orion. "Want my donut?"

"Might as well. Thanks."

The aspirin wasn't helping much. Orion knew from experience that he'd better keep moving, not lie down, which is what he wanted desperately to do. He needed to think, to talk to someone. When he first arrived on the Island, he'd leased the second floor of a building a block off Main Street. He didn't look forward to returning to his empty office where there was no one to talk to. So he headed up Island on State Road and found himself looking forward to getting home to Victoria Trumbull.

Victoria was typing her column for the newspaper with great rapidity using the forefingers of both hands and her right thumb on the space bar. She looked up with a smile, which faded when she saw his face.

"You're hurting." She pushed the typewriter aside.

"Just my back. It'll pass." At her sympathetic voice he already felt marginally better.

"Was the death an accident?"

Orion sat down carefully next to her, keeping his back straight. "He was shot."

"A local man?"

Orion sighed. "You said something about your being a police deputy."

"I've helped our local police chief on a few occasions," said Victoria. "She appointed me her deputy."

"She?" asked Orion.

"Casey, our chief of police. Mary Kathleen O'Neill."

"Ah."

"How did you hurt your back?" Victoria asked.

"I lifted something I shouldn't have."

Victoria eased herself out of her chair and went into the kitchen. "Green tea?" she asked.

"Please, Mrs. Trumbull. I'll get it." He started to get up, but realized he'd better not.

"Sit," she commanded. "By the way, Casey calls me by my first name. You're welcome to, if you'd like."

She brought him a mug of his favorite tea with a plate of graham crackers, and sat again at the head of the table with her own mug. "I know you drink it black, but I've dosed it with honey from Sean's bees. A restorative."

Now that he was inside and warm, the rain was no longer a threat. In fact, when the rain was kept outside where it belonged, it made a pleasing susurration against the silvery-gray shingles of Victoria's house.

He sipped the sweet tea, debating with himself whether or not to tell her about Angelo Vulpone. Victoria sat quietly, drinking her own tea. Suddenly, he said, "Mrs. Trumbull, I knew the man in the trench."

Victoria said nothing.

"Angelo Vulpone. I didn't tell the officers at the scene that I knew him. He was about to become a major investor in my company."

"About to become?"

"He had money, he understood the importance of fiber optics, and he claimed he wanted to invest. Eight million dollars." Orion held his mug in both hands because of the comforting feeling it gave him. He was six years old again, wrapping his hands around a mug of cambric tea at his grandmother's on a rainy afternoon.

"Were you close to him?"

Orion set down his mug. "Not really. I didn't trust him entirely." He helped himself to a graham cracker, snapped it down its perforations, and dipped a quarter piece into his tea. "I'm sure he didn't trust me, either."

"What was he doing here, checking on you?"

"I wish I knew, Mrs. Trum . . . Victoria."

CHAPTER 4

"Rumors fly from one end of this Island to the other faster than your optical fibers will ever carry them." Victoria stood and held the back of her chair. "You've got to go to Casey and explain what you just told me."

Orion shook his head. "I'm distancing myself from any possible connection with Angelo Vulpone and the police."

"I can assure you rumors are already on their way announcing that Orion Nanopoulos knows the identity of the body found on the ball field, and speculation on why you didn't identify the victim." Victoria leaned on her chair. "Why didn't you, by the way?"

Orion ran his hands over his head, smoothing his hair back to the elastic that held his ponytail in place.

Victoria waited.

"I'm sure Vulpone was connected to the mob," Orion said. "Shot in the back of his head, a mob-type execution. I don't want to be identified with this killing. I've got a job to do and a deadline. Do you understand, Victoria?"

"Certainly," said Victoria. "But here are the facts." She moved the chair around and sat again. "Angelo Vulpone will be identified eventually. By dental records, missing persons reports, fingerprints, DNA. And when he is, every contact he's ever had will be unearthed and investigated." She rested her elbows on the table. "When it's learned that you expected him to invest in the project, didn't like him, failed to identify his body, and caused a delay in that identification that cost authorities time and money . . ."

Orion sighed. "I've heard enough."

"Do you happen to be involved with the mob?"

"Good heavens, no."

"Then your delay in identifying Angelo Vulpone will cause someone in the mob to wonder why. You'll have both the mob and the police annoyed with you."

"Is the police station open on Sunday?"

"Casey will be there."

"You win." Orion rose and offered her his hand. "Will you accompany me to the police station, Deputy Trumbull?"

Victoria shrugged into her frayed trench coat, tied a scarf over her head, retrieved her lilac-wood stick from behind the door, and waited in the entry out of the rain for Orion to fetch his car.

When he came around to the passenger side to open the door for her, his entirely pleasant expression had returned along with what looked like a smile.

Orion pulled up in the parking area in front of the tiny West Tisbury police station and held the passenger door for Victoria. The ducks that usually flocked around new arrivals made a few desultory quacks from their shelter under the rosebush. The rain had slackened a bit. Victoria and Orion hurried up the station house steps before the threatening clouds let go again.

When they entered, Casey was on the telephone. She beckoned for them to sit. Victoria took her usual seat, the wooden armchair in front of Casey's desk, and Orion wheeled over the chair from the desk next to the chief's. A nameplate on the tidy desk read SER-GEANT JUNIOR NORTON.

Casey hung up the phone. "I have a feeling that call had to do with something you already know, Victoria. Are you here because of the unidentified body . . . ?"

"Yes." Victoria gave Orion a significant look. "This is Orion Nanopoulos."

Casey and Orion nodded to one another. "Aren't you the fiber-optics guy?"

"That's right," said Orion.

24

"You're installing cable in the trench where the body was found this morning, aren't you?"

Orion nodded.

"Then you know more about the circumstances than I do." Casey picked up her beach-stone paperweight and rubbed its smooth surface absently. "How can I help you?"

Orion leaned forward. "I failed to tell the responding officers at the scene that I knew the victim." He straightened his back amd nodded toward Victoria. "Mrs. Trumbull urged me to talk to you."

Casey flipped the stone from one hand to the other. "Not the state police, Victoria?"

"I'm going through channels," Victoria said primly.

Casey smiled and turned back to Orion. "After I've heard what you have to say I'll call Sergeant Smalley at the state police barracks." She set the stone back on her papers and pulled a yellow legal pad toward her.

"His name is Angelo Vulpone," said Orion. "He owned a construction company in Brooklyn."

"We'll need to notify his family."

"All I know about him is that he has two grown sons in business with him. I don't know their names."

Casey looked up. "How did you meet him?"

"One of my partners, Casper Martin, approached Vulpone about investing in the project, and Vulpone agreed to put in eight million."

Casey whistled softly. "A lot of money. Had he turned any of it over to you?"

"Not yet. We had some negotiating to do first."

"I suppose that's why he was here on the Island?"

"I have no idea," said Orion.

Casey reached for the phone. "I'll let Smalley know we have an ID. You'll need to go to the barracks tomorrow to answer questions, then the funeral home to make an ID."

———

25

The rain started up again while they were meeting with Casey and now it was coming down in torrents. Victoria and Orion hurried to the car.

"Well, Victoria," said Orion, easing his back against the driver's seat, "you were right. If we could figure out how the Island grapevine works, we wouldn't need a fiber-optics system."

Later that afternoon, Orion stopped at his office in Vineyard Haven and called Casper Martin, his partner in New York. The rain poured down steadily.

"Casper, it's Orion."

"What's up?"

"Bad news, I'm afraid."

"Let's have it."

"Vulpone's dead."

"What?"

"Vulpone. He's dead." Orion spent the silence that followed looking down onto the driveway of the house next door. An ordinary two-story frame house, shingled. Tufts of uncut grass ran down the center of the unpaved drive. Puddles in the ruts were pockmarked with rain.

Casper breathed heavily at the other end of the line. "Jee-sus," he said at last. "What the hell? Damn!"

A maroon SUV splashed up the drive and stopped at the side door of the house.

After a long pause Martin said, "What happened?"

As he replied, Orion watched a man get out of the SUV and go into the house, the Sunday paper protecting his head. Orion had never paid much attention to the house next door. Looking from his second-floor aerie, he started to lift his feet onto his desk. His back twinged, and he set his feet down. From the way the man below walked, he was young. Thirties, maybe. That was about all Orion could tell, looking down on him.

As he told Martin about recognizing Angelo, carrying the body on the wheeled stretcher through the mud, and his encounter with Donald Minnowfish, he thought about Angelo Vulpone's sons. Did

Vulpone have daughters? A wife? Orion knew as much about the man next door as he knew about Vulpone, namely, nothing. He told Martin that his ancient landlady had forced him to go to the police.

"She's right, you know."

"Yeah, Casper. I know."

Martin wondered why Vulpone was on the Island, puzzled over who killed him, then added, "There goes a third of our funding," which was what had concerned them both from the moment they knew Angelo Vulpone was dead.

"You knew him better than I did," said Orion. "Know anything about his sons?"

"You mean, will they carry out their old man's intention to invest?"

"Something like that."

"Even if they do, it'll take time," said Martin. "Funeral, grieving, probate. Might take a couple of years."

"We don't have that kind of time," said Orion. "Do they have money of their own?"

"This isn't the best time to ask." Casper Martin stopped talking and Orion said nothing.

Martin broke the silence. "Who killed him, the mob?"

"I haven't a clue," said Orion.

The man next door came out of the house holding an umbrella over a Cronig's grocery bag he was carrying, the kind with paper handles. The bag bulged with something heavy and the handles seemed ready to tear off. He slung the bag into the back seat, closed the umbrella, got into the front seat, and backed out of the drive.

"Vulpone was a stubborn son of a bitch," said Martin. "He wouldn't listen to anyone except those two kids of his. Nobody liked the guy, but nobody hated him, either."

"Someone did. Enough to kill him. How closely was he connected to the mob?"

"Hard to know," Martin replied. "He probably was since just about everyone in the Jersey–New York construction business has dealings with the mob at some time or other."

27

"I assume his killing is mob related," said Orion.

"If so, we'll never know. The question I'm asking is why was Vulpone on the Island? Checking up on the project? The company? You?"

"The head of Public Works told me that Vulpone was asking for me by name last night."

"Probably paying a surprise visit," said Martin, "check up for himself. That would be like him."

"Who told him where we were working? The ball field is not a place you'd think to look for someone installing optical cable. Had you mentioned it to him?"

"I haven't talked to him for a couple of weeks. The ball field operation's come up since then."

"We've got two years to complete a job that should take eighteen months," said Orion. "But I'm learning that with six governments in six towns on this Island and not a single engineer among the lot . . ." He took a breath. "Every meeting I go to has two or three activists in attendance convinced that communicating by fiber optics is going to produce two-headed babies—"

"Okay, okay," Martin interrupted. "We're talking about adding an *extra* two years to educate the populace. We don't have that kind of time."

Orion sighed. "We can complete the project in two, even with town politics. But only with enough capital. You want to see what you can do about that?"

"Yeah," said Martin.

"Vulpone didn't sign anything, did he?"

"Nope. He was too canny."

Orion said, "It shouldn't be difficult to find the money, even now. The communications business is pretty much untouched by recession."

"Yeah," said Martin.

"My best estimate of the total project cost was twenty-four million," said Orion. "You found potential backers for about two-thirds. That leaves a shortfall of the eight million Vulpone had promised."

Looking down from his window, holding the phone against his

ear, wishing he could lift his feet up on his desk, Orion imagined what it would be like to lead a normal life. Coming home with the Sunday paper and sharing sections. The kids reading the comics, he and the wife working on the crossword puzzle together . . .

"I'll see what I can do," said Martin. "There's money out there, only a question of finding it."

After they'd hung up, Orion thought about the man next door and wondered why he'd brought his Sunday paper home and left almost immediately with that Cronig's bag.

CHAPTER 5

That afternoon, contrary to Victoria's prediction of a three-day rain, the sky cleared and the sun appeared. Victoria went out to the garden with her secateurs to snip bouquets of bee balm to put in the two glass vases on the parlor mantel. The elaborately painted vases had been a wedding present to her mother from a rejected suitor. She wondered, briefly, if something more formal than bee balm might be more appropriate, then decided she liked the carefree look of the gaudy, unkempt flowers.

The bee balm was humming with bees, and she felt mildly selfish taking part of their livelihood away. She was snipping carefully, avoiding the busiest flowers, when Sean McBride's pickup truck pulled into the pasture.

She hastily filled a watering can from the garden faucet, set the long-stemmed flowers in it, and hustled over to her front-row seat.

He backed his truck a safe distance from the hives and went around to the rear where he kept his beekeeping gear.

"Morning, Mrs. T. You hear about the body in the playing field?" Sean shook out his white suit. The slight breeze billowed out the legs and arms so the suit looked, for a moment, like his shed skin. Ecdysis, Victoria thought. A snake slipping out of his skin. A crab leaving its hard shell. She envisioned, for an instant, Sean as a nightclub stripper, an ecdysiast, and smiled at the thought. He paused, waiting for her response.

"I'm sorry, I was distracted," said Victoria from her front-row seat.

"They found a body in the playing field this morning." He leaned against the lowered tailgate of his truck and slipped first one foot, then the other into his new skin.

"Yes, I heard. Orion Nanopoulos got a call early."

"Staying with you, is he? How's that working out?" Sean thrust his arms into the sleeves of the white suit and pulled it over his shoulders.

"He seems agreeable. I told him it was to be only a temporary stay."

"I understand Nanopoulos is laying his cable in the trench where they found the body."

Victoria nodded.

"Seems like he knew the guy. Didn't tell the cops."

Victoria felt a wash of pride at the efficiency of the Island grapevine. "He's spoken to Casey, and will be talking to the state police tomorrow."

Victoria shifted on the hard bench. "When you saw him at the Farmer's Market, was that when you first met him?"

"Never seen him before. Heard about him, though. Someone you don't want to mess with." Sean reached into the back of the truck for the next prop.

"He's a perfect gentleman," said Victoria. "Courteous, considerate."

"Figured he would be to you, Mrs. T." He started up the smoker and pumped the handle a few times. Before slipping his hood over his head he gazed at her, light blue eyes focused, not on her, but through her on some distant horizon. Once his hood was in place, Victoria had trouble understanding what he said next, and wasn't sure she heard correctly. It sounded like, "Wouldn't surprise me if he knew more than the identity of the corpse."

"What do you mean?" she asked.

But Sean had turned his attention to the bees and didn't reply.

Early the next morning, Victoria walked to the police station. Casey was standing at the top of the stairs, scooping out feed for the ducks and geese.

"I don't know why I feed them. All they do is make a mess and get in the way." She dropped the scoop back into the galvanized container and snapped the lid into place. "What's on your mind?"

"The investigation into the murder." Victoria climbed the steps and she and Casey went inside. Casey sat behind her desk; Victoria took her usual seat.

"State police problem, Victoria."

"Surely they can use our help." Victoria crossed her hands over the top of her stick.

"We've got our own problems," said Casey.

"Mrs. Sommerville's complaint about the rooster?"

"That's important to her. We've got to deal with it."

"But a man has been shot to death."

"Not our job," said Casey.

"We can contribute a great deal."

Casey stood up. "Victoria, the selectmen asked me to check up on a complaint about kids drinking on the Lambert's Cove beach. That's top priority for me right now. Want to come with me?"

Victoria, too, stood. "I don't think so."

"If you're going to freelance this murder, I'd advise against it, Victoria."

"Thank you for the advice."

"I'll give you a ride home, if you'd like."

"I'd prefer to walk."

"Come off it, Victoria. You know policing. The state cops are in charge. We stay out of their way. I could use your company, checking out the drinking complaint."

"All right," said Victoria, but she yielded grudgingly.

On his way home—Orion realized he was already thinking of his temporary dwelling place at Victoria Trumbull's as home—he stopped at the pie place on State Road and bought a rhubarb-strawberry pie. He set the cardboard box on a newspaper on the front seat, the pie still hot from the oven. Ruby-red juice oozed out between the interlaced strips of golden brown crust.

Victoria was in the cookroom. She looked up from her typewriter when Orion entered. Orion opened the box and she peered in. "My favorite." She pushed her typewriter aside and started to get up.

"You sit still, Victoria," said Orion, feeling very much at home. "I'll serve us."

"How's your back?"

"Much better, as long as I don't think about it."

Two or three bites into the warm pie with appropriate comments about flavor and flaky crust, Victoria told him about Casey's insistence that she stay off the case. "She had no information on what the state police are doing. Have you spoken to Sergeant Smalley?"

Orion nodded. "He understood my situation and drove me to the funeral parlor to ID the body." He paused. "Why call them parlors? As though it's a place to entertain."

"Denial," said Victoria. "What happened?"

"I attested that I recognized the deceased as Angelo Vulpone of Vulpone Construction, Brooklyn, New York, and Smalley drove me back to the state police barracks."

"Did he tell you anything about the investigation?"

"Of course not."

"Identifying the body must have been unpleasant."

"I'd already seen the body at the ball field and knew who he was. They'd cleaned him up a bit." Orion leaned back in his chair. "It's been a full day. Yesterday afternoon, I called my partner, Casper, and we talked about needing another investor now that Vulpone's dead. The problem is, we don't have much time."

"What about Dorothy Roche?"

Orion smiled. "The woman you think is egotistical, self-satisfied, and a social climber?"

Victoria frowned. "Those weren't my words."

"She's agreed to purchase the Ditch Witch directional drill in return for a share in the company."

"I assume you asked a lawyer other than that fraud on Circuit Avenue to look over the agreement," said Victoria.

"You mean Parnell Alsop?"

Victoria looked directly at Orion. "Surely you didn't trust him to draft anything?" At Orion's expression, she added, "Why didn't you ask me about him first?"

"I hadn't met you at the time. Don't look so stricken, Victoria. I work with legal documents and contracts all the time. The contract he drafted was boilerplate."

Victoria looked unconvinced.

"More pie?" asked Orion.

Later that evening, Orion returned from supper and found Victoria in the garden as the light faded. She was kneeling on a device that had handles to lift herself up. Orion noticed that the ends of the handles had red glass reflectors, as though Victoria might want to take the kneeler out on the highway some dark evening.

"I got a call from Dorothy Roche," he said. "The drill is being shipped over day after tomorrow on Ralph Packer's barge. Would you like to—"

Victoria didn't let him finish. "Of course I would." She struggled to her feet. "What time?"

On Wednesday morning, Victoria dressed in clean gray corduroy trousers and a shirt printed with tiny rosebuds for the occasion of the arrival of the Ditch Witch drill. She plucked a straw hat from the selection hanging in the entry, made sure her police deputy hat was in her bag, just in case, and was ready before Orion had finished shaving.

Orion held the passenger door of his fine vehicle for her and she swung her long legs in. He went around to the driver's side, patted the car, and got in. The car was roomy, solid, and luxurious, not like today's models. Victoria sighed and sat back to savor the ride.

They drove to the end of Old County Road and turned toward Vineyard Haven. Along the way, Victoria pointed out the grove of beech trees. She'd written a poem, she told him. If she were to be turned into a tree, like Baucis and Philemon, she hoped it would be a beech. Orion listened with his pleasant expression, although he'd heard Victoria tell the very same story the last time they'd driven into Vineyard Haven together.

He pulled into the Packer's Marine parking area. In the distance, coming around the jetty, a tug was hauling a barge, and on the barge was a magnificent orange machine that glistened in the bright morning.

Victoria held the brim of her floppy hat against the breeze, examining the Ditch Witch drill as the barge drew near. "Isn't Dorothy going to be here?"

"She's supposed to be," said Orion, looking behind him down Beach Road. "This must be her car now."

"A Mercedes roadster," murmured Victoria.

The woman who got out of the car was, as Victoria knew, fifty-ish, fleshy, and a bit over five feet tall. Victoria stood as straight as she could, pushing against her lilac-wood stick to give herself added height.

The woman was enveloped in an aura of musky perfume. She was dressed in a Lilly-something outfit, too young for her, big splashy pink flowers with chartreuse leaves. Her shoes, scarf, and hat, all a horrid shade of pink, matched everything else she was wearing, including the frames of her sunglasses.

Victoria glanced at Orion and knew he was smitten.

The woman's hair, an aggressive metallic auburn, clashed with all that pink. She ignored Victoria, and thrust her small arms out to Orion, who responded with a warm embrace. "Darling!" she cried. "Isn't this exciting! Our very own Ditch Witch drilling unit!"

Orion disentangled himself, apparently recalling that this was not one of Victoria's favorite people. "Dorothy," he said. "You know Mrs. Trumbull, don't you?"

"Of course, darling! Everybody, just everybody knows Mrs. Trumbull. Hello, dear. How nice to see you." She looked up at Victoria and held out a small hand. Victoria took it in her large gnarled one, only slightly concerned that she might crush it.

There was sudden activity at the Packer barge ramp, the sound of powerful engines reversing and churning an awful lot of water. The tug maneuvered the barge next to the ramp with a soft thump. The vehicle aboard wobbled against its wooden chocks. As if by magic, the machine—the Ditch Witch drill and all its accoutrements—was off-loaded onto a flatbed trailer, and without ceremony, the truck attached to the trailer drove off, heading up Island.

"That's it," said Orion, smiling down at Dorothy Roche.

CHAPTER 6

That evening, Elizabeth made supper: lamb chops, Swiss chard from the garden, and tiny new potatoes dug out from under the potato plants. Victoria was unusually quiet.

"How was the arrival of the drilling machine, Gram?"

Victoria set her napkin down beside her barely touched food. "Anticlimactic. Packer's tugboat brought the Ditch Witch drill over. A couple of men winched it off the barge onto a trailer; the men got into the truck and drove off."

"Where to?" Elizabeth finished the last of her lamb.

"Behind Trip Barnes's moving and storage place." Victoria rearranged her knife and fork on her plate.

"Did Dorothy Roche show up for the launching? I guess you'd call it a reverse launching."

"Yes."

"No champagne smashed over its hood?"

Victoria smiled weakly.

"Was she being obnoxious?" asked Elizabeth.

"No. Not at all."

"Are you okay, Gram? You've hardly touched your food."

"Everything looks delicious, but I don't have much appetite tonight," Victoria said. "I'm sorry."

"I hope you're not coming down with something."

"I hope not, too. A week ago I pulled a tick off my middle. I didn't notice until it itched, and by then the tick was well entrenched."

"A deer tick?"

"A tiny one, at any rate."

"Do you want to show me where it bit you?"

Victoria lifted her shirt and pulled down the waistband of her corduroys.

Elizabeth put her hand on a hot red circle on Victoria's side, the diameter of an orange slice. "Here?"

"Yes."

"Oh, Gram. It looks like the classic sign of Lyme disease. A bull's-eye with a dot in the middle."

Victoria tucked her shirt back into her trousers.

Elizabeth remained standing. "We'd better go to the emergency room. You don't want to mess with Lyme disease."

"Tomorrow I read to the elderly at the hospital," said Victoria. "Doc Jeffers is next to the nursing-home wing."

"You sure?"

"I'm sure." Victoria got up slowly and carried her plate into the kitchen.

"Leave the dishes. I'll do them," said Elizabeth.

"Thank you." Victoria climbed up the stairs to bed.

The next morning, Casper Martin called Orion.

"How're things in the city, Casper?" Orion selected a working pen from the jelly jar on his desk and turned to a clean sheet on his yellow legal pad.

"I've got a line on a potential investor."

"Oh?"

"A car distributor with a place on the Vineyard wants to communicate fast from the Island with off Island dealerships. He's willing to invest, but he wants a share in the company."

"What's his name?"

"Paulson. Roger Paulson."

"I've heard of him." Orion noted it on his yellow pad.

"Also, I've located a buddy of Angelo Vulpone's who has a line on a couple of venture capital firms. Says he can come up with eight million within six months."

"What does that mean?" said Orion. "That the guy has contacts? That's no good, Casper." Orion looked down to see the maroon SUV drive up and the same man get out and go into the house. Orion checked his watch. Ten-thirty. What was the guy doing home this time of day?

Casper said, "He's got a track record."

"I don't like it, Casper. Have you met the guy?"

"His name's Finney Solomon, and yeah, I've met him. He claims he was mentored by Angelo Vulpone. Want me to set up a meeting with the three of us?"

"I thought you said Angelo didn't work with anyone other than his sons."

"I didn't know about Finney Solomon at the time."

"Sounds as though he's nothing but a broker."

"Claims he encouraged Angelo to invest with us."

Orion sighed. "Set up the meeting, then. Here at the office at his and your convenience, any time this week or next. I suppose he expects us to pay travel and expenses?"

The man next door came out of the house carrying another Cronig's bag, again slung it into the backseat, got in, and reversed out of the drive.

"He pays his own way, he says."

"Well, that's something," said Orion. "Call me on my cell when you've got it set up. I'll be in the field most of today and tomorrow."

After lunch, Casey helped Victoria stow poetry books in her cloth bag, and carried it out to the Bronco.

"What are you reading today, Victoria?" Casey asked when they were heading toward the hospital.

"It doesn't matter what I read. They're glad to have anything to break the monotony. A voice, a face. I'll read bits and pieces until they fall asleep, then stop."

"You seem down, Victoria. Are you okay?"

"I feel a bit peaked." She pronounced the word peak-ed the way Vineyarders always had. Stripe-ed bass and feeling peak-ed. "Elizabeth thinks I might have Lyme disease and wants me to see Doc Jeffers."

They passed the airport, busy with aircraft landing and taking off. Beyond the entrance, Casey turned onto Barnes Road. A small plane took off over their heads.

Victoria didn't feel up to reading for the full hour. Besides, most of her elderly listeners were asleep. Even on her usually optimistic days, she'd leave depressed after her weekly reading. Today was worse. She put her books back into her cloth bag, shook hands with those who were still awake, said good-bye to the nurses on her way out, and trudged down the long hallway to Doc Jeffers's office.

She slumped into one of the chairs in the waiting area and dozed until she was called.

Doc Jeffers's office was the very essence of machismo. A huge desk made from a thick slice of some forest giant, overblown photos on all four walls of Jeffers with his Harley, Jeffers with his cigarette boat, Jeffers holding a fishing rod standing next to an upside-down shark, Jeffers surrounded by a bevy of women in scanty bathing suits . . .

Jeffers was a large man. He stood when she entered his office and shook hands. Victoria felt almost dainty.

"I don't see you often professionally, Victoria. Sit down." He, too, sat. "What's the problem?" He leaned backward in his massive chair and looked at her over the top of his tortoiseshell reading glasses.

"I'm feeling a bit peaked," said Victoria.

Before she could explain about the tick bite, he said, "After all, you are ninety-two, and you can expect—"

"Don't start that," Victoria said sharply. "I was bitten by a tick last week." She got to her feet in the most sprightly manner she could muster, lifted her shirt, and turned so he could see the red patch on her side.

"Hmmmm," he murmured, leaning over his desk to peer at the hot red spot through his glasses. "Typical bull's-eye. Indicative of Lyme." He sat back. "I'll order blood tests, but I'm putting you on doxycycline right now." He scribbled out a prescription and checked off items on a form and handed them to her, pointing toward the lab. "Blood tests. Don't go out in the sun while you're taking doxycycline, or you may get a wicked reaction." He stood. Victoria stood. They shook hands again, and Victoria trudged back down the hall to the lab, each step a slog through soft sand.

On the way home Casey stopped at Conroy's Apothecary to pick up Victoria's prescription for doxycycline. At home, Victoria took the first of the small pinkish-orange pills and climbed up the stairs to bed, for the first nap she could remember taking, ever.

She was awakened by the phone ringing and slipped out from under the comforter to answer.

"Mrs. Trumbull? This is Dorothy Roche."

Victoria felt a surge of resentment at being awakened by this woman. "Hello, Dorothy."

"I hope I'm not getting you at a bad time?"

"Not at all." Victoria tried not to sound irritated.

"I'd love to have you join me for an informal lunch on Saturday, a spur-of-the-moment thing, if you're free."

"Thank you, but I don't know where you live." It was a weak excuse, but Victoria was feeling muzzy and couldn't think of a good reason to say no decisively. She certainly wasn't going to mention feeling ill.

"I live in Edgartown. I'll send my driver to pick you up. Would eleven-thirty be convenient?"

CHAPTER 7

When Orion came home that evening, Victoria was in the parlor reading with McCavity in her lap.

"I hear you've got Lyme disease," said Orion, easing himself down into the rocking chair. "How are you feeling?"

Victoria smiled. "The Island grapevine's been busy." She stuck a bookmark in her book and set it down. "I'm achy and lack energy. How was your day?"

"Productive," said Orion. "The police released the crime scene shortly after noon, and we were able to lay cable to the end of the trench."

"Did the police give you any indication of how the investigation is proceeding?"

"They're not about to tell me," said Orion. "Starting next Friday, we'll use the directional drill."

"Do you own the machine now, or does Dorothy Roche?"

McCavity slid off Victoria's lap and stalked over to Orion, who patted his lap. McCavity turned his back.

Orion laughed. "Dorothy bought the drill, or is buying it, I should say, as her share in the company."

"Are you comfortable with that arrangement?"

Orion paused. "I may have made a mistake in giving up voting shares in my company. But we drew up a contract and had it looked over . . ."

"By her pal, Parnell Alsop, I suppose," said Victoria.

Orion smiled. "Now, Victoria. Have some faith in my judgment. Dorothy is a remarkable woman. To get where she is, she's had to be smart, strong, and determined."

"The word is ruthless."

Orion shook his head. "You're not being fair to her. She's set up several businesses. She knows what she's talking about." Orion rocked back in the chair.

There was a loud yowl.

The cat had been cleaning himself next to Orion's chair, tail under the rocker.

Orion rocked forward. "Sorry, McCavity."

A yellow blur darted toward the kitchen, briefly glared over its shoulder at Orion, and disappeared.

After McCavity's cusswords had faded away, Victoria asked, "What sort of businesses has Dorothy set up?"

"A limousine service, an office cleaning service, and a catering service."

"Not what I'd call sophisticated businesses," said Victoria. "Does she know anything about fiber optics?"

"She doesn't need to, Victoria." Orion checked behind his chair. "She understands business and finance." He pointed his thumb at his chest. "I know the engineering."

Victoria said, "She's invited me to lunch Saturday."

"Good for her. You may change your mind about her."

Victoria lifted herself slowly out of her chair. "Have you had supper yet? If not, you're welcome to join me."

Orion, too, got up. "I've already eaten, but I'll keep you company." He looked closely at her. "If you'll let me, I'll cook one of the best omelets you've ever tasted."

"That sounds fine. Thank you."

Victoria hadn't been hungry, but when Orion served her a fluffy omelet he'd cooked with a touch of cheese and herbs he'd picked from the garden, her appetite returned.

While she was eating, Orion talked nonstop about the drilling machine. "It can be steered around tough obstacles," he said. "It has so little impact on the surface, it can crawl over turf without disturbing it." He added, "At least, not much."

While she was eating, Victoria heard a description of this re-markable machine. Its spindle speed and torque, its carriage thrust, pullback force, its aspiration, stroke, injection, its battery reserve . . .

Victoria finished her omelet. "Thank you."

Orion took her plate into the kitchen and returned with a small bowl of coffee ice cream. Victoria was glad to listen to Orion without having to talk herself.

"A huge difference in safety and environmental disruption be-tween an open trench and this." He stopped.

"Go on," said Victoria, and tilted her bowl to scoop up the last half-teaspoon of melted ice cream.

"We can set a half-mile of cable in one day in this sandy soil, and the only disruption is the machine parked by the side of the road. Compare that with an open trench."

"Less chance of disposing of a body." Victoria folded her nap-kin and stuck it into her silver napkin ring.

"True."

"Have you had any success in finding the funding you lost with Angelo Vulpone's death?"

"I'm meeting with a man on Monday. He claims he has con-tacts in venture capital firms." Orion must have noticed Victoria's puzzled expression, because he added, "Venture capital firms in-vest in major projects like ours."

"Why don't we go into the parlor where it's more comfortable." She rose and Orion immediately stood.

"Who is this man you're meeting with Monday?" she asked when they were settled in the parlor.

Orion had seated himself in the rocker again. "His name is Finney Solomon."

Despite her nap, Victoria was feeling drowsy and was having trouble concentrating. "Aren't you concerned that investors will take over your company if it's successful?"

"Not if, when." Orion studied his landlady. "Are you feeling okay, Victoria?"

"I feel dopey. The effects of that medicine I'm taking. I like hearing you talk."

Orion changed the subject. "You know just about everyone on the Island, don't you?"

"I don't know many people outside of West Tisbury, at least, not the newcomers."

"You know where my office is?"

"The building with a garage underneath?"

He nodded.

"It was built by an automobile mechanic. I can't think of his name at the moment."

Orion rested his elbows on the chair arms. "Do you know anything about the house next door, the one with yellow siding?"

"He built that house as a rental unit and moved off Island shortly after. The office was vacant for a while."

"I'm interested in the people living in the house. Do you know anything about them?"

"Probably renters," said Victoria. "Why do you ask?"

"I was curious," said Orion. "I've seen a man coming and going. Odd times of day. I haven't seen anyone else."

"I have a Realtor friend who may be able to tell me who they are." Victoria reached for a slip of paper and a pen on the end table. "What is the street address?"

The next morning, Victoria called her Realtor friend, Shirley Jensen.

"Man named Tris Waverley rents it, Mrs. Trumbull. Let's see what else I've got." Victoria heard the clicking of computer keys. "He used Dorothy Roche as a reference." Shirley paused. "Does that help?"

"It does indeed," said Victoria. "Do you know when he rented the place?"

More clicking of keys. "Two months ago."

"That was shortly after Orion Nanopoulos rented his office," Victoria murmured to herself.

"Beg your pardon?" said Shirley.

"Sorry, I was thinking out loud. Thank you so much."

"Don't forget me if you hear of someone who wants a twelve-million-dollar home. I've got a nice listing."

"I'll be sure to," said Victoria.

CHAPTER 8

At eleven-thirty on Saturday, a convertible stopped at Victoria's west door. She had dressed for the luncheon with Dorothy in her green plaid suit with a white blouse and earrings that matched.

The car that pulled up to her door wasn't the Mercedes. It was a Rolls-Royce.

The driver got out and came up the stone steps. He was wearing what passed on the Vineyard for a uniform—white trousers and a blue blazer over an open-necked white shirt. He removed his cap and knocked on the side of Victoria's open kitchen door.

"Mrs. Trumbull?" he inquired. He offered her his arm and helped her into the passenger seat, then closed the door with an indescribably expensive thunk and went around to the driver's side.

He indicated the wide sky overhead. "Will this be too much wind for you?"

"Certainly not." Victoria settled into the leather upholstery and lifted her nose to breathe in the soft air.

The driver, when asked, said his name was Tim, and that he was a graduate student at Tufts working for Ms. Roche this summer. He'd been with her two months now, and he liked working for her, he said. She appreciated beautiful cars.

They drove toward Edgartown, mostly in silence, past the airport on the left, Morning Glory Farm on the right, its parking lot full of people with bags and baskets of fresh produce, past the field where sunflowers would bloom in August, past Sweetened Water Pond. Her grandfather always stopped the horse-drawn wagon there so Dolly could drink. They turned onto Main Street. Late yellow and white roses twined around the picket fence in front of the jail.

Victoria waved regally to the summer people in shorts and knit shirts who gaped at the car and wondered who its celebrity passenger could be. They passed the brick courthouse and the grand Whaling Church, and turned left onto North Water Street.

Dorothy Roche lived in one of the big white whaling captains' houses, each one built to face the harbor. Since the street didn't run parallel to the harbor, each house was at an angle to the street.

Tim pulled into a brick-paved driveway, and Victoria waited for him to open her door. She took his arm and swept up the brick steps, through the door that was opened as though by magic, into a front hall that smelled of lavender furniture polish and camphor.

Dorothy Roche greeted her. This was a Dorothy Roche who differed from the woman Victoria had seen on Wednesday. True, she was short, her hair was that awful metallic auburn, and her face was tight and shiny, as though her skin had been pulled back to her ears. But she was dressed in polite beige slacks and matching blouse. She held out her hands, apparently genuinely pleased to see Victoria.

"I'm so honored to have you here." She released Victoria's hands. "We'll dine alfresco by the grape arbor. But first, I have a request."

Victoria cringed, wondering about this request. She followed her hostess into a room to the left, which turned out to be the library.

"I had an ulterior motive in inviting you here, Mrs. Trumbull," Dorothy said sweetly, looking up at Victoria. "I own a copy of every one of your poetry books, and have read and re-read them with such delight. If it's not an imposition, might you sign them for me?"

Victoria couldn't help but feel a surge of pleasure.

On a polished mahogany table at one side of the large room was a display of her books, the covers protectively encased in archival plastic. There was a fountain pen next to the stack of books, and a chair arranged so she could write comfortably. This attention made her warm a bit more toward her hostess. The Rolls-Royce had started the thaw.

Victoria signed all of the books with, "Best wishes, Victoria Trumbull," and glanced up at Dorothy, who had been watching her with a look of admiration.

"Thank you, Mrs. Trumbull. That means so much to me."

"You're welcome," said Victoria, getting to her feet.

The house was pleasantly cool. Victoria assumed the harbor breezes played in through the big front windows, but they were all closed.

"Central air," Dorothy explained. "It's the only way to protect my wonderful floors and woodwork. And the drapes, of course." The curtain fabric had the same floral design as the wallpaper. Dorothy continued, "I feel an obligation to honor the past of my house."

Victoria thought of her own lived-in house, ancient when Dorothy's was built. Victoria's house thrummed with the sense of earlier generations. There was a mark on a fine mahogany table where a long-ago baby had cut its teeth. The old pine kitchen table sported crescent-shaped hammer marks from a forgotten teenager's carpentry project. She cherished the initials carved on the wavy old window glass in the upstairs bedroom, probably with the diamond from a new engagement ring.

They moved from room to room. The library, front parlor, and formal dining room were all as some decorator must have supposed they looked a hundred fifty years ago. The kitchen, with its high-tech appliances, was an exception.

They went out a side door into the garden. A pond on one side teemed with goldfish. They strolled down a slate path to a grape arbor, where a table was set with linen and Limoges luncheon plates with a whimsical mixture of berries, butterflies, and green leaves.

Overhead, a hinged screen kept grapes safely at bay, protecting anyone seated in the arbor from falling grapes and the yellow jackets that dined on the fermented fruit.

An attractive young woman wheeled out a laden cart.

Victoria was about to say she had very little appetite, when she looked more closely at the cart and decided she was hungry after all.

Courtney, the young woman, served. Dorothy and Victoria talked about poetry, about Victoria's work as a police officer. Dorothy had done her homework, and Victoria felt slightly ashamed that she knew nothing about Dorothy. They spooned up a cold potato soup and talked, moved on to a seafood salad and talked, continued on to crackers, assorted cheeses, and fruit, and talked some more.

The luncheon over, Victoria looked at her watch. A large part of the afternoon had gone by. She'd meant to ask Dorothy how she'd learned about Orion's fiber-optics project and the Ditch Witch drill, and, in some indirect way, how she'd obtained the machine and how she was paying for it. Although, when she looked around Dorothy's house and grounds, money didn't seem to be a problem.

But it was time to go. "Thank you so much, Dorothy."

Tim handed her into the passenger seat and they backed out onto North Water Street and headed out of town through the maze of one-way streets.

On the way, Victoria realized that she had meant to ask Dorothy about Angelo Vulpone's death and find out if Dorothy had any insight on the murder, but the entire conversation had revolved around Victoria, and she, who was usually sensitive to the niceties of polite conversation, hadn't even been aware of the way Dorothy had allowed her to monopolize it. She hadn't gotten to know Dorothy at all, and Dorothy had found out much too much about her.

The luncheon had been pleasant, starting and ending with a ride in the Rolls-Royce. Victoria settled into her seat at the cookroom table and thought about it. The food had been prepared perfectly and served beautifully.

But something she couldn't quite put her finger on left her feeling uneasy. She lifted her typewriter onto the table and removed the cover. She would write a sestina, one that explored reality and perception.

Dorothy's had been a perfect setting. Off to one side a small waterfall trickled musically onto stones set just so around the small artificial pond. Even the shutters on the house were in perfect repair, the shingles a uniform silver. Victoria's had weathered unevenly as she'd replaced patches here and there.

She rolled a sheet of paper into her typewriter and typed the date. She lifted her hands from the keys.

What was it that bothered her so much? It had been a picture-perfect setting with a perfectly charming hostess presiding. The hostess even had copies of all of her poetry books, all of them protected in plastic archival covers.

That was the key, she suddenly realized. Her poetry books. They shouldn't be protected from anything. She'd have felt much better if her books had been thumbed through with dog-eared pages and an occasional penciled note.

Fingerprints and smears and stains meant use.

Victoria gazed out the window at a newly patched section on the side of her own house, yellow and raw, tucked in among the older silvery shingles. Neither she nor her house would ever be as perfectly put-together as Dorothy Roche and her house.

The more she thought about her shabby house and overgrown garden, her lawn with its dandelions and clover and plantain and who-knows-what wild grasses, the more uneasy she felt.

And then it all came together.

Her house was the way a house should be, lived in and loved. Dorothy's house and Dorothy, herself, were phony.

Nothing she'd seen today was real. The house and grounds and Dorothy were all artificial.

This revelation made Victoria feel much better. She turned back to her typewriter and began to write her poem about perception and reality.

On Monday, Orion drove to the airport to meet his partner, Casper Martin, and Finney Solomon, the financier.

The two had flown from New York to Boston and from there in a small plane to the Vineyard. Orion parked his car and strolled over to the gate, where he stood by the chain-link fence that separated people from airplanes, and waited for the Cape Air Cessna to arrive.

It was a little after twelve-thirty, a hot day. A breeze ruffled the grass on either side of the runway and flicked Orion's ponytail around his face.

The plane landed, and the ground crew, one small, dark-haired woman, wheeled a stairway up to the plane. Two passengers disembarked, one after the other, stooping to get through the low door. The first, a man in his forties with carroty red hair, looked around expectantly, spotted Orion, and waved. He turned to the man behind him and said something Orion was too far away to hear. The second passenger, a freshly scrubbed–looking young man, followed him down the stairs and across the tarmac to where Orion stood by the gate, now open.

The ground crew, the same dark-haired woman, wheeled the stairway off to one side, the door shut, and the Cessna taxied away.

"Casper." Orion stuck out his hand and the redhead grabbed it with his, clasping Orion's shoulder with his other hand.

"Good to see you, Orion." Casper let go and turned to the man with him. "Finney Solomon, meet Orion Nanopoulos."

"How're you doing?" The young man thrust out his hand and grinned, showing great white teeth. "Delighted to meet you, Orion."

"Same here." Orion shook hands and studied the man, who, in turn, was studying him with a half-smile. Finney Solomon was taller than Orion, six-one or -two, nice looking without being too much so. Light brown hair cut short, hazel eyes.

"I was shocked to hear about Angelo," said Finney Solomon. "A good friend. Great guy. His wife and kids are devastated. Any word on what happened?"

"Not many clues," said Orion. "Shot in the back of his head, left in the trench in pouring rain. Just a fluke they found his body before they filled in the trench."

"A real loss." Finney shook his head. He looked athletic, a swimmer or a runner or a bicyclist. Something like that. The guy oozed so much trustworthiness, Orion felt uncomfortable.

"We have a lot to talk about," said Orion.

"We sure do," said Finney. "Is there someplace we can talk in private?"

"My office. Do you have any luggage?"

"Just our briefcases and carry-ons," said Casper. "The pilot loaded them into a wing compartment."

"Yeah, that's how it works," said Orion. "The pilots are baggage handlers."

"At the check-in counter they asked how much we weigh," said Finney. "Gives you kind of an odd feeling."

"They do that, too," said Orion.

"There was a woman going on to Nantucket, you could tell she was deciding whether she could subtract a few pounds and still get there safely." Finney laughed.

"Have you been to the Vineyard before?" asked Orion.

"Couple of times, briefly. I took a sightseeing bus tour once. Saw what you could see in three hours. I've been hoping to come back and get to really know the Island."

Orion, who by this time had been on the Vineyard for three months, had walked its roads every day of those three months, and knew he'd seen only a minuscule portion.

The two men picked up their briefcases from the luggage cart and walked with Orion to his station wagon.

"You sit up front, Finney," said Casper. "Better view, and I've seen it before."

"I just can't get over Angelo's death," said Finney. "Things won't be the same without him."

On their way to his office, Orion pointed out to Finney the sights he thought might interest him. The state forest with its stark, silvery snags, the failed venture of a planned forest product, where a rare and hungry fungus growing north of its usual range met up with the red pines grown for telephone poles south of their range. He showed Finney the now-defunct golf driving range that had been a wind farm and before that had been a gravel pit.

Finney Solomon looked with interest. After Orion pointed out the commercial vineyard that had given up and sold out, Finney said, "You're not trying to discourage investors, are you?" He smiled as if to indicate he was only kidding. "I'd like to see that Ditch Witch unit of yours."

"It's on our way," said Orion, passing, without comment, the pick-your-own-berries place that was for sale.

CHAPTER 9

The Ditch Witch drill was parked behind Trip Barnes's Moving and Storage in an area of junked vehicles and construction debris. The rig glistened and sparkled in its surroundings, as out of place as a coat and tie at a clambake. Orion, Casper, and Finney Solomon walked over the rough ground to the rig.

This was Orion's first opportunity to examine the machine closely, and he walked around it, studying it with interest. To him, an engineer, it was perfection. The entire rig was not quite twenty feet long, about seven feet wide, and, on the trailer, about ten feet tall. Compact.

"So this is it!" said Finney. "A lot of action packed into a pretty small package." He smiled down at Orion.

"It'll do the job," Orion said, feeling irritated for some reason. On the way from the airport, he'd done most of the talking. Casper had said almost nothing. Now, Orion could look at Finney directly, see his face and find out who this man was. All he knew was the guy had been a friend of Angelo Vulpone's and claimed to have connections to venture capitalists.

Orion and Finney walked around to the front of the Ditch Witch drill and stood on either side of the trailer hitch, while Casper checked out the rear.

"You have an engineering background?" Orion asked.

"My background is strictly financial," said Finney. "I'm depending on you to tell me what I need to know."

"This is the first time I've been able to examine the rig," said Orion.

"Do I understand an investor bought the rig in exchange for a share in your company?"

"That's right," said Orion.

Finney scratched his chin. "Did he buy it outright?"

"She," said Orion. "Dorothy Roche. She worked out some kind of payment plan with a finance company." He noticed a fleeting skeptical look on Finney's face. "She's wealthy. Lives in Edgartown, expensive cars, expensive house. No question of money." Orion put his foot up on the trailer hitch to relieve his back. "According to her, financing it is the best route."

Finney looked thoughtful. "Sometimes it is. How did she get involved?"

"She apparently has contacts in New York who'd heard about our fiber-optic project. She attended a selectmen's meeting where I spoke and came up to me afterward."

"I'd like to meet her, talk to her. Would you mind calling and introducing me to her?"

"How long are you staying?"

"I'd planned on leaving in the morning, but I can rearrange my schedule to leave later."

"I'll set up a breakfast meeting for you. I'm sure that would work for Dorothy." Orion's back was beginning to ache, so he stepped over the trailer hitch and they moved around to the side of the machine.

"This rig even has cruise control," Orion said.

Finney grinned. "You'd drive this down the road using cruise control?"

"It's not that kind of cruise control," said Orion. "The operator can set the drilling speed and then just monitor the unit while it drills. Less fatigue and increased production."

He showed Finney where the drilling fluid was stored. He pointed out the mud pump. The operator's controls. The pipe rack. They walked partway along one side and Orion was about to point out the new tracks, not a speck of dirt on them, when Finney said, "Impressive. But I've seen enough. Time to talk business."

Casper was tagging along after the other two and spoke up for the first time since they'd stopped at Trip Barnes's. "Finney's right. We've got a lot to discuss."

Orion felt, somehow, as though his machine had been slighted. He'd begun to think of the Ditch Witch drill as his very own, and wanted to show Finney everything. Finney hadn't seen the anchoring system. Orion hadn't yet sat up in the operator's seat. He itched to climb aboard and examine the controls. He turned away and walked over to his station wagon, patted its side, and climbed in.

They drove from Trip Barnes's up Main Street and then over a block to Orion's office, and parked behind the two-story frame building. The three climbed the outside stairs and Orion unlocked the door, which opened onto a large, airy room with skylights and windows on two sides and a drafting table in the center.

Finney Solomon took off his sports coat and slung it over the back of a chair, opened up his briefcase on the drafting table, and the three sat down to business.

"How did you and Casper get connected?" Orion asked.

"Angelo Vulpone was my mentor," Finney said. All three paused for a moment of respect in Angelo's memory. "I knew about your project and after Angelo's death I contacted Casper here." He nodded at Casper, who was sitting to his left. "Angelo was a genius at spotting winners, and he was confident your project was a winner. He said his investment would pay off many times over, big time."

Casper nodded. Orion looked down at the table.

"That's why I'm interested," said Finney. "When Angelo decided to invest in a construction project, it was a platinum seal of approval."

Orion produced several thick folders from a locked file cabinet and spread maps and diagrams and copies of permits in front of Finney, lists of contacts, lists of town officials, lists of equipment owned, leased, or required, budgets, schedules . . .

Finney examined everything. Two hours later he said, "How much additional capital are you looking for?"

"Fourteen million," said Casper.

Finney took out his iPad and worked it with a stylus. "Shouldn't be a problem to raise that." He looked over and saw Orion's doubtful expression. "Believe it or not, it's easier to raise fourteen million than it is to raise fourteen thousand."

"How long will it take to raise?" asked Orion, fishing a notebook out of his shirt pocket.

"Guarantee you'll have money in hand in six months."

"What do you mean by guarantee?"

"You'll have your fourteen million dollars. Period." Finney's voice was flat.

"And your take is?" asked Orion, his pen poised over the notebook.

"A monthly retainer for six months, and two percent of the funds raised."

Orion worked some figures. "Two percent of fourteen million comes to two hundred and eighty thousand, right?"

"That's right."

"And what's your modest monthly retainer?"

"Five thousand plus expenses," said Finney.

Orion scribbled some more. "Thirty thousand." He looked up. "Three hundred thousand plus, for six months work? And I assume you've got other jobs going at the same time as well."

Finney didn't answer.

"That's a lot of money."

Finney grinned. "Fourteen million is a lot of money."

Casper had been silent during this exchange. Orion turned to him. "What do you think, Casper?"

Casper sat where a shaft of sunlight from the skylight struck his hair, turning it an almost fluorescent orange. He was doodling stars and dollar signs on the pad in front of him. "If he can raise fourteen million in six months, it's worth every penny of it."

"If he can't," Orion stood, "we're out thirty thousand plus expenses. Plus time. I want to see the contract."

Finney reached into his open briefcase. "Here it is. Look it over." He slid a green plastic binder, legal size, down the table to Orion.

Orion sat again and glanced at the contract. He turned to Finney. "You brought your CV with you, too, I assume."

Finney shuffled through papers in his briefcase and produced a document in a blue plastic binder. "There's a one-page resume on top. The rest is background."

Orion leafed through the slickly produced document. "We need to think about this for a while. How soon do you need an answer?"

"I'm in no hurry," said Finney. "As you surmised, I have other projects." He snapped his briefcase shut. "You're the ones under time pressure."

CHAPTER 10

Dorothy Roche invited Finney to breakfast the next morning at her house. She'd send her car, she said.

"The hotel is only a few blocks from here," Orion told Finney. "I'll drive you there."

Finney snapped his briefcase shut. "Appreciate it."

"Mind dropping me off on West Chop?" asked Casper.

"Sure. No trouble," Orion said.

"Aren't you staying at the hotel?" asked Finney.

"I'm visiting an old college friend." Casper gathered up the papers they'd spread out on the drafting table and Orion stowed them in the locked file cabinet.

After they settled Finney at the Mansion House, Orion continued up Main Street toward West Chop.

"What do you think?" asked Casper.

Orion grunted. "I'm not impressed."

"He claims he can raise fourteen million."

"So he claims." Orion slowed to let a woman with a dog cross the road in front of them. She waved her thanks.

"Any other suggestions, Orion?"

"You talked to the car dealer, Roger Paulson?"

"By phone. He's a cranky, stubborn guy." Casper gazed out at the glimpses of the harbor through trees. "As I told you, he offered to invest seven million, but he wants a share in the company."

"How did you learn about him?"

"He came to me," said Casper. "He heard about your presentation at the selectmen's meeting and checked up on you and the project."

The West Chop light came up on their right, its beam feeble in the bright afternoon. Orion slowed. "Where's the place you're staying?"

"On the dirt road straight ahead."

"Before we go any farther, let's talk money." Orion pulled over next to the lighthouse. "Can you get Roger Paulson to accept non-voting shares? I don't want any investor taking a percentage of the company."

"You gave Dorothy a percentage."

"That may have been a mistake. I wasn't thinking straight. I should have offered her shares of profits rather than a percentage of the company. But we need the drill and she's buying it."

Casper shrugged. "I'll meet with Paulson, try to talk him into accepting your proposal. But I'm in favor of giving Finney Solomon a chance. He's talking double what Paulson is willing to invest."

"I won't close my mind to Finney. But Paulson has a place on the Island, wants fast communications, and the system will make money for him. Use that approach."

When Orion came home that evening, Victoria was in the parlor reading. Orion sat in the rocker.

Victoria put her book aside. "How's your back?"

"Not bad. How are *you* feeling?"

"The Lyme disease medicine makes me a bit queasy, so I try not to think about how I feel."

"You're on doxycycline?"

"For twenty-one days. Seventeen more to go."

"I haven't talked to you since your luncheon with Dorothy on Saturday. How was it?"

"Lovely. We ate in the garden under the grape arbor."

"Have you changed your opinion about her?"

Victoria thought for a second. Orion was clearly taken with Dorothy, and she wasn't sure how candid she could be. "She was a perfect hostess. Everything was just so."

"But?" Orion rested his elbows on the chair arms and laced his hands together. "You're not answering." His pleasant expression took the sting out of the rebuke.

Victoria reached for the glass of water on the end table. "She's really not my sort, I'm afraid."

"Why so?"

"Everything seemed artificial, almost temporary. Even Dorothy, herself, was playing a role of some kind."

Orion leaned forward slightly. "For example?"

"Her driver and maid are summer help. The house isn't her own. I'm sure it's rented. It's like an expensive hotel. Yet Dorothy pointed out improvements as though they were hers. She's had cosmetic surgery on her face. It was all part of the artificiality."

"For some reason, I was under the impression you'd known her for some time," said Orion.

"Hardly. She was introduced to me at a gallery opening two months ago, and immediately after she was introduced, a more noteworthy celebrity on the other side of the room attracted her attention and she excused herself."

Orion's pleasant expression returned. "Perhaps the luncheon was an attempt to make amends."

"The luncheon was because she believes she can use me in some way. How, I don't know." Victoria picked up her glass and wiped off the condensation that had formed a wet circle on the end table. "If I were you, Orion, I'd be careful. She's not at all what she seems to be."

The next morning, Tim parked Dorothy's Mercedes in the loading zone across from the Mansion House. He crossed Main Street and went into the lobby where Finney Solomon was seated, legs crossed, reading *The Wall Street Journal*.

"Mr. Solomon?"

"Yes?" Finney looked up. "From Ms. Roche?"

"Yes, sir. I'm parked across the street."

Finney arose, folded the paper and tucked it under his arm, picked up his briefcase, then followed Tim out to the car. They drove in silence toward Edgartown. Finney worked his laptop; Tim concentrated on avoiding the early morning summer people who wandered down the middle of Beach Road, talking on their cell phones, figuring, apparently, that since they were on vacation, no harm could come to them.

Finney looked up briefly from his laptop. "What's holding things up?"

"Traffic, sir," said Tim, who knew better than to honk the horn.

They drove through Oak Bluffs, quiet this early in the day, and along State Beach, with banks of wild roses on their right and blanketing the low dunes to their left. Beyond the dunes, the waters of Nantucket Sound shaded from pale green to a rich ultramarine far out. Tim looked over to Finney to see if his passenger appreciated this stretch of the Island, but Finney was intent on his laptop. He stopped typing briefly to answer his cell phone, which had rung with a snatch of *Pachelbel's Canon*, said a short sentence that Tim couldn't make out, and snapped the phone shut.

"Reception is poor," he said to Tim. "Is this usual?"

"Yes, sir," said Tim.

Finney went back to work without further comment.

Tim slowed at the outskirts of Edgartown and inched along in a tangle of cars past the Triangle, past the Stop & Shop, and onto Edgartown's Main Street. Left onto North Water Street and, voilà! Home.

His home, Tim told himself, at least for the summer. In September, the Island would disappear into the mist like *Brigadoon*, not to appear again until next summer.

Dorothy met Finney at the door. She was older than Finney had expected, probably late fifties. Well-preserved, he told himself. Looking at the beautifully maintained house he decided he liked older women.

"I'm delighted you could come, Mr. Solomon," she said. "I see you've brought your laptop. We're going to have a wonderfully productive meeting. You do want coffee, don't you? Or would you prefer tea?"

"Coffee, please," said Finney. "Black."

"Just the way I like mine!" exclaimed Dorothy, clasping her hands under her small chin in a charmingly girlish way. "Courtney will

bring our coffee to us in the garden. And we can be private there."
She smiled up at him. "And breakfast whenever we want. I'm sure
you're hungry?"

He smiled at her. "Sounds like a plan, Ms. Roche."

She pointed to herself and looked up at him. "I'm Dorothy. May
I call you Finney?"

Finney looked down at her and nodded.

They went out the side door, past the fishpond, down the slate
path, and seated themselves under the grape arbor at the glass-
topped table. He set his laptop on the paving.

"Nice," said Finney, leaning back in his wrought-iron chair.
The filtered light coming through the grapevines gave Dorothy's
face an attractive softness. "Peaceful here. How long have you had
this place?"

"It's my summer house," said Dorothy. "Here's Courtney now
with our coffee. Thank you, darling. You can leave the coffeepot on
the table. And Courtney, dear, we'll have breakfast whenever you
have it ready."

"Yes, ma'am," said Courtney, and walked lightly down the garden path toward the house.

"Nice girl. Has she been with you long?"

" 'Woman,' dear." Dorothy patted his hand. "She's a student at
Brown. Why don't we get right down to business."

"Good idea," said Finney, taking a sip of the excellent coffee. "I
understand you're buying into Universal Fiber Optics, Nanopoulos's company."

"I'm acquiring the Ditch Witch horizontal directional drill as
my share in the company. Isn't that a wonderful name for such a
machine!"

Finney glanced up at the safely contained grapevines above
them. "Orion tells me you're financing the rig."

"According to my accountant, that was the most advantageous
way for me to do it."

"Sometimes it is," said Finney cautiously. "How did you hear
about the fiber-optics project?"

"A friend mentioned it. I wanted to learn more." She looked

over the rim of her delicate cup at Finney. "So I went to the selectmen's meeting and heard Orion speak and, well, I was impressed."

"Rightly so," said Finney. "He knows what he's talking about. My friend, Angelo Vulpone—"

Dorothy clasped her hands again. "I'm so sorry. I heard you were great friends. What a tragedy."

"A great loss. Angelo endorsed the fiber-optics project so strongly, we won't have any trouble raising the money we need." Finney took a sip of coffee. "Did you know Angelo, by any chance?"

Dorothy looked away. "Not well." She smiled. "How much do we need?"

Finney was caught off guard by the "we." "The project cost is estimated at twenty-four million. Nanopoulos has commitments for ten, so we need an additional fourteen."

Dorothy gazed at him with admiration. "And you'll be able to raise the whole fourteen million?"

"No problem," said Finney, a bit uncomfortable now that he'd mentioned numbers. But she was part of the company, he told himself, and he felt better thinking that. He lifted his coffee cup. "The best coffee I've tasted in a long time—Dorothy."

"I'm glad you like it, Finney." Dorothy leaned toward him. "You must have wonderful contacts. I'm sure they think highly of you to trust your judgment."

Finney shrugged and started to demur, but Dorothy exclaimed, "Here's our breakfast!"

Courtney was wheeling a serving cart down the path. As it approached, the aroma of bacon and sausage and cinnamon made Finney realize how hungry he was. He hadn't eaten much the day before. He'd been too tense about the meeting with Nanopoulos and his partner.

Courtney lifted the lid of a chafing dish. Two golden omelets oozing melted cheese and topped with chives, and a half-dozen little sausages, and another half-dozen rashers of bacon.

Courtney reached to a lower shelf on the cart where a magnum of champagne was chilling in an ice bucket. Holding the bottle in a linen napkin, she showed it to Finney.

"Good heavens!" said Finney, looking at the label.

Dorothy put her hand on his arm. "If you don't see what you like, just ask," she said, and she smiled.

Courtney eased the cork out of the bottle and poured the champagne into two flutes. "Will there be anything else, madam?"

"No, thank you, darling. That's lovely. We can take care of ourselves from now on." She glanced at Finney. "Can't we, Finney," she added after Courtney had wheeled the empty cart away.

"Perfection," said Finney, raising his glass.

Dorothy held her own glass up. "To the success of a perfect project."

After that, they talked in general terms about the project—general because Finney didn't understand the technology at all and Dorothy apparently didn't, either. Finney made a feeble offer to check some information on his laptop, but Dorothy insisted that could wait. They toasted each other with champagne and served themselves fresh strawberries with thick cream poured on top.

"You must try honey on the strawberries," said Dorothy. "It's Island honey produced by Island bees."

"Island bees," Finney murmured. "I'm allergic to bee stings." He nodded at the screening under the grapes above them. "I'm glad to see you keep your yellow jackets contained." He held up the honey jar to the morning sun.

"Local honey is supposed to alleviate allergies," said Dorothy. "Go ahead, try it."

"I don't think that applies to insect stings." He said again how much Angelo would have liked to be involved with the project and how Angelo thought the project was a winner. This theme was voiced repeatedly throughout breakfast and the magnum of champagne.

"When do you expect to pay off the rig?" asked Finney.

"I'm leaving that up to my accountant to work out," said Dorothy. "I think micromanaging is so unprofessional."

"Very wise," said Finney.

"What do you think of Orion?" asked Dorothy abruptly.

Following the sudden change in topic, Finney had to think a

moment. "I just met him yesterday, but he seems like a competent guy. Intelligent. Certainly knows his stuff. Why do you ask?"

Dorothy toyed with her spoon, making swirls of honey and cream on the bottom of her crystal bowl. "Did he seem, well, I don't like to say anything."

Finney leaned forward and put his hand on top of hers. "If it's anything to do with the company or the project, tell me." He realized how much he enjoyed the company of an older woman, especially a wealthy one.

"Not really," said Dorothy, blotting her mouth with a dainty linen napkin. "I shouldn't have said anything."

"Out with it," said Finney, feeling manly.

"It's nothing, really. I think I'm just overly sensitive, and it seemed to me he's been under a great deal of pressure lately. Please, forget I said anything."

"Of course," said Finney. "A project like this is bound to create a lot of pressure."

"That's right," said Dorothy. "He's such a sweet man; I hate to see the pressure getting to him. I'm sorry, Finney, darling. I shouldn't have said anything."

But when Finney was in the Mercedes on his way back to Vineyard Haven, he spent the time thinking how he could check up on Orion Nanopoulos's mental stability without being too obvious.

CHAPTER 11

While Finney and Dorothy were breakfasting alfresco, Victoria was cutting a bouquet of black-eyed Susans. She happened to look toward Sean's beehives and saw a pineapple-shaped black object hanging from the wild cherry tree. When she looked more closely, she realized the object was a mass of bees in constant motion. She went into the house as quickly as she could and called Sean.

"Your bees are swarming. They're hanging from a branch. What would you like me to do?"

"Nothing. I'll be there shortly."

"I'll keep an eye on them," said Victoria.

"Keep your distance," said Sean.

He arrived ten minutes later.

"Are they leaving the hive?" Victoria asked.

"These are."

"That's the end of the hive then?"

He shook his head. "That's how bee colonies reproduce. Half the hive takes off with the old queen and a new queen develops in the old hive."

"It's alarming to see that many bees in a swarm."

"They're not usually aggressive when they swarm. They've got other things on their minds."

He slipped his legs into the white suit and stuck his arms into the sleeves. "That's not to say they won't attack when they're swarming. They will if they're threatened."

He pulled the suit over his shoulders, zipped up the front, lifted the hood onto his head, and pulled the gauntlets over his hands.

Victoria watched as he held an open wooden box under the swarm and knocked it gently into the box as if it were some exotic fruit he was harvesting. He closed the lid.

Victoria applauded the performance from her seat.

"You've got eight hives now, Mrs. T. At least you will if the bees like their new home." Sean shed his suit and stowed his tools away. Finished, he found a towel in a corner of the truck, and came over to Victoria's bench. She moved over to make room for him.

"Hot work," he said, wiping his face with the towel. "Hear you came down with Lyme disease."

Victoria nodded.

"Join the gang." He held out his hand and she shook it. "How're you doing? That doxycycline make you nauseous?"

"A bit," said Victoria, and changed the subject. "Do you know Dorothy Roche?"

"Hah!" said Sean. "What makes you ask about her?"

"She invited me to lunch last Saturday."

"Lucky you." Sean rubbed his neck with the towel.

"Where does she get her money, do you know?"

He draped the towel around his shoulders. "As far as I know, she doesn't have two cents to rub together."

"She lives on North Water Street."

"Is she paying for it? Or some male friend."

"What do you know about her?" asked Victoria.

Sean reached down, pulled up a blade of grass, and stuck the end in his mouth. "First saw her maybe three months ago at a select-men's meeting."

"Where Orion spoke?"

"She was in the audience acting like some big deal. Talked to him after and they went off together."

"She's investing in his company."

"Yeah? Has he seen the money?"

"She's buying a drill rig as a share in the company."

"She is, hey?" Sean chewed on his grass stem, then tossed it aside. "Has Orion seen a purchase contract?"

74

"Parnell Alsop drew up a contract."

"Him!" Sean spit out a strand of chewed grass, stood up, and stretched. "Gotta go, Victoria. Mrs. Wingfield's got bees in her barn."

"And honey?"

He nodded. "Any progress on the murder investigation?"

Victoria scowled. "I have no idea. They're not sharing information with us." She looked up at him. "Can you save the honey?"

"By the time I get it out of there, if I can melt the wax without burning down her barn, it'll be full of debris. Worthless." He got into his truck, rolled down the window, lifted a hand, and took off.

Finney Solomon stopped by Orion's office after his breakfast with Dorothy Roche. He plopped into the chair he'd occupied the day before and set his briefcase down.

"How was your breakfast?" Orion asked.

"Impressive woman." His speech was only slightly slurred. "Knows her stuff. Excellent taste in champagne." He touched his briefcase with deliberate care. "Whole magnum."

Orion nodded. "What time's your flight?"

Finney looked at his watch carefully. "Three o'clock. Not quite two now. I've checked out of the hotel."

"We'll leave for the airport in a few minutes. Any last-minute odds and ends we need to tie up?"

Finney said, "She's an important member of your team."

Orion nodded.

"You signed the contract?" Finney asked.

"Casper signed it and left it for me to look over. I haven't signed yet."

"No hurry, far as I'm concerned," said Finney, brushing an imaginary crumb off his trousers. "Take your time. I've got a few items to look into."

"Do you need any other information from me?"

"I'm all set," said Finney, getting to his feet.

On the way to the airport, Finney was understandably quiet, and Orion didn't attempt to converse with him.

They pulled into a parking place at the airport, went into the waiting room, and Finney checked in at the Cape Air counter. "A hundred and ninety-seven pounds," he informed the gray-haired woman at the counter before she asked. "Gained two pounds at breakfast this morning."

She smiled and noted his weight.

"I'll be in touch," he said to Orion. "Send me the signed contract so I can get to work." They shook hands. Finney went through the security check, the Cessna taxied up to the gate, and Orion went out the side door of the airport to where he'd parked. He climbed in and sat for a while, waiting until the Cape Air flight left.

He felt vaguely troubled.

Finney had been distant, strange, and it seemed to be something other than the half-magnum of champagne he'd consumed a couple of hours earlier. He'd have to discuss Finney with Dorothy, next time he met with her.

He backed out of the parking space and headed to the office.

Finney felt a bit queasy on the short flight to Boston. He leaned his face against the cool glass of the Cessna's window and shut his eyes. That was a memorable breakfast with Dorothy. What a woman! An experienced woman. A wealthy woman. Finney sighed.

In Boston he made his way to the departure gate. After he'd boarded, he settled into a window seat where he could again rest his face on the cool glass.

Finney Solomon was new at the venture capital game. He had a two-year degree in business from a community college and had interned at a couple of places during that time, a bank and a mortgage firm. Years ago his father had introduced him to the great Angelo Vulpone. He'd been just a little kid at the time and was awed by the powerful man. Once he decided on a career like Vulpone's, he tried unsuccessfully to meet with him, and instead, kept an Angelo Vulpone scrapbook of articles about him. Through the articles, Vulpone became Finney's mentor, at least according to Finney.

Finding financing for Universal Fiber Optics would be a piece of cake, according to Angelo, quoted in a recent business column. High-tech communications was a sure thing, didn't matter what the economy was doing. The only trick to it, Angelo had said, was making sure the right person was managing the project. You needed a man with a combination of brains, expertise, courage, and personality. Plus a degree of cold-bloodedness, a focus on the project so intense that not much else mattered. The columnist had ended by writing that in Orion Nanopoulos, Angelo believed he'd found the right person.

Finney knew nothing about the technology, nor did he care. Orion knew what he was doing. His plan made sense. He'd convinced Angelo that an optical-fiber network for the Island was not just for better cell phone reception, but so emergencies could be dealt with at the speed of light.

But now that he'd breakfasted with Dorothy, he sensed her reservation about Orion. She'd assured him she hadn't meant to say anything negative, and of course, she hadn't. One of his strengths, Finney believed, was his sensitivity to nuances. He'd check around, see what other Islanders thought. He wasn't about to make a decision involving fourteen million based only on that whiff of concern of Dorothy's. The trouble was, he didn't know any Islanders.

When he got back to his apartment in Union City, he called Dorothy. He thanked her again for the delightful respite from his heavy schedule, told her again what a great asset she was to the project. He said, "I'm doing a routine check of Nanopoulos. Can you suggest a couple of Island people I might talk to?"

"Of course, Finney, dear," said Dorothy. "Hold on a minute while I get my address book."

She was back on the phone shortly. "Here are three people who know him well. Denny Rhodes, a West Tisbury selectman; Parnell Alsop, my attorney; and Daniel Pease, the head of the Department of Public Works." She gave him the phone numbers. "I'm sure they'll help you. Call me if you need anything else, Finney, dear."

Finney noted the names and numbers on his yellow legal pad.

CHAPTER 12

The night had turned cool, so Victoria lighted a fire in the parlor. Orion came home to a comforting blaze.

"Would you care for a glass of wine?" he asked.

Victoria set her book down. "Alcohol apparently slows the effects of the doxycycline. I'm not supposed to drink."

"Cranberry juice, then." He turned toward the kitchen.

"Actually, I don't think a small glass will hurt."

Orion returned with two wineglasses and a bottle of Bug Light Red. Victoria told him about the bee swarm and Orion shuddered, almost spilling the wine.

"According to the beekeeper, bees aren't terribly aggressive when they're swarming."

"All the same, I'll keep my distance," said Orion, handing her a glass, half-full.

"Just to be safe, where do you keep your antidote?"

"In my car," said Orion. "An EpiPen. You twist off the cap and jab the cylinder at your thigh."

"Through clothing?"

"It's designed to be used quickly," said Orion.

Victoria said, "I suppose I should have an EpiPen in case a guest is allergic to bees and gets stung."

"I'll get one for you. Once you use it, you're to call nine-one-one." He dropped a log onto the fire, sending up a shower of sparks, and sat down.

"How did yesterday's meeting with the venture capitalist go?" asked Victoria.

"I don't know." Orion set his glass on the small table next to him. "Finney Solomon is young, which isn't necessarily a drawback. But he has nothing to offer. Simply a promise that he'll come up with fourteen million within six months. He expects us to pay a retainer."

"You haven't signed anything yet, have you?"

"Not yet. By the way, he had breakfast with your friend this morning."

"Dorothy?"

Orion nodded.

"What did he have to say about her?"

"Not a great deal," said Orion. "They finished off a magnum of champagne . . ."

"A magnum!" exclaimed Victoria. "That's an entire bottle each. Good heavens!"

"La Grande Dame, according to Finney. That much he told me before he clammed up. I took him to the airport and he didn't say a word the whole way."

"Small wonder," said Victoria. "Where does Dorothy get that kind of money?"

"Family money, I assume," said Orion.

"She's not from old money. I can tell."

"I don't care where the money comes from, Victoria. She's buying the Ditch Witch drill. That's a fact."

"When will you start using it?" She wasn't about to tell him the beekeeper's opinion of Dorothy Roche's wealth.

"Friday," Orion said. "Three days from now."

"It's going to rain," said Victoria.

The next morning, Victoria walked slowly to the police station, each step an effort. She hoped it was the doxycycline and not advancing age. She refused to think about it. Instead, she thought about Dorothy Roche deluding Orion and probably that wealthy Finney Solomon as well.

What on earth was the matter with men that they could be so easily misled by a false smile and a dab of perfume?

Then it occurred to her. Perfume was nothing but a pheromone, a chemical that caused behavioral changes in animals. Including men.

Dorothy was daubing herself with pheromones, a queen bee attracting drones for a deadly mating flight. Victoria stabbed her lilac-wood stick into an anthill without thinking, and the ants hustled to mend the damage. She moved on. Orion was not behaving logically. But how could he behave logically if he was chemically bewitched?

She reached the police station, not even aware of the cars that had passed on the Edgartown Road, or the lowering sky. When the ducks dozing under the rosebush got to their feet and gathered around her, she snapped out of her reverie. She'd brought stale bread, as usual, and shook it out of the paper bag onto the grass, then folded up the bag and tucked it into her pocket. She climbed the steps to the station house, entered, and dropped into the armchair in front of Casey's desk.

"Morning, Victoria. How are you feeling?"

"All right," said Victoria without enthusiasm. "Can you look up the background of someone for me?"

Casey studied her. "Who do you need looked up?"

"Dorothy Roche."

"Oh, her." Casey swiveled to face her computer and entered keystrokes. "What do you need specifically?"

"Is she as wealthy as she claims? If so, where does she get her money?" Victoria put both hands on the top of her stick. "Orion said she'd established several businesses. Can you find information on those?"

Casey concentrated on the computer for a few minutes. "Interesting." She angled the screen so Victoria could see. "Here's a picture of Dorothy Roche. A television actress."

"That's not her," said Victoria, examining the image of the pretty, dark-haired teenager on the screen.

"Didn't think so," said Casey.

"Are there other Dorothy Roches listed?"

Casey typed in more keystrokes. "A few long gone."

"May I use your phone?"

Casey pushed the instrument and the directory across the desk. Victoria found the number for her Realtor friend.

"Hi, Mrs. Trumbull. How can I help you?"

"Another favor to ask. Dorothy Roche was the reference for Tris Waverley, who's renting that house I asked about. She lives on North Water Street. Does she own the house?"

"Hold on."

Victoria heard the sound of computer keys. "She's renting it. Came in May, signed a lease to mid-September."

"Do you know who she used as a reference?"

"Bruce Vulpone, her TV producer. I didn't realize she's a TV actress."

"Can you tell how she's paying her bills?"

More clicking of keys. "Everything's being charged to the studio's production account. The house, car rental, servants, everything. What a life! Anything else?"

"That's it for now. Thank you."

"Let me know if you need anything more."

Victoria pushed the phone back across the desk. "Could you look up another person for me, a Bruce Vulpone?"

"Any relation to the murdered man?" asked Casey.

"I don't know."

Casey worked with her computer. "A lot of Bruce Vulpones. Can you narrow it down?"

"New Jersey or New York, a television producer."

"Bingo!" said Casey. "Bruce Vulpone, owner of Triple V Cable TV. Vulpone's Vampire Venture."

"Is he related to Angelo?"

Casey shrugged. "An awful lot of Vulpones in New Jersey. I'll see if I can find a connection between them, but I can't spend any more time on this today."

That same morning, Finney Solomon, holding a dish towel–wrapped plastic bag of crushed ice against his forehead, sat down to call the three people Dorothy Roche had suggested as references. The first call he made was to the head of Public Works, Daniel Pease.

Engines chugged and whined in the background before a voice came on the line. "Dan'l Pease speaking."

"Mr. Pease, this is Finney Solomon. I'm a potential investor in Orion Nanopoulos's fiber-optics company. I'm calling a few people who've worked with him, who know him, to find out what they think of him. That kind of thing."

Someone shouted above the engine noise. Finney couldn't make out the words.

"Yeah?" said Dan'l.

"You worked with Orion. What's your impression?"

"He's okay," said Dan'l.

"A good manager?"

"He's fine."

The engine noise got louder and it was difficult for Finney to hear. "He work well with his employees?"

"Yup."

"They like him?"

"Yup."

"Any problems with him?"

"Look, Mr.—I didn't get your name. It looks like it's about to rain and I'm right in the middle of something and can't talk to you now. Sorry." And Dan'l disconnected.

Finney got up and went into his kitchenette, drained the meltwater out of the plastic bag, wrapped it back in the dish towel, sat down again at the table he used for a work space, and reapplied the ice pack to his forehead.

He wrote "Daniel Pease" at the top of his yellow pad and under that noted, "Questioned DP about problems with ON, declined to answer."

Next he called Denny Rhodes, West Tisbury selectman.

"Orion Nanopoulos? He's a nutcase," said Denny.

Finney held the ice pack and phone awkwardly between his left hand and shoulder and wrote with his right.

"Anyone who thinks he can get consensus from the six towns on this Island has got to be out of his mind."

Finney scribbled.

Denny Rhodes went on. "Six towns. Eighteen selectmen, except Oak Bluffs has five, so that's twenty, six highway departments, six conservation commissions, six planning boards, six zoning boards, six town administrators. Every town's got a police department, fire department, library, and school. Every last damn town official is in a power struggle to be top frog in this small pond. You think Nanopoulos is sane? If he's sane now, he won't be in six weeks, working with the clowns on this Island. Guaranteed."

Denny's voice got louder. Finney moved the receiver away from his ear, and the ice pack slipped and fell on the floor. He continued to write as fast as he could.

"Furthermore," said Denny without waiting for a comment from Finney, not even waiting for an assurance that Finney was still on the line, "not one of them has any technical background, except Tim Osmond, the shellfish warden, who has a master's degree in marine biology. Not engineering. The shellfish warden is about the only town official Nanopoulos doesn't have to deal with. They'll probably insist that he check with the six fence viewers."

Finney interrupted. "Fence viewers?"

"Damn right. Twelve. Two in each town, all elected. Not one has a technical background. It's all liberal arts, yoga, horses, and house painting. Not one has any idea what fiber optics is. To them, you're talking coconut husks. You think he's going to get to stage one? He's outta his mind."

"Fence viewers," said Finney weakly. "Thanks."

"Anytime," said Denny. "Glad to help."

Finney wrote "out of his mind," and underlined it three times. As he disconnected, water dripped from his face onto his yellow pad. He brushed the melted ice off with his forearm, smearing the ink. "Damn!" he muttered.

CHAPTER 13

Orion was working on company finances when Casper arrived the next morning. "How's your college buddy?"

"He's got a nice place overlooking Vineyard Sound." Casper settled onto one of the chairs by the drafting table. "Once we sobered up after an evening of reminiscing about the good old days we found we had nothing in common."

Orion pulled up the chair by the window and sat down. "That's the way it goes," he said. "Are you planning on leaving the Island today?"

"I have an appointment to meet with Roger Paulson later. Any suggestions?"

"I don't want to give away a voting share in the company. I'm adamant about that."

Casper got up and headed for the door. "I'll let you know how the meeting goes."

Roger Paulson lived on Chappaquiddick in a new house overlooking Edgartown Harbor. Casper drove onto the ferry for the minute-and-a-half ride. Now a separate island, Chappaquiddick had been connected to Martha's Vineyard by a narrow barrier bar until the ocean broke through the bar, forming a channel with wicked tidal currents. On the other side he drove along a maze of sand roads until he came to a white fence that surrounded Paulson's property. A discreet sign on a gate requested that he press a button to gain admittance, which he did. A buzzer sounded, the gate swung open, and Casper drove the quarter-mile to the huge house with its glittering windows. He pulled into a parking area next to a Lexus, got out with his attaché case, and looked up at the house. A grand staircase led up a half-flight to the ground floor, where a dark-haired man stood, wearing khaki slacks and a yellow knit shirt.

"Come on up," the man said. "Martin, right?"

"Yes, sir," said Casper, mounting the stairs.

They shook hands, firm grips. Roger Paulson was shorter than Casper, who wasn't tall. Paulson was in his mid-fifties and trim, with dead black hair and clear blue eyes that studied Casper.

"Come in. Can I fix you a drink?"

"No, thanks," said Casper, entering into a foyer that looked like the lobby of an expensive hotel.

Paulson led him into a vast kitchen off the foyer. "We can sit here at the kitchen table. Much more relaxed."

Casper noticed the commercial stove, the stainless-steel refrigerators. "Nice kitchen."

"I'm a great cook, you know."

"No, sir. I didn't know that, Mr. Paulson."

"Call me Roger," Paulson said, sitting at the head of a large table inlaid with intricate patterns of dark wood. "We're not formal. I suppose you were called Red."

"Yes, sir." said Casper. "In elementary school. Always hated it." He took the chair at right angles to Paulson and set his attaché case on the floor next to him.

"Kids called me Shorty. Same kids wouldn't dare, now."

"Kids can be mean," said Casper.

Paulson sat forward. "You have something to show me."

Casper brought out the prospectus he and Orion had worked on and handed it over.

Paulson slipped on reading glasses and turned pages, examining each one. The scope of the project, personnel, schedule, permits required and obtained, the budget. He went over budget items one by one without saying a word.

Casper, seated stiffly at first, relaxed slightly. From the kitchen he could see a large dining room with a banquet table. An archway at the end of the dining room led into what was probably a vast living room. Floor-to-ceiling windows overlooked the harbor, and Casper could see powerboats kicking up curling wakes.

Paulson looked up from his study of the budget. "They're not supposed to do that, you know."

"Sir?"

"No wakes in the harbor. Kids. Gotta go fast, get wherever they're going as fast as they can." Paulson put his glasses back on and continued to read. At last he set down the prospectus and pushed it to one side.

"What do you want from me? When we talked earlier on the phone, we mentioned seven million."

"Yes, sir. The total amount of financing we need is twenty-four million." Casper cleared his throat. He hated asking for money. "We hope you're still interested in investing the seven million we talked about earlier."

Paulson leaned back in his chair and twirled his glasses. "As I recall, and correct me if I'm wrong, we discussed my investing seven million in exchange for twenty-five percent . . ." He held up a hand as Casper started to correct him. "Don't interrupt me. You negotiated that percentage down to twenty percent. Am I right?"

"Yes, sir."

"You had to discuss this with your partner, of course. I assume you're back with a counteroffer? Stop calling me 'sir,' by the way."

"Right," said Casper. "Mr. Nanopoulos refuses to give away a voting block in the company."

Paulson laughed. "Hardly giving away. Seven million?"

"You would be getting a guaranteed return on investment," said Casper, warming to his talk. "Fiber-optic cable will carry information to and from your dealers and distributors at the speed of light."

"I know what it can do," said Paulson. "What makes you so sure your company is the right one?"

This seemed, to Casper, like the right time to bring up Angelo. "You may have heard of Angelo Vulpone."

Paulson narrowed his eyes. "Yes, I've heard of Angelo Vulpone. He's dead now and good riddance. My wife committed suicide because of Angelo Vulpone."

"I'm sorry," said Casper, stricken. "My God."

"Angelo Vulpone," repeated Paulson. "Before he was exterminated I understand he endorsed your project. He put it in writing?"

Casper said nothing.

Paulson stood up. "Leave the prospectus with me. I'll look it over again. But let me tell you," he stabbed a finger at Casper, "if I put seven million into your company, I'll want a voting share. Twenty-five percent."

Casper stood.

"That's firm." Paulson set his glasses on the table and held out his hand. "Nice to meet you, Red."

Casper, still upset over the "Red" dig and even more upset by Paulson's wife's suicide, called Orion on his cell phone but got no signal. He then drove to the office.

Orion looked up as Casper came through the door. "Do I dare ask how it went?"

"Arrogant bastard. He's back to demanding twenty-five percent of the company and voting shares."

"You told him he was the one who'd benefit?"

"I did."

"Well, Casper, you tried."

Casper tossed his attaché case onto a chair. "I should've called him 'Shorty.'"

"Say what?"

"I'm taking the five o'clock flight."

"You tell him Angelo Vulpone planned to invest?"

Casper nodded. "Paulson's wife committed suicide. He claims Angelo Vulpone was responsible. I didn't ask why."

"No, of course not."

Casper picked up his attaché case and left. His footsteps faded away down the outside stairs.

Early on Friday morning, the inaugural day for the Ditch Witch drill, Orion left Victoria's early. The rain that had been threatening for a couple of days had held off. But now, as Victoria had predicted, the sky darkened and the smell of rain was in the air. By the time he was halfway to Vineyard Haven, drops were spattering his windshield. He told himself it wouldn't make much difference. The directional drill was a lot less messy than a trenching excavator. He straightened his back and shuddered as he thought of carrying the corpse of Angelo Vulpone through that sea of mud.

He stopped at the ArtCliff Diner for breakfast before heading to the ball field. At the edge of the field he parked and slipped on his foul-weather gear.

The drill was on its trailer, two-thirds of the way across the field, where the route of the fiber-optic cable diverged from the town's drainage trench. Orion hiked along the line of red sandy clay that filled the trench. Fine misty rain beaded up on his jacket.

Several men, including Dan'l Pease, stood around the drilling unit.

Dan'l nodded to him. "How's it going?"

"We'll see," said Orion.

"Got a call Wednesday from some guy asking about you."

"Who was it?"

"Didn't get his name. Cell phone reception is lousy here, as you know."

"What was he after?"

"He was fishing around, trying to determine whether you were crazy or not. Damn near told him you were, but I hung up on him instead."

Orion flipped his jacket hood over his head. The rain was coming down in earnest. "Was it Finney Solomon?"

"Never caught the name. I'd like to see how that drill rig of yours works out."

"We'll start her up any minute, now. In this sandy soil, we should be able to drill a half-mile today."

"Can't hardly beat that," said Dan'l. "Watch out for that pressurized sewage pipe somewhere around where you'll be drilling." He waved an arm toward a section of the field not far from the rig.

"No problem," said Orion. "My foreman, Mike, is operating the rig. I checked the installation maps and charts. We're well clear of its location."

"Wouldn't trust those maps."

"I never do. That's why we're drilling fifty feet from where the line's supposed to be, and three feet below it."

"That ought to clear it all right. The maps aren't that far off." Dan'l turned his back on the rain and wiped a hand across his face. "At least, not usually."

When the rain began, Victoria was at the police station. She hung her raincoat on a hook next to Casey's yellow foul-weather jacket.

"Orion is using the drilling machine for the first time today," Victoria said, sitting in her usual chair.

"If it weren't so wet today, I'd watch," said Casey.

"There'll be other times, I'm sure." Victoria leaned forward. "Any news on the Vulpone investigation? It's been almost two weeks."

"I haven't heard anything. My best guess is the state guys called in the FBI, since it may be a mob killing."

"I'm sure they're wrong," Victoria said. "The murder is more likely to be related to Orion's cable project. He's dealing with money and power-hungry people, and either one is cause for murder."

Casey shrugged. "Money and power fits the mob." She got up from her desk. "We need to check out another of Mrs. Sommerville's complaints." Casey took down Victoria's raincoat and her own oilskin. "This time it's about loud music at the Old Ag Hall."

"What loud music?"

"The contra dance group."

"Fiddle and harmonica? Heavens! She's just lonely."

"We'll talk to her then. After that we can make our rounds and I'll get you home in time for lunch."

Casey shrugged into her own musty smelling jacket. WEST TISBURY POLICE was stamped on the back in large black letters. Victoria put on her own coat, picked up her lilac-wood stick, and followed Casey to the door.

"I've never known such a rainy July," said Casey, peering out at the water pouring off the roof.

"It's good for the garden," said Victoria.

"How about your bees?"

"It's not good for them, according to Sean, the beekeeper. They have to contend with mildew."

"Don't we all," said Casey, examining a spotty patch on the sleeve of her jacket.

In his apartment in Union City, Finney Solomon stood up and stretched. He'd been working the phones for the past couple of days with zero success. The venture capital firms he'd contacted wanted a signed contract from Orion before they'd even talk to him, and they wanted to know more about Finney's credentials than he cared to tell them. Orion *must* sign that contract.

He had to get some air. It was raining on Martha's Vineyard. They could use rain here in Jersey. His stuffy apartment was over a photographer's studio and consisted of two rooms with only one window. The window opened onto an air shaft shared by a burlesque theater's fire door. The air shaft began, or ended, in a roof a few feet below the windows. On warm days like today the roof sent up a scent of hot tar, stale cigarette smoke, and urine.

He closed the window to shut out the stench, gathered up the *Wall Street Journal* he'd picked up at the Mansion House, and descended the flight of wooden stairs that led to the sidewalk. Heat rose from the concrete, distorting its rough surface. He turned left, avoiding eye contact with a group of teenage boys in tank tops and baggy pants hanging out in front of the theater, and headed to the overlook, five blocks away. It was only three o'clock, but early Friday commuting traffic streamed past with the dissonant music of tires, brakes, horns, stereos, warbling fan belts, screeching metal . . .

He waited at a corner for the light to change. When it did, he started across. A horn blared and he leaped out of the way. An angry voice shouted, "Watch where you're going, buddy!" He shook the folded-up *Journal* at the disappearing car and shouted back, "I had the right of way, asshole!"

Was it just Tuesday he'd been reading this same copy of *The Wall Street Journal* in a chauffeured Mercedes that floated him along polite roads to that garden of wealth?

He reached the overlook, angry and hot and sweaty and dusty and reeking of exhaust fumes. His head pounded with a combination of the traffic he'd escaped from and the rejections from the firms whose money had seemed so promising, so close, so easy to access.

He found an unoccupied bench, tore out an inside page from the *Journal,* and used it to wipe the seat before he sat down. Below him the Hudson River bore every sort of vessel, from container ships and ferries to small sailboats. Across the river the golden city shimmered in the afternoon heat haze, a magical place of vast sums of money. One of these days that's where his office would be, directly opposite where he now sat overlooking the river. Money. He would buy a trophy house; no, he'd *build* a trophy house on Martha's Vineyard. Money, that's all it took. He would have that money. Angelo Vulpone had taught him well.

As the pounding in his head subsided, he thought about his future with Universal Fiber Optics. In his imagination he took over the company, that easy producer of money. He visualized taking charge, easing Orion out of the picture. Orion might have more than a problem with stress. The head of Public Works had evaded his question. And Denny Rhodes had outright said that Orion was out of his mind. A nutcase. If Orion was crazy, should he be running the company?

Fourteen million dollars, that was Finney's goal. He couldn't gamble on a nutcase. This was his first big one. Fourteen million. A sure thing, Angelo had told that reporter. With Angelo's endorsement the money was there. Just needed a reliable guy heading the project.

Or a reliable woman?

Finney brightened. In his mind, he saw himself running the project. If Dorothy were the titular head of UFO, that would be a doubly sure thing. A female CEO, one with her own money, heading a multimillion-dollar project.

Yes! Finney thrust a fist into the air, startling a nearby pigeon into flight. The pigeon had been strutting toward and away from him for several minutes, easing closer and closer to a possible food source.

Dorothy wouldn't need technical know-how. He took out his pen and jotted some notes on the margin of the *Journal*. He'd call that lawyer, the last of the three references Dorothy had suggested, simply a formality, find out what he thought of Orion's mental health. Then he'd call Dorothy, broach the subject of her taking over Universal Fiber Optics. In his mind, Orion was already out of the picture. Better to have all the pieces in place, the paperwork done before breaking the news to Orion. No telling how an unstable guy would react to a woman taking over his company.

He looked across the Hudson to Manhattan, golden and sparkling, and decided not to wait any longer. Investors would not put money into a project run by a nutcase.

Finney kept thinking about Dorothy Roche as CEO of Universal Fiber Optics. What a fine woman. An older woman. An intelligent woman. A rich one. That was key. Money.

He got up from the bench and started walking back to his rooms over the photography studio. How long before he could afford a house like Dorothy's? Six months? A year? Cars, chauffeur, maid. No cockroaches.

Friday's traffic had thinned out while he was at the overlook. Couples out for an evening drive along the Palisades had replaced the frenetic drivers racing toward the suburbs and the Jersey Shore.

Dorothy Roche as CEO, Finney Solomon as financial wizard. Finney could see the fiber-optics project take off under his management. Angelo was quoted as calling it a gold mine, and Angelo was infallible when it came to money.

CHAPTER 14

On their way to pacify Mrs. Sommerville, Victoria brought up Dorothy Roche again. "She's power hungry and she's not who she claims to be."

Casey said nothing. She eased around a farm truck loaded with baled hay.

"I'm sure she knew Angelo," Victoria continued. "Angelo's brother, Bruce, is paying all her bills."

"That doesn't mean she knew his brother." Casey crossed over Mill Brook on the narrow bridge and turned left onto North Road. "We're almost at Mrs. Summerville's, Victoria."

"I'll just bet she knew Angelo," said Victoria.

Orion hadn't planned to stay on the site, but he wanted to watch the drill at work, to run it, in fact. He drove the unit off the trailer and tested the various operations. Sweet. Reluctantly, he turned the controls over to Mike Collins, his foreman, who'd waited, not too patiently, for his turn. Barring any unforeseen accidents, underground fiber would be installed throughout Tisbury in six months.

Off and on throughout the day, Orion thought about Victoria and her Lyme disease, and as the afternoon wore on, he became increasingly worried about her. Around four, he called out to Mike, "I need to get home. Go ahead and shut everything down at five. Looks like we're clear of that sewer line now." He shouted to his crew above the sound of the machine. "Good job, guys. Have a great weekend. See you Monday."

On his way home, he picked up a container of quahog chowder and grabbed a bag of oyster crackers, enough for Victoria, Elizabeth, and himself, and propped the container upright among the tools on the floor of his car.

Victoria was in the cookroom, scribbling a poem on the back of an envelope, her typewriter pushed to one side.

"How are you feeling?" Orion asked.

She looked up with a smile. "Do I smell chowder?"

"You do."

"Then I'm feeling much better, thank you."

Orion set the container on the kitchen counter.

"Elizabeth is working the late shift. She won't get home until after midnight." Victoria started to get up.

"Sit still," said Orion. "How was your day?"

"Mrs. Sommerville thinks up complaints so we'll call on her." Victoria snapped the cover onto her typewriter and set it on the floor. "How was the Ditch Witch unit's first day?"

"Good," said Orion. "No problems so far, knock on . . ." He reached into his pocket and brought out his cell phone. "Nano-poulos here." A long pause. "I'll be there in fifteen minutes." He closed the phone and put it back in his pocket, frowning. "Guess I spoke too soon."

"A problem?"

"You might call it that. Ten minutes of five on a rainy Friday night, we hit a sewer line, a plastic line carrying raw sewage under pressure."

"Ouch!" said Victoria.

" 'Ouch' is right. The line was three feet below where it was supposed to be and more than fifty feet south of where it was supposed to be and we drilled right through it. What are the chances of that happening?" He grabbed his still-wet foul-weather gear from the rack in the entry. "Guess you'll have to eat alone."

"You'll want a shower when you get home," said Victoria. "I'll put out fresh towels."

Orion arrived home shortly before two in the morning. Victoria was asleep in her chair, her mouth open, snoring gently. Orion hated to wake her. He dropped his wet and smelly clothes into the washing machine, sure she would forgive him for using it this one time, and took a long, hot, welcome shower. He wrapped himself in one of her thick towels, climbed up to his attic room, where he tugged on a clean shirt and sweatpants, and came down to put his chowder in the microwave to heat.

In the parlor he gazed down at Victoria, touched that she'd waited up for him. Softly, he asked, "A cup of hot cocoa, Victoria?"

She awoke with a start, smacked her lips, and brushed her hand over her mouth. "What time is it?"

"Almost two in the morning."

"I didn't mean to fall asleep. I want to hear how you made out with the sewer pipe." She smoothed her corduroys over her knees. "Hot cocoa would be nice."

"The sewer pipe is taken care of. I'll tell you all about it." The microwave beeped. "My chowder's ready."

"I'm afraid there's not much left."

"There's plenty."

Victoria yawned, got up stiffly, and took a few steps to limber up. The fire she'd lighted earlier had died down to glowing coals. She thought about leaving it for the night, then decided Orion might like the comfort of a fire. She wadded up newspaper, added kindling and a few small logs, and waited until it relit itself with a swirl of smoke and a snap of flame. By the time Orion returned, the fire was blazing cheerfully.

"Just what I needed." He handed her the cocoa, then stood with his back to the fire spooning up his chowder.

She wrapped her hands around her mug. "How in the world did you fix it?"

"I called Dan'l Pease, who heads Public Works. He shut off the pumps to stop the flow of sewage." Orion set his soup bowl on the small table next to his chair and sat down. "The guys working for me had to cancel their Friday-night dates and they hand-dug six feet down in the pouring rain to the break in the line. They worked knee-deep in sewage, cut out the section we'd drilled through, spliced in new plastic pipe, and filled in the hole."

"They deserve medals," said Victoria.

"They deserve good-sized bonuses, which they'll get," said Orion, stirring his thick soup. "Thanks for waiting up. After an evening like this, it was good to get home and see the lights on and you snoozing in your chair."

On Saturday, Elizabeth made a late breakfast. Orion retold his night's adventure.

Victoria said, "I haven't had a chance to tell you, Orion. I've got information about your man next door."

Orion looked up from the blueberry pancakes he'd heaped on his plate.

"He's renting, he's apparently single, and the reference he gave to the Realtor was Dorothy Roche."

Orion went back to his pancakes. "I'm not surprised. A wealthy woman like that has workers who need housing."

"He rented the place a week after you rented your office and garage."

Orion studied her. "What are you trying to tell me?"

"Dorothy isn't who she pretends to be."

"I know how you feel about her, Victoria."

"It's more than feelings. I have proof that she's not who she says she is."

Orion got up from the table, pancakes half-eaten, and took his plate into the kitchen. "I'm off to work."

Victoria pushed her chair away from the table. "You're dealing with millions of dollars. Casey checked for Dorothy on the Internet, and—"

"I'm really not interested in what you and Casey think about Dorothy. Thanks for breakfast." With that, Orion left, shutting the door firmly behind him.

"Sounds as though you touched a nerve, Gram," said Elizabeth. "What were you about to tell him?"

Victoria folded up her napkin and set it beside her plate. "The only Dorothy Roche Casey could find is a teenage television actress who acts in vampire films made for preteens by a studio run by a Bruce Vulpone. The Dorothy we know is charging everything to that same television studio as though she is the actress."

"Why won't Orion listen? He's a reasonable guy."

"Pheromones," said Victoria.

Orion, frustrated by Victoria's bias against Dorothy Roche, buried himself in work. He slept on his office cot on Saturday night. For the past couple of days he'd neglected his paperwork, and it had piled up—permit applications from various boards in all six towns, requests from the *Island Enquirer* for information, state and federal government forms to fill out, and constant adjustments to the budget spreadsheet. By Sunday night, he'd reduced the pile considerably. Fortunately, he and Donald Minnowfish had become coffee drinking buddies, and the tribal antiquities representative seemed to have forgotten about the permits he'd demanded. Nevertheless, Orion insisted on a tribal member being present whenever they worked.

Occasionally he'd look down on the driveway of the house next door, but only when he was at the desk where the phone was. At one point he saw the SUV pull up and the guy enter the house. Big house for a single guy.

For the most part, Orion forgot about the man next door. He sorted papers and spread them out on the drafting table in the center of the room. He finished with most of the paperwork and concentrated on the budget.

The budget worried him. He'd had to adjust the figures constantly as the project moved along. After suffering much too long with it, he called his partner on Sunday night.

"Don't you believe in taking a day off?" Casper asked. "I'm sitting here with my feet up, drinking a Scotch and watching the game. Time you did the same."

Orion snapped. "I'll take time off when we fund this."

"That's why we're talking to Solomon," said Casper.

"Listen to me, Casper. The guy smells."

There was a long pause before Casper responded. "What's the problem?"

"I've been over his resume and researched what I could on the Internet. He makes what are essentially clerical positions—and there are too many of them—sound as though he was project manager. He's listed start-ups I can't find any record of. I haven't checked all his references and don't intend to. I'm not even sure the guy knew Vulpone. As you, yourself, said, Vulpone worked only with his two sons." Orion glanced outside. Light from his window reflected off the hood of the SUV. "Contact investors yourself, will you, Casper? Don't go through Finney."

Casper sighed. "I'll see what I can scout out."

"Tell you what," said Orion. "I'll talk to Paulson, see if he'll give up his demand for voting shares."

"Good luck with the bastard. Seems to me the prospectus you developed covers every possible question anyone can ask."

"You signed that contract of Finney's, right?"

"I didn't see how we'd lose. But I'll defer to you."

"Let's table the contract for a week," said Orion. "Maybe things will sort themselves out by then."

CHAPTER 15

Victoria was writing her column for the *Island Enquirer* when the phone rang on Monday morning.

"Mrs. Trumbull, my name is Primo Vulpone—"

"One of Angelo Vulpone's sons?"

"Yes, ma'am, the elder."

"My condolences. I didn't know your father, but I know how difficult it must be for you to have lost him."

"Thank you, Mrs. Trumbull."

"How can I help you?"

There was a long sigh at the other end of the line. Victoria waited. "I'm not sure where to start, Mrs. Trumbull. The police don't seem to be doing anything about his murder, and I'm told you might be of assistance."

"The police have very little to work with," said Victoria. "How did you get my name?"

"Father was planning to invest in a fiber-optics project on Martha's Vineyard, headed up by an Orion Nanopoulos. My brother and I got in touch with Mr. Nanopoulos and he suggested we talk to you."

"To me?" Victoria asked, astonished.

"Mr. Nanopoulos said you're associated with the police in some way, but are not restricted by their regulations."

"Well," said Victoria, not knowing what else to say.

"We understand you're a deputy officer with access to the police, that you know everyone on the Island, are related to most of them, and are not afraid of anything."

"Good heavens," said Victoria.

"We'd like to talk to you, my brother and I. May we come by?"

"Are you calling from New York?"

"No, ma'am. We're here on the Island, calling from Alley's Store."

"That's only a short way from here." Victoria looked at her watch. She had her column to finish, but that could wait. She was curious to know what the Vulpone brothers thought they could learn from her. "I'll put fresh coffee on," she said, and gave them directions to get to her house from Alley's.

The coffee hadn't finished dripping into the glass pot when a bright red sports car skidded to a stop in the drive, and two men, dressed entirely in black, unwound themselves from the low-slung vehicle. Victoria went to the door to greet them.

The driver, the shorter of the two, whipped off his wraparound sunglasses and smiled at her, a charming smile with dimples and white teeth set off by olive skin. He was a young man, probably in his early thirties.

"A Ferrari," she said after she introduced herself. "Are you Primo?"

"I am. And this is my brother, Umberto."

The extremely tall slender man who'd emerged from the passenger seat was an elongated version of his older brother. He'd already taken off his sunglasses. He bowed slightly.

"I didn't realize . . ." Primo said, then started over again. "From everything we've learned about you, I expected a much younger woman." He stopped, clearly uncomfortable. "In her twenties, perhaps. I didn't expect to find an elegant woman in her sixties."

Victoria smiled. "Thank you."

"I see you know fine cars, Mrs. Trumbull," said Umberto. His nose, in fact both of their noses, were every bit as large as Victoria's own—great beaks that began at the level of their eyebrows and arched out regally.

"Please, come in," said Victoria. She led the way into the parlor. Primo followed her, and Umberto trailed behind, ducking his head to clear the door frame.

The two waited until she'd seated herself and then they, too, sat, Primo on the sofa next to Victoria's wing chair, Umberto on the rocker.

"I'm so sorry about your father. His death under such circumstances must be especially difficult for you."

"Thank you," said Primo. He sat forward on the stiff sofa, his hands clasped between his knees.

Victoria served coffee to the two men—boys, really—and sat again.

Primo lifted his mug to her in a kind of salute. "Thank you for seeing us, Mrs. Trumbull."

"Of course," said Victoria.

"As I told you on the phone, my brother and I," he nodded at Umberto, "are not at all pleased with the progress the police are making in their investigation of our father's death."

Umberto looked up. "They've made no progress at all."

Victoria said, "It's my understanding there were few, if any, clues. Your father's body was found, entirely by chance, at the bottom of a six-foot-deep trench in a foot of water. It was raining when they found him, and had been raining all night, washing away any footprints."

She looked from one brother to the other. Dark brown eyes looked back at her. The two seemed priestlike in their somber black slacks, tieless black shirts buttoned up to the throat, black blazers. Black, wavy hair, and intense dark eyes in gloomy faces. There'd been only that brief smile of Primo's when she'd recognized their Ferrari, to see how handsome he was.

They waited politely for her to finish speaking.

"The police believe your father was assassinated. That his death was likely to have been mob related."

Primo set his mug down on the coffee table. "Father had mob connections, of course. Everybody in the construction business does."

"At least in Jersey and New York," said Umberto.

"But this was not a mob killing," said Primo. "First off, Father knew how to work with the mob. It's like a union, you know, you pay your dues, obey the rules, and they'll protect you."

Umberto nodded.

Primo continued. "Secondly, the mob wouldn't follow Father to some remote island to kill him. They'd have taken him out at his favorite restaurant or his business office. Not here."

"What was your father doing here on the Vineyard?" asked Victoria.

Primo shrugged. "We have no idea. He was interested in this fiber-optics project of Mr. Nanopoulos's."

"But it wasn't like him to go into the field like that," said Umberto. "He'd have ordered someone else to do that for him. He wouldn't travel if he didn't have to."

"The entire setup is wrong, Mrs. Trumbull," said Primo. "We'd like to hire you to look into it."

"I'm not an investigator," said Victoria.

"We've investigated you," said Umberto with his first smile, a delightful duplicate of his brother's.

Primo said, "We need someone who knows the Island and its people."

"What if the killer is not from the Island?" asked Victoria.

"We trust you'll recognize the marks of a stranger," said Primo. He reached into an inside pocket in his blazer and brought out a checkbook.

Victoria held up her hand. "Wait. I need to think about this."

"We've already made out the check, Mrs. Trumbull. It's for a thousand dollars, as a retainer. We'll cover any expenses you incur and will pay for your time at five hundred dollars a day. Is that reasonable?"

"No, not at all!" said Victoria. "I can't possibly accept—"

"Make it seven hundred and fifty, Primo," said Umberto, sitting forward.

Primo flushed. "I didn't mean to insult you, Mrs. Trumbull. We'll pay your rate, whatever it is. Seven hundred and fifty? Eight hundred? Plus expenses, of course."

"Let me think about this," said Victoria.

"Nine hundred, Primo," said Umberto, gesturing with his hands.

"Stop!" said Victoria. "This has nothing to do with money. I don't have—"

"A secretary, Primo," said Umberto. "Mrs. Trumbull should have a secretary."

"Personal assistant," said Primo. "Would that make it easier for you, Mrs. Trumbull? To have a personal assistant to handle the paperwork and phone calls?"

Victoria sat back in her chair. If she weren't taking that doxycycline and feeling less energetic than usual, she'd be better able to tell these intense young men that she didn't want their money, that she knew nothing about tracking down a killer, and didn't wish to learn how to do so. They were watching her with dark eyes.

"Very well," she said. "I'll do what I can."

Primo leapt to his feet, bent over her, and kissed her on both cheeks. "Thank you! We'll put a car at your disposal."

"I don't drive," said Victoria, lifting her nose into the air. She still resented losing her license simply because she'd backed into the Meals on Wheels van.

"Of course you don't," said Primo, stepping away in horror. "We'll provide you with a driver, of course." He tore the thousand-dollar check out of its leather binder, placed it on the coffee table, and set a nearby stone on top of it. Victoria had picked the stone up on the beach just the other day, a lucky stone with a broad white stripe around it.

Umberto looked at his watch and stood up. "We have forty-five minutes to catch that ferry, Primo, and we need to be in line a half-hour before sailing time."

Victoria struggled to her feet, feeling inadequate, put upon, and outmaneuvered. If it weren't for that Lyme disease, she'd have straightened out those two young men.

Umberto, too, bent down and kissed her on both cheeks. He carried the tray with its empty coffee mugs back into the kitchen. Victoria followed. For one of the few times in her life, she had no idea what to say.

Both Primo and Umberto flashed her their identical charming smiles and headed outside toward their bright red car.

"We look forward to hearing from you, Mrs. Trumbull," said Primo, blowing her another kiss. *"Cara mia!"* He thrust his arms into the air.

"Ciao!" said Umberto.

While Victoria watched from the top of the stone steps, hugging her arms around herself, the two slipped back on their wraparound sunglasses. Primo slid behind the wheel, Umberto folded himself into the passenger seat, and the Ferrari squealed out of Victoria's drive in a spray of sand as though competing in some kind of Island grand prix.

CHAPTER 16

After spending an uncomfortable weekend sleeping on his office cot, Orion awakened, groggy from working late. He met his crew at Five Corners, the busiest intersection on the Island, where five roads came together. Vehicles disembarking from the ferry met traffic heading in a snarl of different directions. For the most part, Island drivers waited their turns. Visitors from off Island plunged ahead into the mess, not understanding Vineyard traffic protocol.

This was the morning the Ditch Witch drill was to bore under that busy intersection.

Orion engaged the services of two off-duty Tisbury police officers to direct traffic, should the drilling hold things up at some point. Actually, it wasn't the work that held up traffic, it was drivers slowing to ask why the cops were there.

Orion stood on the corner of State Road and Water Street, where drivers were likely to stop with questions. He was dressed, as usual, in jeans and a plaid shirt. He wore a hard hat and leaned on a shovel. A horn honked. A Subaru pulled over. The driver lowered the window and leaned over. "Say, buddy, what's going on?"

Orion stepped over to the open window, his pleasant expression in place. "They're laying a fiber-optic cable under the road, sir," he said.

"Yeah? What's it for?"

"Better communications."

"About time. Tell the boss good luck."

Orion touched the brim of his hard hat with two fingers. "I'll do that."

The driver gave him a thumbs-up and moved on.

By nine o'clock the drill head had crossed under State Road. The crew removed it, attached a device that grabbed onto the cable, and pulled it back through the hole that had been bored only a few minutes earlier. Orion dismissed the police with thanks, and went back to the drill. He and Mike spread out the map on the now mud-caked treads to recheck their next job site.

While they were studying the map, Orion's cell phone rang. He fished it out of his pocket. "Nanopoulos."

"Orion, it's Amanda. We have a problem I don't want to discuss on the phone."

"I'm at a good stopping place," said Orion. "I'll be there in ten minutes."

Mike glanced up questioningly.

Orion shrugged. "My bookkeeper. I probably didn't sign a check. Be back within the hour."

After noon on Monday, while Orion headed to the bookkeeper's office, Victoria and Casey made their rounds.

"Angelo Vulpone's sons visited me this morning."

"Yeah? What did they want?"

"They hired me to solve their father's murder."

"The police are working on it, Victoria."

"Not fast enough, apparently. I was sympathetic."

"A murder takes time to solve. You know that. Evidence has to be processed. Interviews."

They passed the mill pond, turned toward the cemetery.

Victoria said, "I can't understand why that man is so thick headed about that woman."

"Who are you talking about?"

"Orion Nanopoulos and that woman. I've only half-jokingly blamed his behavior on pheromones."

"You've got bees in your—"

"Perfume is pheromones, scientifically concocted to make some man lust after a woman. Aftershave cologne, too. Pheromones designed to seduce some unsuspecting woman."

"Wow!" said Casey, glancing away from the road with a smile. "You're really steaming, Victoria."

"Orion's not stupid."

Casey slowed around Dead Man's Curve. "I gather 'that woman' is Dorothy Roche."

"We know," Victoria said, "the Dorothy Roche renting that house is not the Dorothy Roche she claims to be."

"However, she lives in Edgartown."

Victoria stared straight ahead.

Casey went on. "Edgartown is not in our jurisdiction. And, as far as I know, no one has complained about her."

They passed Whiting's fields and the New Ag Hall on the left, and crossed the bridge over Mill Brook.

"How can I contact the real Dorothy Roche's television station?" Victoria asked.

"When we get back to the office, I'll check the Internet. There'll be someone at the studio to contact."

Victoria settled back in her seat. "What is she trying to do? Take over Orion's company? She doesn't have any money, as far as I can tell. It's all outrageous fakery."

"I'll treat you to a cup of chowder," said Casey.

Victoria glanced at her. "You're not listening to me."

"I am. When we get back to the station house, I'll contact the television studio that shows her films or whatever they are."

"Chowder sounds good," said Victoria.

Orion drove to the bookkeeper's office in a small house off Spring Street in Vineyard Haven. He parked in her driveway and went to the back door. Amanda Medeiros opened the door. She was a stout woman in her early fifties with flyaway, prematurely white hair and pale blue eyes.

"Come in, Orion. I need to show you something."

"I'm afraid I've been distracted over the past few days. Must have forgotten to sign—"

"No, not that. Come into my office."

Orion bent over and untied his boots, kicked them off, and followed her, stocking-footed, across her white-tiled kitchen floor and into her office, with its hand-knotted, beige wool rug.

Her office overlooked a compulsively neat garden, where blue and white petunias and pink geraniums were neatly bounded by a plastic edge.

Orion thought briefly about trudging into Victoria's parlor with his boots on. Perhaps he should leave them in her entry from now on. But perhaps not. Victoria's floors were meant to be trod upon.

"You'd better sit down, Orion," said Amanda, beckoning him to an armchair upholstered in cream and pink satin stripes. Orion eased himself down. Amanda sat and opened a manila folder, the only item on her desk, and picked out the top papers. She swiveled to face him.

Orion rested his elbows on the arms of his chair, his feet flat on the floor. He noted with relief that his socks were clean.

"It was my understanding, Orion, that Ms. Roche's investment in Universal Fiber Optics was a piece of equipment called a 'Ditch Witch horizontal directional drill' for which she was to get a twenty percent share in the company."

"That's right," said Orion.

"She was to pay for the equipment."

"That's right."

Amanda handed him the papers without a word.

Orion took them from her and studied the top one. He looked up. Amanda sat with arms folded across her ample bosom, watching him with those light eyes.

"A bill for payments on the rig?" asked Orion.

"That's right." Amanda said. "Billed to your company. Not paid for or billed to Ms. Roche. I paid the bill, not having all the information I should have had."

"This must be a mistake," said Orion, slapping the paper with the back of his hand.

"I don't think so. Check the next page."

Orion slipped the first page underneath the papers he held. He read the page Amanda had indicated. He read it a second time. He looked up at her again.

"You see what I mean?" Amanda uncrossed her arms and leaned on her desk.

"She owns the title to the drill rig, and Universal Fiber Optics has been paying for it."

"I hate to say this, but I warned you against her," said Amanda. "I thought she was just a frivolous, stupid bitch." Amanda heaved herself out of her chair, hands propped on her desk. "But she's not. She's a crafty, scheming, conniving, evil bitch."

Orion set the papers back on Amanda's desk with great deliberation, and plopped back into the satin chair.

"My God!" He ran both hands over the top of his head. He smoothed his mustache and dropped his hands into his lap. "I've been a fool."

"I guess," said Amanda. She sat down again. "Any thoughts on where we go from here?"

"Yes," said Orion, standing up. "I have a very good idea where we go from here."

Chapter 17

On Monday afternoon, Finney called Dorothy Roche to sound her out about taking over as CEO of Universal Fiber Optics. In his mind, the company was no longer Orion's.

"Finney, darling," Dorothy said after he broached the subject, "We need to talk, face-to-face. Get back here to Martha's Vineyard as soon as possible. Tomorrow."

"I'll have to go over my schedule." Finney laid the phone down and reached into the cardboard box where he kept his unpaid bills and checkbook. Was there enough in his account to pay for another flight to Martha's Vineyard?

He paged through the checkbook. The answer was no. His monthly check from one of his clients was due in two weeks. When it came, the check would barely cover the stack of bills in the cardboard box, and the client was beginning to dither. Finney did not need the police on his back. The only way he could afford airfare was to put off paying the credit card bills, even though the finance charges were already killing him.

Fourteen million dollars.

He could raise that easily, if only would-be investors would listen to him. When Nanopoulos signed that contract, he'd get a monthly retainer, and six months from now, the finance charges would seem like nothing. What the hell. Charge the airfare on the latest credit card he'd gotten in the mail and had never used. That's what he'd do.

"Dorothy," he said, picking up the phone. "Sorry I had to put you on hold. Another call. Tied up with a mega deal that I expect to close at the end of the week. I can get a flight out of JFK on Friday afternoon."

"Make it Wednesday, darling." Dorothy's voice was silky. "We have a lot to discuss. Let me know what flight you'll be on, and I'll have Tim pick you up at the airport. Why don't you stay at the Harbor View? It's within walking distance of my house."

The elegant Harbor View was absolutely out of the question. Finney said quickly, "I prefer the Mansion House." His gut churned when he thought of the hotel bill. "All right. Wednesday, then. I'll give you a call with the flight number after I've taken care of my other affairs."

Orion turned off Main Street, parked in back of his place, climbed the outside stairs, and let himself into the light, airy office. He could see the neighbor's SUV in the driveway. He looked at his watch. Three o'clock.

According to Victoria, Tris Waverley had rented the place after Orion had rented his own office. He'd used Dorothy Roche as reference. After meeting with Amanda, Orion's infatuation with Dorothy had chilled.

He needed to meet Tris Waverley, this mysterious neighbor of his before he confronted Dorothy. In his present mood he was quite capable of murdering her.

He retraced his steps down the outside stairs, walked across the driveway, and knocked on the side door. Until now, his only view of Tris Waverley had been the top of his head, usually covered by a baseball cap. He knocked again, harder. Footsteps pounded down wooden stairs and the door was flung open by a tall, thin, comfortably homely man wearing thick glasses and a Red Sox baseball hat.

When he saw Orion, the guy swallowed and his Adam's apple rose and fell. "Help you?"

Orion held out his hand. "I'm your next-door neighbor, Orion Nanopoulos. About time I said hello. Tris, isn't it?"

"Sure. Yeah." They shook. Tris's hand was limp and damp. "Waverley. Tris Waverley. Nice to meet you."

"Here for the summer?" Orion asked pleasantly, wiping his hand on the seat of his pants.

"The summer. Yeah." Tris leaned awkwardly against the door frame, blocking the entrance.

"I've got a couple bottles of Sam Adams in my office fridge. Why don't I bring them over."

"I'm in the middle of something . . ."

"An hour, then," said Orion. "Give you time to get to a stopping place."

The guy swallowed again. His glasses had steamed up. "Why don't I come over to your place in, say, forty-five minutes."

"No way. My place is a mess." Orion was compulsively neat and his office was anything but a mess. "I'll bring the beer over in forty-five minutes. Give you time to hide whatever it is you're working on."

"Look, I . . ."

Orion turned, said over his shoulder, "Nice to meet you, Tris," and walked away.

He went back to his office and got on the Internet, something he'd meant to do earlier. He keyed in Tris Waverley. The ElecTris Web site popped up with a picture of Tris and Marylou Waverley and a list of products and services the company offered. Surveillance was on the list.

Orion started to pick up the phone to call Casper, but thought for a moment. He set the phone back into its cradle and reached into his pocket for his cell.

Casper answered.

"Bad news," said Orion. "Dorothy owns the title to the rig. The bills have been sent to us."

"We've been paying them?"

"Amanda's got authority to pay anticipated bills. She knew we were acquiring the drill. Eight thousand a month."

Casper said, "Where does that leave us? What does the contract with her say?"

Orion shifted through papers on his desk. "Says that Dorothy agrees to acquire a Ditch Witch horizontal directional drill in return for a twenty-percent share in the company."

"Anything say she's putting up the money?"

Orion took a deep breath and let it out slowly. "The word 'acquire' doesn't actually mean she'll pay, does it?"

"You plan to talk to her, Orion?"

"As soon as I hang up I plan to strangle her. Which brings up another possible problem."

"I'd better sit down," said Casper.

"The renter next door used Dorothy as reference. He owns a shop in Quincy that does electronic surveillance."

"You're on your cell phone, I take it," said Casper. "They're not entirely safe, either, you know."

"Safer than the landline. You have my cell number."

"You plan to speak to Dorothy before strangling her?"

"Face-to-face," said Orion.

"Call me after you straighten this out. Don't do anything rash. It may be a simple misunderstanding."

"Unlikely," said Orion, and hung up. He decided the call to Dorothy didn't matter, and used the office phone.

"Dorothy," he said.

"Darling!" said Dorothy. "What can I do for you?"

"I'd like to stop by for a chat."

"That's sweet, darling. Come for a drink this afternoon. Wait a minute." Orion heard the rustle of papers. "Not this afternoon. What about Friday?"

"Can't do it. What about tomorrow?"

"Tuesday, hmmm." More rustling of pages. "Thursday is the best I can do. Around five, would that be convenient?"

"It will have to be," said Orion.

He spent the next half-hour going over his log of phone calls to determine what sensitive information he'd been feeding Tris Waverley next door.

Most calls were to Casper. They'd discussed finances. He'd shown concern about Finney Solomon. No real problem. The setup was too obvious. Dorothy was smart enough to know he could detect the surveillance. Unless she was smarter than he thought. Did she want him to know he was spied on?

Orion checked his watch, gathered up four bottles of Sam Adams and an opener, and headed for Tris Waverley's.

CHAPTER 18

Tris Waverley ushered Orion into the kitchen, a bleak place with yellowing appliances and flickering overhead fluorescent lights, a chrome-legged table with a chipped green Formica top, and two chairs. The refrigerator, which had been humming loudly, shut off with a shudder. In the silence that followed, Orion heard a steady drip.

In an attempt to be light he said, "If that's hot water, I hope you're not paying the utility bill."

"It's the cold," said Waverley.

Orion set the Sam Adams on the table and took the chair closest to him, the one with the fewest cracks in its stiff, marble-patterned vinyl seat.

Waverley was leaning against the sink.

"Nice place," said Orion, shifting his feet to a less sticky spot on the linoleum. "You're here for the summer?"

"Right," said Waverley.

"Working vacation?" Orion slid a bottle and the opener across the table. "Have a seat. Help yourself."

"Thanks." Waverley sat awkwardly on the chair that matched Orion's and pried off the bottle cap.

"I hear you're in electronics," said Orion.

"How'd you hear that?" Waverley ran a hand up and down the cold bottle.

"Word gets around this Island." Orion opened his own beer. "A working vacation means surveillance, I gather."

"Look, Mr. Nanopoulos, what I do is confidential."

"Call me Orion. We're neighbors, after all."

Waverley lifted his beer and drank.

Orion said, "Is your sister running your store now?"

Waverley took another swig and set the bottle down. He stood again. "I'm afraid I don't have time to chat. I gotta get back to work."

"I don't think so," said Orion, leaning his chair back on two legs. "How much is Ms. Roche paying you?"

Waverley choked on his swig of beer. He breathed in and started to cough.

"You okay?" asked Orion, still leaning back in his chair, hands in his pockets.

Waverley coughed some more.

Orion set his chair down on all four legs and leaned forward slightly. "Want a slap on the back?"

Waverley shook his head.

"Lift up your arms. Sometimes that clears your air passage," Orion said.

Waverley turned his back to Orion and lifted his arms.

"I'm going over to Dorothy's for drinks on Thursday, as you probably heard," said Orion.

Waverley coughed again and sat down. "Who *are* you?"

"Not a friend of hers, apparently."

"Look, I do what I'm hired to do." Cough. "I'm not the bad guy in this." He adjusted his glasses.

Orion looked for a recycling container, didn't see one, and left his empty bottle on the table. "I think we know who the bad guy is. Might as well continue to monitor my calls. Only my landline, not my cell?"

Waverley, still seated, nodded slightly.

"She paid you yet?" asked Orion.

"A retainer."

"Has the check cleared the bank?"

"Cashier's check."

Orion nodded. "Better collect what she owes you before you let it go too long. She pay your rent?"

"Yes."

"I'd make sure she does, if I were you, since your name's on the lease." He stopped at the door and turned. "You can have the rest of the beer."

On Wednesday, Dorothy's chauffeur met Finney's flight, direct from New York. A cool breeze whispered through the fence as the attendant opened the gate. Finney was the only passenger to disembark.

Tim greeted him. "Morning, sir. Want to stop at the Mansion House before going on to Ms. Roche's?"

"Please," said Finney.

"Any luggage, sir?"

Finney held up his gym bag and attaché case. "Short trip."

"We're parked right over there." Tim indicated the Mercedes near the gate. "Have a good flight, sir?"

"Fine," said Finney, preoccupied with his expenses.

"Nice weather we've been having," Tim said as they drove away from the airport. He looked in the rearview mirror. "You don't get weather like this in Boston in July. Hot and steamy there, according to the radio."

"Umph," said Finney, and Tim shut up.

At the Mansion House, Finney registered for one night, went to his room and washed up, and took a manila folder out of his briefcase. He checked his image in the large mirror by the door, turning sideways to see how he'd appear to Dorothy from that angle, then went down the stairs and out onto the hotel's porch. Tim was parked across Main Street and opened the passenger door. Finney got in.

They drove the familiar route to Edgartown, past the shipyard, the fuel oil tanks, the canoe rental place. They crossed the bridge over the opening into Lagoon Pond, past the hospital, and past the Oak Bluffs Harbor.

Wild roses formed a fragrant pink, red, and white border on either side of State Road. It was still early in the morning, but cars already were parked on the beach side of the road. Bathers and sun worshippers unloaded coolers and umbrellas, picnic baskets, radios, and towels.

Edgartown was scented with roses. Yellow, pink, and white blossoms covered white picket fences in front of white painted captains' houses.

They turned onto North Water Street, and Finney's resentment rose. Why couldn't she have invited him to stay at her place? She certainly had enough room.

"Here we are, sir." Tim opened the door. Finney emerged, too busy with his thoughts to acknowledge Tim. He went up to the big front door and lifted the brass knocker.

"Darling! I didn't expect you so soon. How was the flight? Have you had breakfast?"

"An easy flight, thanks. I didn't have time to eat."

"Well, we'll take care of that right away." She led him down the front hall and into the library where a wide window overlooked the garden. A couch and two comfortable armchairs faced a fireplace at the other end. Floor-to-ceiling bookcases lined the walls.

"I'll ask Courtney to get us something to eat, and while she's fixing it, we can talk." Dorothy bustled out of the room. Finney stood by one of the bookcases, examining the titles. The books, most of them leather bound, included fiction, biographies, and scientific treatises on obscure subjects. They were arranged by size, not by subject.

He barely had time to glance at the books when Dorothy returned. "There, now. Make yourself comfortable, darling."

"Impressive library," said Finney.

"I'm glad you like it." She seated herself in one of the armchairs and Finney sat across from her in the other. She said, "How are the prospects with the financiers?"

Finney patted his folder. "Only a matter of time."

"We don't have much time, Finney. Have you impressed upon them the importance of our project?"

"They understand. But as you well know, those of us with money have it because we're careful with it. Orion has the contract, but hasn't signed it yet."

Dorothy smiled. "Are you sure he should sign it?"

Finney shifted uncomfortably in the soft chair. "I don't know. I called the references you suggested, and, well . . ." He left the sentence unfinished.

"Since I'm his partner, I ought to be able to sign."

"It requires his signature, I'm afraid."

Dorothy pouted. "What was your impression after talking with the references?"

This was an area in which Finney felt more comfortable. "The answers I got were guarded, naturally. The head of Public Works said he didn't want to talk about Nanopoulos, and the selectman claimed Orion was, to quote him, 'out of his mind.'"

"Oh dear," said Dorothy, clasping her hands under her chin. "I was afraid of that. Poor Orion has been under such stress. I had a feeling he might even be suicidal."

"Really!"

"Such a shame. He's such a bright man."

Finney cleared his throat. "I've decided I need to remain on the Island for a few more days." Now was the time Dorothy could offer to let him stay in her house.

"Good idea," said Dorothy.

Finney cleared his throat again. "I thought of trying a bed-and-breakfast, getting to know the Island."

"I'm not sure that's where you'll find the investors. But you know best." She frowned. "Do you have any thoughts about this deplorable situation?"

"You mean about Orion?"

She nodded.

"It's clear that he must step aside," said Finney. "Away from the stress that's driving him so, so . . ."

"You needn't go on. It's too pitiful."

"I think we're on the same page, Dorothy. I believe you should talk to Orion."

She nodded.

"For his own health," said Finney. "We'll be custodians until he can take over again."

"You're so perceptive." Dorothy looked up at the sound of the wheeled cart coming down the hall. "Here comes our breakfast. You must be starving."

While Finney and Dorothy were plotting against him, Orion was waiting in line for the three-car ferry to take him over to Chappaquiddick to meet with Roger Paulson.

The ferry docked, the chain was lowered, and Orion drove on board, the first car. The captain slid wooden chocks in front of his tires, collected his fare, and headed out across the harbor. Through his windshield, Orion had a disconcerting view of open water.

"Pretty rough today," he called out to the captain.

"Since the ocean cut through, the current's unpredictable. May take five minutes to cross."

"Using more fuel?"

"You got it."

They angled into the slip on the Chappy side and Orion drove off the ferry. He found his way to the gate to Paulson's property, and was buzzed in.

As he drove down the long approach to Paulson's mansion, he noticed two stocky, reddish bay horses with light muzzles and upright manes cropping the pasture grass. He slowed to look more closely. The horses had stripes on their legs, almost like zebras.

He drove slowly, thinking about the horses. He parked and Paulson greeted him from the top of his stairway.

"Fine car you've got there," said Paulson.

Orion patted the side of his Chevy. "It's been good to me. I understand you know cars."

"Largest distributorship on the East Coast. C'mon up." Paulson indicated the stairs.

"Impressive," said Orion, looking up at the high roof. "Both the distributorship and your house. You've put a lot of work into both, that's obvious."

"I started at the bottom, washing cars at a dealer's. Worked my way up," said Paulson, leading the way into the kitchen. "Put in eighteen-hour days, seven days a week."

"You deserve this." Orion gestured with his hand.

"Sit down," said Paulson. "Your partner says you're not interested in releasing voting rights. I have to tell you, if I'm shelling out seven million, I want a say in how the company's run."

"Understandable," said Orion. "I took the same route you did, shoveling stable manure, grooming horses, sweeping floors in an engineering firm, and hitting the books at night school. Twenty-four/seven."

"You like horses?" asked Paulson.

"I do," Orion said.

"Got a couple of my own out there." Paulson gestured to the pasture where the horses stood, nose to tail.

"They're beauties," Orion said. "Przewalskis."

"You do know horses." Paulson grinned. "Not many people recognize them. Most are in zoos."

"Horses were my first love."

"Not anymore?"

"I took a few too many falls," said Orion. "It's a young man's profession." The horses broke apart and trotted out of sight. "Let me ask you this, Paulson. In your business, have you given investors a say in your company?"

"Hell, no."

Orion smiled. "We think alike. I understand you had some dealings with Angelo Vulpone."

Paulson stood up and went to the window. "My dealings with Vulpone have led me to be cautious. Damned cautious."

"I understand he was responsible for your wife's—"

"Stop!" said Paulson. He turned and sat down again, his face dark with barely controlled rage.

Orion moved away from the subject of Angelo Vulpone. "Universal Fiber will be a moneymaker."

"I don't doubt it." Paulson folded his arms over his chest. "I'm not interested in making money. I'm interested in running your company." He looked at his watch.

Orion noticed and stood. "I've taken up enough time."

"I was checking to see how close to lunchtime it is. Care to join me? We'll talk about horses, not business."

CHAPTER 19

The following afternoon, Thursday, Orion arrived at Dorothy's a deliberate half-hour late. Dorothy was waiting for him at the front door.

"Darling, you're late, bad boy!" She was wearing black velvet trousers and a low-cut, long-sleeved silk blouse.

A scent wafted toward Orion, conjuring up a field of wildflowers, a girl running toward him.

Pheromones, Victoria had said. Chemical bewitchment.

"Come in, darling," she murmured.

They moved from the foyer into the library, and there, sitting by the fireplace, was Finney Solomon. He stood.

"You know Finney, of course," said Dorothy. "He flew in from the city yesterday."

"Certainly. We met at my office." He turned to Finney. "Are you staying at the Harbor View?"

Finney's smile was feeble. "I decided to stay at a bed-and-breakfast in West Tisbury. Meet more natives that way." He extended his hand. "How's it going?"

Orion shook the hand. "Great."

"Finney has good news," Dorothy said.

"Always like to hear good news," said Orion.

"I've gotten a lot of interest," Finney said, still standing by his chair and not looking at Orion. "I can't get any action, though, until you sign that contract."

"I'm sure you have plenty of other work to keep you busy. We can wait on the contract."

This was Orion's first time in the house on North Water Street, and it was as Victoria had described it, an expensive hotel. Not a personal touch anywhere.

Dorothy slipped into the easy chair. "Have a seat, Orion." She indicated the couch that faced the fireplace, where three white birch logs were stacked artistically on polished brass andirons.

She leaned toward him. "You wanted to talk to me. Business? Or pleasure. The latter, I hope."

"Business," Orion said. "First, that is." He smiled.

Finney cleared his throat.

"I hope you're not going to scold me." Dorothy pouted and sat back, relaxed. "I haven't paid as much attention to our company as I should have, now that I'm part owner."

Orion was determined not to show his irritation. "Things are going well." He turned to Finney. "Angelo's death must be tough on you."

Finney gazed thoughtfully at the fireplace.

After a pause, Dorothy sat up and clapped her hands. "What am I thinking! Drinks," she said. "What would you boys like? I believe I'll have a glass of white wine."

"That sounds fine," said Orion.

As she bustled away a sense of longing trailed her.

Neither Orion nor Finney spoke. They stared at the never-to-be-burned logs in the pristine fireplace.

Dorothy returned a few minutes later carrying a tray with a bottle of white Burgundy, three delicate, long-stemmed glasses, and a plate of crackers and cheese. She set the tray down on the coffee table in front of Orion.

He opened the wine and poured.

"Cheers, darlings!" She held up her glass. "To my two favorite men and the success of Universal Fiber Optics!"

They chatted about wine and the weather. Orion didn't intend to bring up the subject of Ditch Witch equipment ownership with Finney here.

"Finney is such an asset to our company," said Dorothy, taking a small sip and smiling at Finney. "He's wealthy in his own right, you know."

Finney looked down. Dorothy smiled. Her smile had lost its girlish charm.

"Finney mentioned the contract." Orion turned to Finney. "I understand you discussed it with Dorothy?"

"Finney's raising the funds we need," said Dorothy.

"It's unethical to discuss the finances of my company with anyone until I sign that contract, Finney."

Finney stared at the fireplace.

"He's not only told me about the contract, he showed it to me," said Dorothy.

"You had no business doing that, Finney."

Dorothy brushed aside his remark. "I suppose I should sign it, too, since I'm a partner."

Orion folded his arms across his chest to hide his shaking hands. Hands he wanted to wrap around that pink throat. A partner in his company? He'd see about that.

Finney stood. "If you'll excuse me, Dorothy, I have some business to attend to."

"Tim will drive you to wherever you're staying now."

"Thanks. I'll see you tomorrow."

"Call me, and I'll have Tim pick you up. Plan on staying for supper. Courtney will fix something yummy."

After Finney left, Dorothy said, "That was rude of you to talk to Finney that way."

Orion said nothing.

"He's really quite brilliant. We can't antagonize someone as wealthy as he is. Our company . . ." She chatted about her plans. Orion was having difficulty controlling himself. Her plans! None of her plans involved installing fiber-optic cable. What was she thinking? She stopped talking and eased to the edge of her chair, a bit closer to him. "You're being awfully quiet, darling. Are you pleased with the Ditch Witch drill?"

"Let's talk about that."

"Why so serious? Are you feeling all right?"

In truth, Orion was on the verge of throttling her. He knew exactly where to place his thumbs on her throat. She'd look up at him and smile, thinking what? That he was about to kiss her? What a fool he'd been.

"There's a mistake on the title," he said calmly, tucking his hands into his armpits. "The finance company made it out to you."

Dorothy set her glass on the small table next to her.

"We need to correct it." Orion reached into an inside pocket of his denim jacket and drew out an envelope.

"I'm really not clever about things like that," said Dorothy. "Have some cheese, darling. It's artisanal goat cheese and," she pointed to the plate in front of him, "these are organic caraway rye crackers from Wisconsin."

Orion withdrew a sheet from the envelope and stood. "Here's the title change. Sign here," he pointed. "I'll take care of the rest."

"According to my lawyer . . ." Dorothy paused. "He should probably look at this."

"No need," said Orion. "It's according to our agreement. From now on, bills go directly to you."

"I don't know, Orion. My financial advisor . . ." Dorothy stopped and looked up at Orion.

He continued to hold the change-of-title form out to her. She continued to ignore it.

"The accountant will bill you for the past invoices she mistakenly paid." Orion slapped the paper on the palm of his hand. "I'm sure you didn't intend to have the company make those two payments."

"Darling, there's some mistake." She nudged the cheese platter closer to him. "Do try this."

"When you've signed the title over to the company, we'll complete the paperwork making you a partner."

"You don't understand," Dorothy said. "I acquired the machine, darling. That's in the agreement we all signed. It said nothing about my paying for it." She moved closer to him. "That agreement makes me your partner." She brushed aside the papers he'd set down. "You simply must accept the fact that we're partners. Universal Fiber Optics will make us millionaires." Her voice hardened. "You understand, don't you?"

CHAPTER 20

It was after seven-thirty, still light, when Orion found himself on the road back to Vineyard Haven. When he left Dorothy's, he'd driven robotically around Edgartown. He was not sure how he'd gotten away from the house on North Water Street. He had no recollection of saying good-bye to Dorothy. Somehow he'd negotiated the lanes that led out of Edgartown and wound up on the long stretch of road with Nantucket Sound on his right, Sengekontacket Pond on his left. He wasn't aware of the mellow evening light, the pastel colors of the Sound, the Canada geese circling over the marsh, honking as they settled in for a peaceful night. Bathers, packing up their belongings.

Orion, the soul of patience, the epitome of inner strength, the archetype of composure, drove back to his office, climbed up the outside steps, unlocked the door, and closed it carefully behind him.

He then hurled a tall glass vase against the wall, where it broke into glittering splinters. He heaved a ceramic paperweight at a framed certificate and before the shards fell to the floor he pitched the wine-bottle lamp filled with sea glass, still plugged into the wall socket, against the door. The bulb burst with a flash of bright light and the bottle dropped to the floor, releasing a cascade of green, brown, and white sea glass.

Orion brushed broken glass off his chair with a piece of cardboard, dropped down onto the seat, put his elbows on the drafting table, and his head in his hands. Goddamn that Dorothy. How in hell had he messed up so thoroughly?

He was too preoccupied to hear footsteps on the outside stairs. At first he didn't hear the knock on his door. The insistent pounding finally registered on him.

"Police!"

"The door's not locked," Orion snapped. What in hell were the police doing here?

Broken glass scritched across the floor as the door was shoved in. Sergeant Smalley and a state trooper, both in uniform, stood on the doorstep, silhouetted by the garish colors of sunset. They looked around at the chaos.

"What do you want?" Orion demanded.

"Looks like a war zone in here," said Smalley, glancing from one shard-covered surface to another.

"Come on in." Orion felt exhausted, foolish, and apprehensive. Had they found her body so soon? "Have a seat," he said.

"Mind telling me what happened here?" asked Smalley.

"Stupid," said Orion, shaking his head. "I don't want to talk about it. What do you want?" he asked again.

Smalley stepped into the room. "Where've you been?" The trooper was behind him.

"Where've I been? Why do you want to know?"

"I'll ask the questions," said Smalley, hands behind his back, feet slightly apart.

"Edgartown. North Water Street."

"What were you doing there?" Smalley asked.

"Seeing someone."

"Who, please," said Smalley.

"An associate." Orion started to sweat. They'd found the body. They knew he'd killed her.

"Name, please. Who were you seeing in Edgartown?"

Orion said nothing.

"Mr. Nanopoulos?"

"Dorothy Roche."

The trooper was taking notes.

"What time did you get to Ms. Roche's?"

"Five-thirty," said Orion.

"How long did you stay?"

"An hour." Orion checked his watch. "I just got back."

"It's after seven-thirty now."

"I drove around."

Orion heard the sound of pen on notebook.

"You go directly to Ms. Roche's from your office?"

"Yes." Looking down, Orion noticed that Smalley's boots were so highly polished they reflected the colors of the sunset behind him. "Have a seat," Orion offered again.

Every chair was covered with broken glass.

"No, thanks."

Orion stood, took his handkerchief out of his pocket. "I'll clear some of that off."

"Don't bother," said Smalley. "Sit down again. You left from this office. What time?"

"Do I need a lawyer?" Orion asked.

"I don't know," said Smalley. "Do you?"

"For God's sake, are you arresting me?"

"No. At the moment, you're free to answer or not. Where were you before you left here to go to Ms. Roche's?"

The trooper looked up from his notebook.

Orion took a deep breath. He glanced at his hands.

Smalley repeated each word deliberately. "Where were you before you left here to go to Ms. Roche's?"

"I was in the field, working with the drill rig."

"Where do you keep the rig?"

"Behind Trip Barnes Moving and Storage."

"That where you were working?"

"No." Orion stroked his mustache. "We've been working at Five Corners."

Smalley remained in the doorway, hands behind his back, feet slightly apart. "You know the man next door?"

"Tris Waverley?"

Smalley nodded.

"Met him a couple of days ago."

"Where was that?"

"At his place."

"What did you and Waverley talk about?"

Sweat trickled down Orion's back. "What?" he asked.

"What did you talk about?" Smalley repeated.

"His business, electronics. He's here on a working vacation. We had a beer." Orion wiped his forehead with the handkerchief he was still holding. Smalley watched.

"He say what the working vacation entailed?"

"Not exactly." Orion couldn't meet Smalley's eyes.

"Not exactly," repeated Smalley. "What do you mean by not exactly?"

"I asked if he did electronic surveillance."

Behind Smalley, the trooper coughed. Smalley didn't seem to notice. "Why did you ask that?"

"I figured someone had hired him to check on me."

"Why would someone do that?" Smalley had not moved. The sun had set. The trooper was in shadow.

Orion swiveled his chair and looked down on the driveway. Waverley's SUV was gone.

"Mr. Nanopoulos?"

"I'm engaged in a multimillion-dollar project that a lot of people would like to know more about."

"Who, in particular?"

Orion allowed himself a grim smile. "You'll wring that information out of me one way or the other, won't you?"

"Let's get back to the question," said Smalley. "Who did you think was paying Waverley to spy on you?"

Orion swiveled.

Smalley waited.

"Dorothy Roche hired Waverley."

"Did Waverley tell you that? Or Ms. Roche?"

"I confronted him with it and he admitted it was Dorothy Roche."

Smalley turned to the trooper behind him, said something too low for Orion to hear, and turned back to Orion. "What relationship is Ms. Roche to you?"

Orion knew he'd have trouble saying it. "A partner." He swallowed. "In my company."

The phone rang. Orion looked at it without moving.

"Answer it," said Smalley.

Orion picked up the receiver. "Nanopoulos here."

"Casper Martin here. Why are you being so damned formal all of a sudden?"

Orion glanced at the cops. "The state police are here, questioning me."

"What about? What's going on?"

"I don't know. What are you calling about?"

"Never mind," said Casper. "Not that important. It can wait. Call me when you're free." Casper disconnected.

The word *free* echoed in Orion's mind.

He stood again. "What now, Smalley, taking me in?"

"Not at the moment," said Smalley. "I'd appreciate your not leaving the Island for the next couple days."

"Are you going to tell me what this is all about?"

"I suppose it won't hurt." Smalley turned to the trooper again before he answered. "This afternoon we found the body of your neighbor."

"My neighbor?" Orion dropped into his chair. "Who?"

"Waverley. Your neighbor. Tris Waverley."

"Dead?" Orion felt himself go white.

Smalley moved quickly toward him. "You okay?"

"I don't know," said Orion. "What happened?"

"Found his body in a beat-up old truck next to the carcass of a dead skunk. Next to that drill rig of yours, Trip Barnes's place. Strangled."

After Smalley left, Orion sat in his cleared-off chair and looked down at the driveway where Tris Waverley had parked his SUV. He'd met the guy, challenged him, frightened him, even, and now Waverley was dead.

Why?

He looked around at the mess he'd made and cursed himself. What had come over him? He'd dealt with worse blows than the one Dorothy Roche had delivered. Damnation.

Had he killed her? He still didn't know. Wouldn't one of the students who worked for her have called the police by now? Could he expect a second call from Smalley? He couldn't go through that icy questioning again.

He saw, in his imagination, that pink throat, his fingers squeezing the miserable life out of her. He shuddered. He flexed his fingers.

He couldn't go home to Victoria and confess what an ass he'd been. Not yet.

He didn't feel like cleaning up. Served him right to have to think about the mess for a while.

He had to get away, go where the noise level would block out Dorothy Roche and the fact, the awful fact, that he'd lost control. Not only of himself, but, it seemed, of his company.

He wasn't much of a drinker, but right now he craved the companionship of people who did drink.

He turned out the lights, locked the door between him and the mess within, and trudged down the outside stairs. The last time he'd descended those stairs he'd gone to confront Dorothy Roche. Now Tris Waverley was dead. His last view of the world that long-dead skunk at his feet.

He headed for the Rip Tide Bar and its conviviality. He nursed a beer for an hour and left before the serious drinkers had one too many. He didn't want to hear their maudlin talk of unpaid bills and cheating partners.

He returned to his office and brushed the broken glass off the folding cot. He'd face Victoria in the morning.

But that night he tossed and turned on the narrow cot, as much as his sleeping bag allowed. Who'd killed Waverley and why? The cops suspected him. That was for sure.

He recalled the red curtain that had dropped in front of his eyes—was it yesterday? He recalled holding his hands out in front of him like claws, the expression on Dorothy's pasty face. He remembered all that.

And then he was driving along that stretch of beach with roses on either side. A gull swooped down to pick up a clam it dropped on the road and he'd swerved to avoid it.

Perhaps he had a few hours of freedom before Smalley's footsteps marched up the outside stairs again. This time . . . He didn't want to think about this time.

He went back to Waverley, a two-bit shopkeeper Dorothy hired because that's what he was, a two-bit shopkeeper, a not very bright guy scratching out a living. Why him?

The sleeping bag had twisted around his legs as he tossed from side to side. He'd gone to bed in all his clothes except for his boots, which he'd set neatly on the floor at the foot of the cot. He got up, shook out the sleeping bag, smoothed it out, and slipped back inside it.

His mind flashed back to Dorothy. Who was she, anyway? Victoria had seen through her from the start. He hadn't listened. And then, he thought, he couldn't have killed her. He wasn't a violent man. His way of dealing with a problem was cerebral, not brutal. Then he thought of the destruction around him.

He'd killed her. He knew he had.

With that, he fell asleep, and when his face relaxed, it assumed its normal pleasant expression.

CHAPTER 21

Sean, the beekeeper, showed up at Victoria's kitchen door early Friday morning as she was taking a blueberry pie out of the oven.

"Come in," she called.

"Brought you some honey."

"Thank you." Victoria set the pie on a rack to cool. Purple juice oozed through Xs in the golden brown top crust. "Do you have time for coffee?"

"I'll make time." He sat down at the table.

Victoria noticed his expression. "What's the matter?"

"One of the hives looks like it swarmed. I can't find the swarm."

"Where would they go?"

"Not far, usually." Sean scratched his head. "Scouts go out to find a site for a new hive and the swarm waits till the scouts return."

"That's quite civilized," said Victoria.

"Pheromones," said Sean.

She eased a wedge of pie onto his plate.

"They wouldn't settle into a new hive before the scouts come back, Mrs. T. They'd do what you saw the other day, attach themselves to a branch temporarily."

Sean finished his pie and put his plate in the sink. "I'm going out to look again."

"I'll help," said Victoria.

While they were in the west pasture searching the thick cedar trees for the swarm, Orion drove up.

"Good morning," Victoria said. "I've missed you."

"Bad news, Victoria. Tris Waverley is dead."

Victoria backed up to her bench and sat. "What happened?"

"One of Trip Barnes's crew found his body near where the drilling unit was stored. He was strangled." Orion ran his hand over the top of his head. "Smalley showed up at my office yesterday evening. Tris and I had talked over a couple of beers a few days ago."

"I didn't realize you'd met him."

"Met him Monday. Dorothy hired him to tap my phone."

"Let's go into the house," Victoria said.

As they walked around the flower border, Orion told her how Dorothy had outmaneuvered him.

They crossed the rutted drive.

"She deliberately wrote that contract in an ambiguous way." Orion grimaced. "Go ahead and say it."

Victoria shook her head.

"I was ready to kill her. The next thing I knew, I was on the road home."

"I don't know what to say," said Victoria.

"After I got back to my office, the police arrived."

"*Had* you killed her?"

"I don't know."

Victoria stood up. "I'll call her house and find out."

A few minutes later, she returned. "Dorothy's in bed, having her morning coffee." She sat down. "This means you'll still have her to deal with."

"I suppose I'm relieved," said Orion.

The next morning, Victoria was up early. Elizabeth was sleeping in, so Victoria and Orion breakfasted together.

"What sort of hindrance is she?" Victoria asked.

"The company has been paying for the drill, something we didn't anticipate. Eight thousand dollars a month."

Victoria made a whistling sound.

"Aside from that," Orion said, "her partnership is a nuisance. She views it as an opportunity to spend money, when we're doing everything we can to work within budget."

"I wish I could think of some way to help."

Orion bit into a piece of toast and grinned.

"You have something in mind."

"A thought just came to me." He said nothing else, and Victoria didn't ask.

When they finished eating, Orion gathered up the dishes and took them into the kitchen. "I've got to clean up the mess I made." He told her what he'd done. "Stupid."

"I'd say you controlled yourself pretty well, smashing pictures and lamps instead of Dorothy."

"I'll be home early," said Orion, and Victoria smiled at his mention of home.

She watched her tenant from the cookroom window as he walked slowly to his car. It was difficult to imagine her life without this decent man in it. She ached to think of him cheated by that woman.

Orion reached his car and patted its side. He tugged open the door. Immediately, he threw his arms across his face and fell backward. A cloud of bees hovered around him. Victoria got up from her seat in a hurry, burst out through the kitchen door, flew down the stone steps, and rushed out to him without even thinking of her stick.

Orion was writhing on the ground.

The antidote. She had to get that, and quick. Orion gasped for breath. His face was white. The antidote was in the glove compartment. A syringe holding epinephrine. She wrenched open the passenger side door, snapped open the glove compartment, seized the EpiPen.

How to use it? She rushed around the back of the car to where he lay on the ground, twisting off the cap as she went. She must be careful not to trip and fall. Orion was not breathing. She took a deep breath, as though she willed him to breathe with her, lifted her arm, and jabbed the device into his thigh with all her strength, through his heavy jeans and muscles.

"Please, please work." She prayed.

Almost immediately, Orion gasped. He opened his eyes.

"I'll call nine-one-one." Victoria reached into his pocket for his cell phone, something she'd never used before, and punched likely buttons.

The Tri-Town Ambulance was there in less than five minutes, Erica in the passenger seat, Jim driving.

"Nice going, Mrs. Trumbull," said Erica. "Anaphylactic shock comes on fast."

They strapped Orion onto a stretcher and loaded him into the ambulance. Jim helped Victoria into the back and slammed the door. She sat next to Orion, whose color was returning. The ambulance took off, lights flashing.

When Victoria could move close enough to talk to the EMTs she said, "I'm sure he was stung by at least a dozen bees." She braced herself as the ambulance passed around the car ahead of them. "I saw a cloud of insects around him. He put his hands up to protect his face."

"You knew he was allergic?"

"He tells everyone he works with how to use his EpiPen in case he gets stung. He's out of doors a great deal."

"He'll be okay."

Victoria sat back on the bench and watched Orion, who looked almost normal. His eyes were open and he smiled.

Erica leaned over the seat. "We'll give you a ride home, Mrs. T., once we're sure he's okay."

"Thank you," said Victoria. "I can't imagine how those bees got into his car."

Victoria used the emergency room phone to call Sean while she waited for Doc Yablonsky to treat Orion.

"I'll go over to your place right away and clear the bees out of his car," Sean said.

"Do you suppose that's where the swarm set up their new hive?"

"Unlikely," said Sean. "His car wasn't there when the swarm went missing."

"Oh," said Victoria. "You're right."

The doctor came out into the waiting room while Orion was putting his shirt back on.

"Saw your poem in the latest issue of *The Lyric*, Mrs. Trumbull," he said. "Nice sestina." Before Victoria could comment, he continued, "Powerful. Moving," and he handed her his card, which had a silhouette of a dancer with his arms outstretched. The card read, "G. William Yablonsky, MD," and under that, "Poetry, Theater, Medicine." Victoria tucked his card into her cloth bag, while the doctor continued his dissertation on the shortcomings of modern poetry, which, they agreed, neither he nor Victoria understood.

Orion came out of the examining room, buttoning his shirt. He stood waiting for a break in the mostly one-way conversation. Doc Yablonsky was leaning against the high counter, an elbow resting on it, hands clasped, one ankle crossed over the other.

"I've tried sestinas myself. Never could get that complicated rhyme scheme to work for me."

"Doc?" asked Orion.

"Those sapphics of yours are remarkable. 'Sapphics on Greek Isles.' Clever title."

Orion coughed.

Victoria said, "I believe . . ." She stood. "I look forward to reading your work, Dr. Yabov . . . Yabnov . . ."

"Call me Bill." He grinned and turned to Orion. "Oh, sure. You're fit as a fiddle. I'll give you a prescription for a new EpiPen. Make sure it's handy for the next time."

"Right," said Orion. "How many stingers were there?"

"I didn't remove any. Didn't find any."

"No stingers at all?" asked Orion. "That's odd."

"There were a dozen swellings on your head, neck, and hands, but no stingers. A heavy dose of venom, even for someone who's not allergic. Wonder it didn't kill you." Doc Yablonsky, at least four inches taller than Orion and thirty pounds heavier, slapped Orion heartily on the back, almost felling him. "Guess your number hasn't come up yet." The doc then turned to Victoria, and, still talking poetry, walked her and Orion to the waiting ambulance where Jim and Erica were engrossed in a game of cribbage. Jim stowed the cribbage board and cards behind the front seat, climbed down from his perch, went around the vehicle, and opened the back.

"Would you mind waiting a minute?" asked Doc Yablonsky. Erica had shifted from the passenger side into the driver's seat and was about to start the engine. The doc reached into the large front pocket of his white lab coat and brought out a weather-beaten book, its jacket torn and blotched with what looked like raspberry jam or blood, the pages dog-eared, frayed, and soiled along the edges. He turned to Victoria, who was waiting for Jim to help her into the back of the ambulance, and held the battered book and a pen out to her. "Would you mind very much signing this for me, Mrs. Trumbull?"

Victoria eyed the well-read volume of her poetry with delight. "I'd be honored," she said.

CHAPTER 22

On Monday, Orion drove to work as usual. Sean's truck pulled into the west pasture and Victoria stopped what she was doing to watch him work.

"Mornin', Mrs. Trumbull."

"Good morning to you."

Sean unfolded his white suit. "How's the patient?"

"He left this morning as though nothing had happened."

"Lucky you were there."

Victoria watched Sean spread out his suit. "How did the swarm get into Orion's car?"

Sean tugged the suit around his shoulders. "You mean, since his car wasn't there when the bees swarmed, right?"

"Exactly."

"Fact of the matter is, they weren't my bees."

Victoria shifted slightly on the hard wooden bench. "How can you tell?"

"You really want to know?"

"Yes, of course."

He zipped up the suit. "They were yellow jackets, not honeybees."

"Good heavens." Victoria stared at him. "How did they get into his car?"

"Left his car unlocked that night."

"Everyone does," said Victoria.

"Couple of overripe apples on the seat."

"Yellow jackets couldn't materialize overnight."

Sean smoothed out his hood and looked at Victoria with his far-seeing eyes. "Not on their own."

Victoria realized she'd have to wait for him to explain at his own pace.

"Someone dropped a yellow jacket nest into his car along with the apples."

"How could anyone get hold of a nest? I thought yellow jackets lived underground."

"They build nests under eaves. Gray papery masses."

"That takes someone with nerve to detach."

Sean shrugged. "Gloves and a long-sleeved shirt, put a big paper bag over the nest, scrape the nest off with a spatula, and close the bag, quick."

She thought about the killer wasps and shuddered.

Sean placed the hood over his head. Victoria could barely hear him. She thought he said, "Someone allergic to insect stings, good way to kill him."

After Sean left, Victoria went back to her typewriter. She'd finished her column when a dark green Bentley pulled up. A uniformed chauffeur emerged from the driver's seat and came to her door.

She greeted him. "Primo, why the uniform?"

Primo lifted his cap in a deferential flourish. "I'll be driving you, Mrs. Trumbull."

"What happened to your Ferrari?" she asked.

"We thought it might be too conspicuous."

"And you don't think a Bentley is conspicuous?"

Primo looked down. His breeches, tucked into polished boots, matched the car. "We thought you might be more comfortable in a sedan."

"Good heavens!" Victoria said. "Where's your brother?"

"He's vetting personal assistants for you."

"What am I going to do . . ." Victoria realized she was out of her element. "Well, come in. We need to talk."

Primo's boots made new-shoe squeaks as he climbed the steps. He followed Victoria into the cookroom and she sat down heavily. How was she going to solve this problem of too many helpers with too much money trying too hard?

"All right," said Victoria. "I need information."

Primo sat down. "Of course, Mrs. Trumbull."

"Tell me about your father. What was he like? Did he have brothers and sisters?"

Primo set his hat in his lap. "My father was the eldest of eight children. He had one brother and six sisters. His brother was the youngest."

"Are they still living?"

"Only my father has passed away, bless him." Primo crossed himself.

Victoria felt a surge of sympathy. "I'm so sorry."

"Thank you."

She waited a respectful moment before asking, "What do your aunts and uncles do for a living?"

"My oldest aunt is a nun, the other siblings are married with families."

"And your uncle?"

"Uncle Basilio and his wife have no children. He owns a television studio near Secaucus." Primo folded his hands on the checked tablecloth. "He calls himself Bruce. My father was displeased with that, his brother denying his Italian name."

"Our names are important to us."

Primo stood. "If you'd like, I'll make tea."

Victoria nodded. She counted up the number of days she must continue taking the doxycycline. Three more. It had seemed an interminable amount of time. Three days from now she'd be in a better frame of mind to withstand the blandishments of these young men. In the meantime . . . Well, she'd never ridden in a Bentley.

Primo returned a few minutes later with tea and oatmeal cookies he'd found in her cupboard. Victoria hoped he hadn't noticed the flour moths flitting around in there.

He set the tray down and Victoria poured.

"Tell me about your uncle's television station."

"Uncle Basilio, that is, Uncle Bruce, produces and broadcasts live music and drama."

"What kind of drama?"

"Made-for-TV movies geared to preteens. Ten- to thirteen-year-olds."

"That seems an awfully specialized audience."

"That age group is a huge market, Mrs. Trumbull, with access to a lot of disposable income. Uncle Bruce's channel carries more advertising than most TV channels."

"What kind of movies does he show?"

"Vampire and horror movies."

Victoria set down her mug. "Vampires? Horror movies?" She loved vampire movies.

"I hope I haven't offended you, Mrs. Trumbull."

"No, no. Go on."

"Vampires are big business these days. Preteens love fantasy, magic, slimy creatures crawling out of sewers. That sort of thing."

"Are you familiar with any of the actresses in your uncle's movies?"

Primo shuddered. "I haven't seen any of his television shows for years. I'm much too old for vampires."

Much too old? Victoria sipped her tea. "Does the name Dorothy Roche mean anything to you, Primo?"

He shook his head. "I'm afraid not."

"Could you find out for me, without alerting your uncle, if she performs in any of his movies?"

"Certainly, Mrs. Trumbull." Primo took a small leather notebook from an inside pocket of his uniform jacket, uncapped a black-and-gold fountain pen, and noted the name.

"If she does, can you get a photograph of her?"

Primo made another note and put his pen and notebook away. "I gather this should be entirely confidential?"

Victoria nodded. "How successful is his studio?"

"Very successful," said Primo. "My uncle's income from the studio didn't match my father's, but it yields him three or four million dollars annually."

"Three or four *million*?" Victoria was aghast. "Your father earned more than that?"

"Three times what Uncle Bruce earns, twelve million, more or less. Uncle Bruce was jealous of my father."

A bee flew in through the open door and made its way into the cookroom, where it bumbled against a windowpane.

"That's a honeybee," Victoria said. "Bring me a glass. I'll trap it and you can let it out."

Once the bee was released, she asked, "Is your uncle connected with the mob?"

"I don't know," said Primo. "My father dealt with the mob. Most construction companies in New York and Jersey do. Uncle Bruce isn't in construction, though."

"The mob has control over many entertainment facilities, I understand."

"I suppose you're right," Primo said. "Uncle Basilio recently got involved in some kind of side business that seems to bring in as much as his television studio."

"Mob connected?" asked Victoria.

Primo shrugged. "I have no way of knowing. He's secretive about the business. But he makes sure we know how much money he's making. Vulgar, my mother says."

"How *is* your mother?" Victoria asked.

"My father's death is a terrible shock, of course. But she's a very strong woman. And she's got Umberto and me."

"Were you close to your father?"

"I respected him. He trained my brother and me to take over his business, but we weren't close like father-sons."

"Tell me more about your uncle."

"Uncle Basilio always competed with Father. He wanted a bigger house, a more beautiful wife, more money. It goes on and on." He stopped, his expression clouded. "Not anymore." He sat up straight. "The fact that he has no children is a terrible blow to his ego."

"And your aunt, what about her?"

Primo looked down at his cooling tea. "Aunt Maria Rosa. She's all right."

"You don't sound enthusiastic."

"It's this way, Mrs. Trumbull." He paused. "It's . . . that is . . . Uncle Basilio, Uncle Bruce . . ."

Victoria nodded.

"He's involved with another woman," Primo blurted out.

"I should think you'd be upset with your uncle rather than your aunt."

"My aunt won't confront him."

Victoria wasn't sure what to say. She asked, "Do you know who the other woman is?"

"I saw him with her at a restaurant, but I have no idea who she is." Primo finished his cookie and washed it down with a few more sips of tea. "Aunt Maria Rosa was the most popular girl in Uncle Bruce's class. I've seen photographs of her when they got married. Amazing green eyes. She was quite beautiful."

"But?"

"Well, she's kind of let herself go."

"She knows about the other woman?"

"Oh, yes. She knows all right."

"Where are you staying, Primo?"

"At the Harbor View, Mrs. Trumbull." Primo stood. "I've booked a suite there for three weeks."

"July into August? That will cost a fortune."

"Mrs. Trumbull, we are hunting down my father's killer. No expense is too great." He followed Victoria into the kitchen. "The car and I are at your disposal."

Victoria smiled. She was beginning to accept the fact that the Bentley Flying Spur was her car, at least temporarily. "Let me get my hat and bag," she said.

CHAPTER 23

Primo parked the Bentley at the small West Tisbury police station and held the door for Victoria. "Would you like me to go in with you, Mrs. Trumbull?"

"No, thank you, Primo. I won't be long."

Casey, on the phone, looked frazzled. She waved a hand, and Victoria perched on the edge of her usual chair and waited for the chief to get off the line.

When she did at last, Casey swiveled her chair around to face her deputy. "What can I do for you, Victoria?"

"I came in to see what progress we're making on the Angelo Vulpone investigation."

Casey leaned back and sighed. "Victoria, it's not 'we.' The state police have everything under control. That call was from them."

"From Sergeant Smalley?"

"None other."

"What did he have to say?" asked Victoria.

"No progress, witnesses, or evidence. Too much mud."

"Angelo Vulpone's sons have asked for my help," said Victoria. "They believe the police aren't doing enough."

"The cops are working their tails off. And the Vulpone sons think you can solve this?" Casey rose from her chair. "Keep your nose out of this investigation, will you?" She set her hands flat on her desk and leaned toward Victoria.

Victoria's face flushed. She stood. "Thank you." She rose from her chair and marched straight to the door, shut it firmly behind her, descended the stairs with straight-backed dignity, and headed for the waiting Bentley.

Casey immediately burst through the door after her and called from the top of the steps. "Sorry, Victoria. I shouldn't have said that." She paused. "A Bentley?"

Primo was holding the door open for Victoria, whose back was plumb-line straight, her face a bright pink.

"Victoria?" said Casey, hurrying down the stairs as Primo shut the car door. "I didn't mean it that way," she said to the closed door and tinted window that showed only her own reflection.

Primo, from the driver's seat, said, "Mrs. Trumbull?"

Victoria held up a regal hand. "To Orion's office."

As Primo reversed out of the station's oyster shell parking area, Casey faded away behind them, standing at the foot of the station house steps.

Primo glanced in the rearview mirror at Victoria, whose mouth was set in a firm line.

"Would you like to talk about it, Mrs. Trumbull?"

There was a second's pause. Then Victoria said, "The idea! The very idea! Treating me like a ten-year-old."

"Yes, ma'am," said Primo, who obviously wasn't sure what had happened in the police station.

"And furthermore, according to her, the police are doing nothing about your father's death. Nothing whatsoever. Blustering to cover up their lack of progress."

"Yes, ma'am."

They drove in silence down Old County Road past the school, past Whippoorwill Farm.

Victoria stroked the fine leather seat next to her. "We'll show those amateurs how an investigation should proceed."

Primo glanced again in the rearview mirror.

"First, to Orion's office," she said.

Primo stopped at the stop sign at the end of Old County Road. "I'm afraid I don't know where his office is."

"Ah," said Victoria. "Of course." She sat up straight and gave him directions. Her color had reduced itself to two bright pink blotches high on her cheekbones, looking much like war paint.

They found Orion, not at his office, but on Water Street near the Steamship Authority dock. He was studying a map he'd spread out on the hood of his car, his reading glasses in place, and he was pointing out something with a steel ruler to a bearded young man standing next to him. He looked up quizzically as the Bentley pulled up. He removed his glasses and, glasses in one hand, ruler in the other, studied the vehicle with its tinted windows that gave no clue as to who was inside.

Victoria lowered her window and came into view.

Orion's pleasant expression turned into a broad grin. "Good afternoon, Victoria. Last time I saw you hitchhiking, you were in a dump truck." He stood back to examine the car from a distance. "You've risen in the world."

A breeze lifted a corner of the map that was on the hood of Orion's car, and he weighted it down with the ruler.

The bearded young man said, "I'm heading to the Black Dog for coffee, Orion." He leaned toward Victoria's open window. "Can I get you anything, Mrs. Trumbull?"

"Not I, thank you," said Victoria. "We'll be here only a few minutes."

"Green tea for me," said Orion, reaching into his pocket for money. "No sugar."

After he left, Victoria introduced her chauffeur.

Primo slipped out of the driver's seat, went around the front of the car, and offered a hand to Orion.

"Primo Vulpone, Mr. Nanopoulos."

Orion's eyebrows rose. "Angelo's son?"

"Yes, sir." Primo removed his hat.

"My condolences. A difficult time for you."

"Thank you. I understand you knew my father."

"Not well. I'd discussed business matters with him. I'm sure we'd have become well acquainted in time."

"He was most impressed with you, Mr. Nanopoulos, your business acumen, and your technical knowledge."

"Thank you," said Orion.

The breeze fluttered the map, shifting the ruler across the hood of the car. Orion picked up the map. "I understand you've engaged Mrs. Trumbull to investigate your father's death."

"My brother and I have, yes, sir. Your suggestion."

Orion rolled up the map and tapped the end to straighten it. "Let me know if I can help."

"Thank you."

"We're on our way to see Elizabeth," said Victoria.

Orion grinned. "If I were riding around in a Bentley, I'd want to show off, too."

Victoria raised the tinted window.

Orion turned to Primo. "A fine vehicle."

"Thank you," said Primo. "I've been admiring yours, too. It must be twenty years old and is in superb condition."

"I'll let you drive it sometime," said Orion.

"I'd be delighted. And would be pleased to return the favor," said Primo, settling his hat on his head and getting back into the driver's seat.

From Orion's work site, Primo drove Victoria to the Oak Bluffs Harbor, but Elizabeth was in the harbor launch checking mooring lines and couldn't leave, so they drove home again, and Victoria dismissed her chauffeur.

Orion, at least, appreciated her car and driver.

The next afternoon, Victoria tried to finish her column, but couldn't concentrate. Her mind was full of unconnected thoughts. Finally, she decided that news of the town could wait. The murder of Angelo Vulpone couldn't. For that matter, neither could the murder of Tris Waverley. Nor the attempt on Orion's life. Were the three—two deaths and a near death—connected in some way?

She pushed her typewriter aside, reached into the drawer of the telephone table for a lined yellow pad, and started to make a list.

The first item on her list was, "Why was Angelo killed? Why was he on the Vineyard? He seldom traveled, according to his sons."

After that she added Tris Waverley. Strangled. Not like Angelo's death. Was there a connection?

Then, why would anyone attempt to kill Orion, and with wasps? What a bizarre weapon. The would-be killer had known that Orion was sensitive to bee stings.

But, of course, Orion made sure everyone knew so they could treat him promptly in case of a sting.

The killer must also have known Orion's habits, where he parked his car and his schedule.

But Orion's schedule was erratic at best. Even she was never sure when he'd be home. The killer must have been watching her house and drive. It gave her a strange feeling to think that someone might have been spying on her.

Orion hadn't told her much about Finney Solomon, the venture capitalist from New York. He was connected to Angelo Vulpone in some way. How did he figure in this?

She was sure the pieces were all there, but she couldn't think how they fit together. Were there missing pieces that would make everything clear?

The only common element seemed to be Orion. Angelo Vulpone and Orion. Tris Waverley and Orion. Dorothy Roche and Orion. Bees or wasps and Orion.

She thought for a moment, her pen suspended in midair, then went back to work. The name Dorothy Roche was next on her list. There were two Dorothy Roches, a television actress and a false Dorothy Roche, who lived a phony life on North Water Street.

If the television actress worked for Uncle Bruce, Angelo's brother, perhaps Uncle Bruce had set up the false Dorothy Roche in the North Water Street house out of sight of his wife, Aunt Maria Rosa. Uncle Bruce could charge the false Dorothy Roche's expenses to his business as though the actress had incurred them, since he owned the studio. The setup seemed much too elaborate for a love nest though, and too visible. Why would he have chosen the Vineyard? Victoria made a note along the margin of the yellow pad to ask Primo and Umberto if they'd seen Uncle Bruce on the Island at any time.

Again, the only connection was Orion.

While she wrote, a silver Mercedes pulled into her drive and parked under the Norway maple. Her first thought was that Primo had returned with yet another car. She'd commented on the Bentley's conspicuousness, and perhaps he'd taken her seriously.

But when the driver's door of the Mercedes opened, Dorothy Roche stepped out and locked the door behind her with some sort of remote-control device.

Victoria quickly lifted the tablecloth, put her list underneath, and smoothed the cloth down over it. She watched Dorothy approach and opened the kitchen door.

"Mrs. Trumbull. I hope I'm not disturbing you?"

"Not at all. Come in." Victoria stepped aside. This was a visit that deserved a certain formality. She led the way to the parlor through the long dining room. She could suddenly see her house through the eyes of a stranger. A battered upright and out-of-tune piano was at the west end between two windows. Late-afternoon sun sparkled on the small panes through a coating of salt spray blown in from the sea. Against one long wall was her great-grandmother's horsehair couch, its worn and cracked faux-leather upholstery covered by faux-fur fabric that Elizabeth had found somewhere. Facing her great-grandmother's two-centuries-old couch was the overstuffed sofa she and Jonathan had bought, their first furniture purchase after they married.

To Dorothy, whose taste ran to designer decor, this comfortably muddled home must seem jarring, with its furnishings ranging from the seriously old to the armchairs Elizabeth had picked up at the West Tisbury dump.

She glanced back at Dorothy as she led the way into the parlor.

"Charming," Dorothy said, her smile firmly in place.

Once Dorothy was seated on the elaborately carved parlor sofa, Victoria realized it was late enough for drinks, and she got up again.

"I'll be right back with sherry, Dorothy."

Dorothy shifted in her seat. "Is there anything I can do to help?"

"I won't be a minute. Make yourself comfortable." As she said that, Victoria realized no one could possibly be comfortable on that stiff couch.

In the kitchen she started to get out the bottle of Amontillado, then put it away and instead brought out the cooking sherry from the cabinet by the stove. She placed the bottle and two glasses on a tray, and carried it into the parlor, poured two glasses, and handed one to Dorothy.

"Thank you so much," said Dorothy. "How sweet of you."

Victoria held her glass, not wanting to taste the sherry, and waited to hear what this visit was all about.

"Interesting decor," Dorothy said, gazing around the room. "So . . . so . . . authentic!"

Victoria smiled. In the future, she'd have to use the word *authentic* with respect to this house. It fit, somehow.

Today, Dorothy wore a beige pantsuit and brown turtleneck shirt that had the effect of making her metallic red hair look less awful. She took a sip of the cooking sherry, cleared her throat, looked at the glass, and set it down. Victoria tried not to smile.

"Mrs. Trumbull, I'm sure you're wondering why I'm here," she began, clearing her throat again.

Victoria took a sip of her own sherry. It was, in truth, dreadful. She felt a tinge of guilt. She could easily have served the Amontillado. "I was about to issue you an invitation," she said.

Dorothy shook her head. "You don't owe me a return invitation, Mrs. Trumbull. I came to ask you a favor."

"Oh?" Victoria set her glass down.

"I don't know if Orion told you, but I'm now a partner in his company. Angelo Vulpone . . ."

Victoria stiffened at the mention of the dead man.

". . . was about to invest a large sum of money in Orion's and, of course, *my* company," she looked up from the sherry glass she'd been staring at, "before he, ah, died."

"Yes."

"I'm concerned about Orion, Mrs. Trumbull."

"In what way?"

"He's under a great deal of stress, and, well, I don't know how to say this. I worry about some of his decisions."

Victoria edged forward. "What are you talking about?"

"I know he's concerned about money and his schedule, and, of course, I don't know him as well as you do, but I sense he may—how can I say this?—he may be having some sort of mental problem."

"Orion? A mental breakdown?" Victoria reached for the sherry bottle. "Would you like a bit more?"

Dorothy shook her head.

Victoria was beginning to wish that she had served the Amontillado after all. No one would take a second or third sip of this stuff, let alone enough to loosen one's tongue. She would like to know what this woman wanted of her, and Dorothy, sober, was too shrewd to slip up.

Dorothy looked down at her glass.

Victoria stood again, gathered up the two full glasses, and set them on the tray. "I have some much better sherry. This is awful, isn't it? Would you prefer Scotch? Or bourbon? I think we do need to talk."

Dorothy smiled. "Scotch, please. On the rocks."

"Right," said Victoria, and strode into the kitchen with the tray of un-drunk cooking sherry.

Chapter 24

Dorothy Roche had shown up at Victoria's around five in the afternoon. Two hours later, she was still there. Victoria had set the bottle of Dewar's Scotch Whisky on the coffee table in front of Dorothy, who was now pouring herself a third glass. Victoria had hoped Dorothy might loosen up with a drink or two, but this was better than she had expected. Dorothy was quite garrulous.

"Don't you see, Mrs. Trumbull, the man's under tremendous stress. Something's wrong with him."

"Really," said Victoria. "Please tell me more."

Dorothy seemed to have some goal in mind, but Victoria hadn't been able to figure out what that goal might be.

Dorothy's conversation slipped into a first-name basis. "I met with Finney Solomon this morning, Victoria. I don't believe you know him."

"I've never met him." Victoria had served herself a weak Scotch two hours earlier, but hadn't touched it. It didn't seem in character for this tightly controlled woman to allow herself to talk too much. Puzzled though Victoria was, she felt satisfaction in seeing Dorothy a bit tipsy.

"He's raising fourteen million for our company. That's quite a lot of money, as you can imagine, Victoria."

"Yes, indeed."

"Finney is wealthy himself. He has to be very sure of the management of our company, you understand, in order to present it in the best light to our investors."

"Of course."

"Finney talked to a number of people who know Orion, and

Finney is convinced that Orion is—well, I don't quite know how to put it." She sipped her Scotch and peered with barely focused eyes over the rim of her glass.

"Who did Finney talk to?" asked Victoria.

"Several people." Dorothy waved vaguely. "One of them said Orion is crazy to attempt to do what he's doing. Another refused to even talk about Orion."

"Who did you say these people were?"

"Various people. We have other concerns as well."

"By 'we' do you mean Finney and you?" Victoria asked.

Dorothy set her glass down on the coffee table with a clink. "I mean everyone who's interested in the project."

Victoria nodded. She'd pushed too hard. She tried a new approach. "Do you think the project is a mistake?"

"No, no. Not at all!" said Dorothy, looking confused. "Everyone who knows anything about fiber optics says it's a gold mine. That's what Angelo said. A gold mine!"

"Angelo?" Victoria tried not to show her surprise.

"Angelo Vulpone," said Dorothy. "He planned to put a lot, and I mean a lot, of money into the project."

"I didn't realize you knew him."

"Well," said Dorothy, picking up her glass. "I did know him at one time, you might say." She giggled. "Of course, I didn't know him all that well. Angelo was a big man, not fat, exactly, but . . . yeah, you could call him fat. He had sex appeal even though he was . . ." She set her glass down. "Oh, hell. Actually he was a filthy fat bastard slob."

Victoria sat back to absorb that bit of information.

Dorothy stirred her Scotch with a finger. The ice had melted but she didn't seem to notice.

"Do you think someone else should take over the project?" Victoria asked.

"I knew you'd understand. Orion is a lovely man, but . . ."

"You and Finney would be the management team, then."

"You do understand. Finney has an extensive background in finance, even though he's awfully young."

"How old is he?"

"Oh, I'm sure he's older than he looks." Dorothy leaned forward unsteadily. "Actually, he doesn't look much older than twenty-something. But he's a financial genius, Victoria. The Mozart of money." Dorothy giggled again.

"I'd love to meet him. You think that with your management experience and Finney's financial ability, you could manage the whole fiber-optics project? Who would deal with the engineering aspects?"

Dorothy waved a hand in front of her face. "One really doesn't need to know the nuts and bolts of a project to manage it, Victoria. But we've thought of giving Orion an honorarium for coming up with the idea."

"Generous," murmured Victoria.

Dorothy hiccuped. "Pardon me."

Victoria handed her a napkin.

"Thank you. Basically, it's simple, Victoria. Orion is unstable. Investors want their money to be safe."

The sun was dropping quickly in the west. Golden light streamed through the windows. Victoria lowered the shade so the light wasn't in Dorothy's eyes.

"You said when you first came, that you had a favor to ask of me," said Victoria.

"It's sensitive." Dorothy patted her lips with the napkin. "I feel a teensy bit uncomfortable asking you."

"Please, you needn't feel uncomfortable."

Dorothy wadded up her napkin and set it on the edge of the coffee table. The napkin dropped to the floor. "Well, Orion lives here and you see him every day."

"What is it that you want me to do? I'm sure you know you can trust me."

"Absolutely, Victoria." Dorothy looked down at the napkin on the floor and picked it up. "We need to convince Orion that it's time for him to step down." She crushed the napkin. "Would you do that? Talk to him about resigning?"

So that's what the past two hours had been leading to, thought

Victoria. Dorothy expected her to convince Orion to drop out of his own company. Orion, the madman. She looked at her watch and stood. "Lovely talking with you, Dorothy."

"Likewise, Victoria." Dorothy, also rising to her feet, knocked over her glass. Victoria quickly mopped up the spilled liquor with a napkin before it dripped down onto the books on the shelf underneath.

Dorothy hadn't noticed. "I know we can count on you. He's certifiable."

"I want to hear more, Dorothy, but it will have to wait for another time."

"I need to use your ladies' room, Victoria."

"Of course. Follow me," said Victoria.

Victoria thought of Dorothy driving in her present condition, and while she was in the bathroom, Victoria called Primo.

"I've got the information you need, Mrs. Trumbull. Dorothy Roche acts in Uncle Bruce's television dramas."

"I suspected as much. Do you have a description of her?" Victoria carried the phone into the kitchen, out of Dorothy's hearing.

"I told the studio I was a thirteen-year-old fan and asked for a photo. They e-mailed me a full-color, signed picture of her."

"Clever of you."

"She's quite beautiful," said Primo with a sigh. "Long straight black hair, dark blue almond-shaped eyes."

"Does she play vampire roles?"

"I think she's more likely the victim."

"I told you about this woman who claims she's Dorothy Roche, didn't I?"

"Yes, ma'am."

"She's here, now. Would you drive her to her place on North Water Street?"

"I'd be delighted, Mrs. Trumbull."

"I'm afraid I'm responsible for her condition."

"No problem. Almost any place on North Water Street is close to the Harbor View. No trouble, at all."

"She said she knew your father. Get her to talk about him, if you can. I have a feeling she's your Uncle Bruce's close personal friend."

"I gather I should remain incognito?"

"That would be wise."

"I'll be there in fifteen minutes."

Victoria thanked him and hung the phone back in its wall cradle as Dorothy emerged, swaying just a bit.

"If I can only remember where I left my car . . ."

"My chauffeur will take you home. You can have someone pick up your car tomorrow." Victoria added with satisfaction, "He's driving the Bentley this evening."

"Ooooh!" said Dorothy, plopping onto a kitchen chair. "What's *he* like?"

"A perfect gentleman."

"I don't want a perfect gentleman," pouted Dorothy, but Victoria had gone into the parlor to clear away the remains of the Dewar's and didn't answer her.

In a short time, Primo arrived. He escorted Dorothy to the Bentley, gently unstuck her arm from his, and settled her into the rear passenger seat.

From the window in the library, Victoria watched the taillights disappear into the shallow swale that marked the edge of her property.

"Lovely evening, Mrs. Roche," Primo began.

Dorothy leaned forward a bit. "Darling, please call me Dorothy. Besides it's not Mrs., it's Ms."

"Did you have a good afternoon with Mrs. Trumbull?"

"She's so clever," said Dorothy, settling back into the soft leather upholstery. "I simply hinted at something, and she understood exactly what I was talking about. What's your name, darling?"

Primo said, "Charles."

"Have you driven for Victoria a long time?"

"Yes, indeed," said Primo. "Years."

Dorothy perked up a bit. "What do you think of her?"

Primo thought of Victoria's deep-set eyes and the spots of war paint on her cheeks, and knew he had to lie. "She's a sweet, gentle, old lady. Extremely wealthy, but quite eccentric."

"Wealthy, is she? You'd never guess."

"I shouldn't be telling you this." Primo looked in the rearview mirror. "But she owns a large villa in Provence, and a ranch outside Santa Barbara."

"Really!"

"Mrs. Trumbull tells me you're a famous actress. Would I have seen any of your plays?"

Dorothy ruffled her metallic hair. "I'm in television, darling. It's Charlie, isn't it?"

"Charles," said Primo, keeping his eyes on the road, his attention on his passenger. "Television. How exciting that must be. I can imagine the lights, cameras, action. Cables snaking over the floor. Crew with earphones." Primo glanced up again and was afraid he'd gone too far. "I'd love to see some of your work. What studio are you with?"

"Vulpone's Vampire Venture," said Dorothy. "I'm sure you never heard of it."

Primo had expected to hear his uncle and his name, but still it took him by surprise. "Vulpone," he murmured.

A deer darted out from the undergrowth by the side of the road. Primo braked. The deer bounded across in front of them. The car stopped abruptly, throwing Dorothy forward.

She screamed. "You almost killed me!"

"Sorry, ma'am. Are you all right?"

"Of course I'm not!"

He pulled over beyond Willow Tree Hollow, thought for a moment, and decided pouring her a nip wouldn't hurt, and might even help. He leaned over the front seat. "The Bentley has a nicely appointed bar, er, Dorothy. Would you like something to calm your nerves?"

She fanned herself with her hand. "You wouldn't happen to have Scotch, would you?"

"We have a nice single malt."

"Oh, my dear!"

Primo, grateful that he'd stashed The Macallan out of reach, went around to the back of the car and opened the trunk, uncased the bottle from its velvet-lined mahogany box, and poured a shot into a silver cup. Setting the cup down on the sandy shoulder, he recapped the bottle, slipped it back into its case, locked the trunk, opened the passenger door, handed the cup to Dorothy, got back into the driver's seat, and continued on toward Edgartown. He checked the rearview mirror. Dorothy was studying the silver cup. She touched her tongue to the Scotch, smiled, and took a tiny sip.

"You said Vulpone Studios," said Primo, getting back to the subject of who this Dorothy person really was. "You must meet a lot of interesting people. Have you ever met Mr. Vulpone, himself?"

"Met! Darling," a throaty laugh. "I certainly have met Mr. Vulpone."

"He must be an important man," said Primo. "Owning a television studio. I bet not many of the actresses have met him. You must be famous."

"Well," Dorothy took another small sip, "he does like the way I perform." She giggled.

A shudder passed over Primo. "I guess actresses get paid pretty well, at least famous ones like you."

"We have per-rog . . . perks."

"Nice long vacations, I guess," said Primo with a sigh. "I've always wanted to be an actor. Do you suppose Mr. Vulpone would be willing to look at my resume?"

"He'd adore you, Charlie."

"Charles. Do you know how I can reach Mr. Vulpone?" Primo held his breath. "What's his first name?"

"Bruce. Scotch." She held up the silver cup. "He'd appreciate this. Scotch with Eye-talian. He's more Eye-talian than Scotch. *Passionato*, you know."

Primo winced. He'd found out the information Mrs. Trumbull

needed. Now, he wanted to get this appalling woman out of his nice car before she . . . He didn't care to finish the thought.

Then he would take a long hot shower in his room at the Harbor View and think about Uncle Bruce, Aunt Maria Rosa, and this awful Dorothy person.

CHAPTER 25

The evening turned chilly. Victoria was lighting the parlor fire when Orion came home. She tossed the spent match into the blazing paper and got to her feet.

He sniffed. "Smells like a barroom in here. Who've you been entertaining?"

"Dorothy Roche."

Orion stroked his mustache. "I think I need to sit."

Victoria told him about Dorothy's attempts to dismiss him from his own company.

Orion laughed.

"You need to take her seriously, Orion."

"I am taking her seriously."

"She claims Finney called a number of people who said you were out of your mind."

"Two people," said Orion. "Denny Rhodes, the selectman, and Dan'l Pease, head of Public Works."

"Finney's telling everyone that you're 'certifiable,' according to Dorothy. They're slandering you, Orion. Isn't this going to influence your would-be investors?"

"Until I sign that contract of his, Finney has no business contacting investors on behalf of Universal Fiber Optics. And I have no intention of signing that contract."

"Dorothy is determined that she and Finney will take over your company."

Orion's face set. "Dorothy Roche and that twerp will not take over my company."

"What about the Ditch Witch drill?"

He stood with his back to the fire, facing Victoria. "I have my own ideas for dealing with Dorothy Roche."

Victoria glanced up in time to see an odd expression on Orion's usually pleasant face. She almost felt sorry for Dorothy. When she looked up again, Orion's expression was pleasant as always.

"Your fires are perfect, Victoria," he said. "You'll have to show me sometime how you build them. Feels good on a chilly evening like this."

Victoria still felt a chill from that fleeting expression, and she thought of the false Dorothy, and she wondered what was about to happen to her.

The next morning, Tim picked Finney up at his bed-and-breakfast. A Rolls? Finney didn't know cars, but this had a woman taking off into space as a hood ornament.

Courtney led him to the library of the North Water Street house, where Dorothy sat. She looked ghastly.

"Are you ill, Dorothy?"

"I have a terrible headache. Come in."

"I'm so sorry."

The library light was subdued, and Dorothy's back was to the window. He sat facing her where he could see out into the garden. Sunlight sparkled on the water spraying up from the fountain, casting rainbows onto the ceiling.

"I met with Victoria yesterday," said Dorothy, holding a hand to her forehead. "We're on a first-name basis now."

Finney nodded.

"I asked her to convince Orion to step aside."

"You're a woman of great diplomacy. Nicely done."

Dorothy untucked a lace hankie from her sleeve and held it to her mouth. A sweet fragrance wafted toward Finney, evoking a faint childhood memory. She moved the hankie aside. "You must get your investors to commit themselves, Finney. And soon. Perhaps if you put in two or three million of seed money, that will encourage others."

Finney cleared his throat and returned to the present. "Orion hasn't signed my contract. Until he does, no one will commit to anything."

"What are you telling them?" Dorothy leaned forward and her handkerchief fluttered to the floor. "We can't have them contacting Orion directly."

"I realize that, Dorothy."

"I want you to meet with Victoria Trumbull this morning. I explained to her our concerns about Orion, but she needs to hear it from you."

Finney shifted. The bright sun pouring through the library window was blinding him and casting Dorothy's face in shadow. No "darling." No offer of breakfast this morning, something Finney had counted on.

"Why don't you call to introduce us," said Finney.

"I don't want you to seem closely connected to me."

"I assume your chauffeur will drive me?"

Dorothy sighed. "I just realized, Victoria's chauffeur brought me home last night in her Bentley and I left my Mercedes in her drive."

"A Bentley? Mrs. Trumbull has a Bentley?" Finney shifted again to see Dorothy's face. She looked haggard. "I gather you drove the Mercedes."

Dorothy didn't answer.

"Will you call Mrs. Trumbull?" asked Finney.

"I suppose that makes sense." Dorothy got up slowly. "Tim will drive you to West Tisbury in the Rolls. Bring the Mercedes back after you've spoken with Victoria."

Victoria recognized the Rolls-Royce when it pulled up to her kitchen door. Tim, Dorothy's chauffeur, opened the passenger door for a tall young man, then got back into the car, and departed.

So this was the Finney Solomon who, with Dorothy, was to take over Orion's company. Victoria studied him as he looked around before he climbed the steps to her entry. As Dorothy had said, he was very young looking. Much too young to have contacts that would hand over fourteen million dollars on his say-so. But then,

Victoria didn't know a great deal about the psychology of investors.

He had short, light brown hair, and as he came closer, she could see his eyes were light, hazel or green, she couldn't quite tell. He had broad shoulders and a narrow waist and hips. He wore tan slacks and a navy blazer over a white knit shirt, and he carried an attaché case.

She went to the door to greet him.

"Mrs. Trumbull?" He held out his hand.

"You must be Finney Solomon. Come in. I've heard good things about you."

"And I of you," said Finney with a broad toothy grin. "Dorothy tells me you own a Bentley. I suppose you must have it garaged?" He was clean-cut, nice looking, but not handsome, and he wasn't at all what Victoria had expected.

Victoria wasn't sure she should mention Primo's name. As a friend of Primo's father, Finney might know him. So she said what was becoming more and more comfortable. "My chauffeur has taken the car on an errand. Please. Come in."

"Wonderful cars," said Finney, wiping his clean shoes on her worn doormat.

This Finney Solomon oozed confidence and honesty and trustworthiness. Victoria could see why investors might write out million-dollar checks to a project presented by him. She led him into the cookroom, where her work was spread out on the table, an old portable typewriter and a drift of notes penciled in her distinctive scrawl.

"I write a news column for the *Island Enquirer*," Victoria explained, moving the typewriter and her notes aside. "I understand you were Angelo Vulpone's friend."

Finney glanced past Victoria and out the window. "He was my mentor. I've known him since I was a boy."

"That couldn't be too long, then." Victoria smiled.

"More than a decade," said Finney.

Odd how his saying *decade* seemed to imply a greater length of time than *ten years*. Victoria said, "I'm sorry for your loss."

"Thank you."

"What can I do for you?"

"I simply wanted to meet you," said Finney. "You have a reputation on the Island for being a mover and shaker."

"I know where a few bodies are buried."

"I understand you're with the police force."

"I'm a police deputy," Victoria said, smoothing the tablecloth in front of her.

"I'm impressed. The police department is fortunate to have the benefit of your knowledge and expertise."

As proud as she was of being associated with the West Tisbury Police, this flattery was a bit too blatant. Victoria got to her feet. "You look as though you could use a bite to eat. I believe we have some leftover muffins and cold coffee from breakfast."

"Great!" said Finney. "Can I get them?"

Victoria smiled as this grand financier morphed into a hungry teenager. She was still under the enervating effects of the doxycycline, and told him where to find everything. "You'll want to heat the coffee in the microwave."

"I'll do it. Can I bring you anything?"

"More coffee, please. There should be plenty."

Plates clattered, a drawer opened and shut, the microwave dinged, and Finney returned with a basket of muffins, plates, and mugs of coffee. He waited for Victoria to serve herself, then dug in as though he hadn't eaten for days. A very young man, Victoria decided. She smiled at Dorothy's description of this Mozart of money.

"Okay if I take another?" Finney asked, his hand hovering over the basket.

"Help yourself. If they're not eaten today, they get tossed out to the crows." Victoria pushed her plate to one side. "Now, tell me why you've come to see me, besides the fact that I'm a mover and shaker."

Finney finished his muffin before he answered. He brushed crumbs from his hands onto his plate. "That was wonderful, Mrs. Trumbull. Thank you." He assumed a serious and mature expression. "As you probably know, Angelo planned to invest in Universal Fiber Optics."

She nodded.

"With his death, the company doesn't have the needed capital."

"I understand you propose to raise that money?"

"Well, we've run into a problem." He leaned his forearms on the table. "One of Orion's partners—"

"Dorothy Roche," Victoria interrupted.

"She and I feel that Orion is no longer the right person to head the company." He looked at Victoria with sincerity. "Technically, you couldn't find a better person. He's got a nationwide reputation, actually a worldwide reputation, as an engineer."

"But?"

"He's over his head, Mrs. Trumbull." Finney held Victoria's gaze. She was determined not to look away first, and he finally dropped his eyes. "He needs to step aside. We'll keep him on as a consultant, of course."

"And you and Dorothy would be the managers."

Finney sat back again, relaxed. "She'll be chief executive officer, and I'll be chief financial officer."

"I see," said Victoria. "What do you expect of me?"

"You have influence over Nanopoulos. We're sure you can convince him to step aside. Let new blood take over."

"Interesting," said Victoria. "If you have a copy of your resume with you, I'd like to see it."

"Certainly." Finney opened his attaché case, extracted a blue plastic binder, and handed it to her.

Victoria turned to the first page, a summary of his work experience. Then the second and third. There were fifteen pages in all. After she'd studied them, she glanced up at Finney, who was looking both eager and expectant.

"I don't know a great deal about finances," she said. "Tell me what you did in this position," she pointed to an entry on one page, " 'assistant to financial officer of Blake and Brown.' What did the company do?"

Finney cleared his throat. "They manufactured paper and plastic products."

"Such as?"

"Decals, that sort of thing."

"Bumper stickers?"

"Well, yes. That, too."

"Is Blake and Brown a printing company?"

"That was one of their functions," said Finney.

"How large a printing firm is it? How many employees do they have?"

"I'm not sure, exactly." Finney squirmed slightly.

"As many as twenty employees?"

"Probably not that many."

"As many as five?" asked Victoria.

"It's hard to say," said Finney.

Victoria turned a page. "Tell me about Osborne, Steere, Williams, and Devons. I've never heard of the company, but then, I'm not really knowledgeable about finances. It sounds like a law firm."

"It is," said Finney, enthusiastic again. "You're absolutely right."

"Your resume says you were assistant to the partners. What was it that you did for the firm?"

"Whatever it was the partners needed. Research, paperwork, that sort of thing. Courier."

"You worked as a messenger?"

"Well, I did that, too." Finney blotted his face with his napkin.

Victoria went through one job after another that Finney had listed. She put the resume aside. "Tell me, Finney. Have you done much fund-raising?"

"Certainly," he said, sounding indignant.

"What are some of the organizations?"

"I can't recall all of them. They're in my resume."

Victoria flipped through the resume. "I noticed a Boy Scout Troop in Hoboken. Yours?"

He nodded.

Victoria changed the subject. "How long have you known Dorothy Roche?"

"I met her when I came to talk to Orion."

"And how did you first meet Angelo Vulpone?"

Finney took a sip of his by-now cold coffee. "My father and

Angelo were both in the construction business. My dad took me to see him, and, well, the rest is history."

"He must have been a wonderful man."

Finney nodded. "A great teacher."

"Had he talked to you about the fiber-optics project?"

"He planned to invest in it heavily."

"So you said." Victoria pushed her own coffee mug aside. "I suppose you know Angelo's family well."

"Not well. He was a private guy."

"Did you know Angelo's brother, Basilio?"

"I heard mention of a brother."

"He owns a television studio called Vulpone's Vampire Venture. Does that mean anything to you?"

Finney shrugged. "I don't know. I didn't know that's what Angelo's brother does."

Victoria looked at her watch. "Finney, I'm afraid my time's up. I have to finish my column for the paper."

"I hope you'll talk to Orion?" said Finney.

"Yes, indeed I will," said Victoria. "Thank you for coming by."

CHAPTER 26

Finney thought about his meeting with Victoria on his way to Edgartown. He felt as if he'd lost a Ping-Pong match, although he couldn't quite put his finger on why.

Mrs. Trumbull didn't act like someone with money. But according to Dorothy, rich Island eccentrics liked to pretend they were ordinary folks.

How nice it would be to pretend you were poor when you had a chauffeur-driven Bentley at your disposal.

Mrs. Trumbull was interested in his resume and his answers to her probing questions. She'd gone over every item, and he felt he'd answered in a straightforward way. She assured him she would talk to Orion.

Since he wasn't having success with venture capital firms, perhaps he could get her to invest three or four million. He shuddered at the thought that Dorothy expected him to invest. At the moment, twenty dollars would stretch his budget. As he passed the airport, he thought about the best way to approach Mrs. Trumbull.

He shrugged to loosen the tightness in his shoulders. In a few minutes, he'd be talking to Dorothy, and he needed to be in control. She'd been distant this morning. He reached into his jacket pocket for his tin of mints and popped two into his mouth.

By the time he reached the outskirts of Edgartown, the mints were half-dissolved and he'd convinced himself the meeting with Victoria Trumbull had gone well.

Since Orion hadn't yet signed the contract, the next step was to suggest that Dorothy invest. Two or three million from her along with three or four from Mrs. Trumbull should loosen the purse strings of other investors. Nothing like an infusion of seed money.

He chewed up the remaining slivers of mints before he turned onto North Water Street so he wouldn't have to think about them when he met with Dorothy, and he brushed any possible crumbs of Victoria Trumbull's muffins from the lapels of his navy blazer.

Now he was ready to act his financier part.

He turned onto North Water Street and was almost abreast of Dorothy's house when he looked over to his left.

Orion's car was parked in Dorothy's space.

Why was Orion here? Finney parked next to his Chevrolet and followed Courtney to the library. Dorothy and Orion were sitting by the fireplace. She didn't look any better than she had earlier. Perhaps worse.

Orion stood and they shook hands. Orion sat again, leaned back comfortably, and crossed his ankle over his knee. His smile made Finney uneasy.

"Have a seat," said Orion, gesturing to a third chair, a straight-backed, rush-seated antique.

Finney glanced at Dorothy.

Dorothy waved vaguely at the chair and he sat.

"I've been telling Dorothy about an opportunity for the company," Orion said. "A way to attract investors, draw attention to our project." He smiled and Finney shivered.

Dorothy's expression didn't tell him anything. She sat primly in her chair, surrounded by bright red chintz roses.

Orion continued pleasantly. "I'm sure Finney's not heard about the annual auction. Would you like to tell him about it, Dorothy?" He turned that smile in her direction.

Dorothy shook her head.

Orion turned to Finney. "The auction is held every summer to benefit the Outstretched Palm Fund." He rested his elbows on the arms of his chair.

"Outstretched Palm?" asked Finney, bewildered. He looked at Dorothy, whose expression was not helpful.

"Forbes's wealthiest, film celebrities, socialites, movers and shakers," at this Orion smiled again at Finney, "money, power, influence, in a congenial setting. People you already know, Finney."

"What about them?" Finney asked, still bewildered.

"They attend the auction," said Orion. "For Island charities, of course. The rich and famous come to be seen, to bid," he rubbed his thumb and forefinger together.

"To bid?" asked Finney.

"A movie star may contribute a dinner with the star cooking and serving. A TV anchor may offer a luncheon cruise on his yacht. That sort of thing." Orion turned to Dorothy. "Tell Finney what you're offering."

Dorothy stared at the never-to-be-burned birch logs.

Orion said, "She's offered the winning bidder a ride on the Ditch Witch drill. She'll drive it."

"Oh?" said Finney, looking from one to the other.

"The drilling unit can travel at speeds up to two miles an hour," Orion said to Finney. "Right, Dorothy?"

Dorothy was now staring down at her hands, which were crushing the scented hankie in her lap.

"Great publicity," said Orion with enthusiasm. "The Outstretched Palm coordinators want Dorothy to drive the winner from the Yacht Club to her house on North Water Street and serve luncheon for twenty-five of the high bidders' friends. This will put Universal Fiber Optics on the map. And you, Finney"—he turned to him—"will have an opportunity to meet even more movers and shakers."

"We need to keep a low profile," murmured Dorothy.

"Nonsense. This is a great contribution. We've already ordered a pink hard hat for you. And a pink safety vest."

Finney, doubtful at first, was warming to the idea. This would lure investors. "He's got something. Let's make it luncheon for fifty. Drive up the bids. Only someone with money will bid, and that someone will have a dozen friends dying to invest in UFO."

"But . . ." Dorothy looked her age.

Finney stood. "That's brilliant!" Demonstrating the drill to investors, Mrs. Trumbull's three or four million, Dorothy's two or three million—well, it was simply brilliant. "What do we need to do to get this going?"

"I've already spoken to the organizers. Some of the biggest names on the Island. Dorothy's already signed up." Orion smiled again. "I knew she'd be thrilled. I'll call tomorrow to let them know the luncheon is for fifty, not twenty-five. Splendid, Finney."

Shortly after Finney left for Edgartown in the Mercedes, Primo arrived at Victoria's in the Bentley.

"Good news, Mrs. Trumbull." He stood at the kitchen door, grinning. "Umberto has hired an assistant."

Victoria dropped onto a kitchen chair. She rested her head on her hand. "Primo . . ."

"You'll love her, Mrs. Trumbull. We've booked her a room at the Harbor View."

"She's not from here?"

"We thought it unwise to hire an Islander. Everyone seems to be related, and everyone seems to know everything before it happens."

"But . . ." She sighed, defeated. "Who is this person?"

"You wanted to know about a television actress?"

Victoria was aghast. "You haven't hired the true Dorothy Roche have you?"

"No, no. Better than that. We know your interest in the true and false Dorothy Roches is to be confidential."

"You'd better tell me whom you've hired."

"Her younger sister, Virginia!" said Primo with a triumphant smile.

"How old is Virginia?"

"Eighteen. Two years younger than Dorothy."

"Virginia Roche?"

"Virginia Carroll. The true Dorothy's name is Dorothy Carroll. Dorothy Roche is her stage name."

Victoria was having trouble concentrating. One more day of doxycycline. Presumably, the Lyme disease would be eradicated from her system along with the dismal effects of the doxycycline.

She could go out in the sun again and concentrate. She could stand up to her two young men. Then she thought about the Bentley. Independence has its price.

"When does Umberto return?" she asked.

"He's here on the Island, settling Ginny—Virginia, that is—into her quarters."

Victoria sighed. "Does Virginia play Scrabble?"

Primo was still standing at the door. "I'll ask." He took out his notebook and pen.

"Don't you want to come in and sit down?"

"I can't stay, Mrs. Trumbull. Besides, there's a nice breeze coming through here."

"Did your father ever mention a Finney Solomon?"

Primo shook his head. "Never heard of him."

"Might you have seen him at your father's office? He's tall, light hair, hazel eyes. About your age."

"Father never mentioned a Finney Solomon."

"Finney claims Angelo Vulpone was his mentor and taught him what he knows about finance."

Primo looked astonished. "Father mentored some kid?"

"That's what Finney claims."

Primo shook his head vigorously. "My father trained Umberto and me to take over his business. He was very close-mouthed. He would never have discussed his business outside our family. Never."

"Would he have given a young man advice on finance?"

"Never. My father wouldn't tell anyone anything that might in the future put him in competition with us."

"According to Finney, your father told him Orion's company was a gold mine."

Primo looked baffled. "Who is this character?"

"He claims he's got a degree from Hudson College."

"That's a community college in Jersey City. He's got a two-year associate of arts degree?"

"It looks that way," said Victoria. "Finney's held a number of clerical jobs that he's inflated on his resume to sound like positions of great responsibility."

"It's true my father was planning to invest in Universal Fiber Optics. I heard him call it a gold mine. But how did this Finney latch onto that?"

"I can't imagine," said Victoria.

CHAPTER 27

Aunt Maria Rosa, contrary to what Primo believed, had not passively accepted her role as betrayed wife. She knew full well what her husband Basilio was up to and with whom he was doing it, and she bided her time.

She'd learned about Basilio's activities in December, six months before her brother-in-law, Angelo, was killed.

This is how she learned. The phone rang. She answered.

"Mrs. Vulpone?" An unfamiliar female voice.

"Speaking," said Maria Rosa.

"Your husband's cheating on you with some bimbo."

"Who is this?" asked Maria Rosa indignantly.

"A friend," and the friend hung up.

Maria Rosa's first reaction was anger. Who was this *strega*, this bitch, who'd called? She hadn't recognized the voice. My Basilio is a good man. He's a good provider. He goes to church. He's a caring father. And he's a . . . She paused. He's a faithful husband.

She thought about the anonymous call. Who could that caller be? Unfamiliar voice. What had she hoped to prove by that call? Maybe she was jealous. Basilio was, after all, a good provider, caring father. But then she thought about the faithful husband bit.

Now that she thought about it, he *had* been working a great many late nights recently.

But the television business was demanding, why shouldn't he work late? And furthermore, he was involved in a new business venture.

Then, too, he'd been going out of town more than usual. Which was understandable, new business and all.

But, she was embarrassed to even think this, there was a certain lack of performance by a normally lusty male.

Stress of his job, she told herself. Maybe she'd let herself go a little. She ought to take off a few pounds, maybe pay more attention to her clothes. But her hair was as dark as it had been when she was at Notre Dame High, and now, with that stylish streak of silver, she looked distinguished. People still commented on the unusual color of her eyes, a clear emerald green.

But, then . . .

What reason did that person have to call her, anyway?

After her anger at the caller cooled somewhat, she decided, out of curiosity, to look up private investigators in the Yellow Pages. A half-page ad cried out at her in bold capital italicized letters: **CHEATING SPOUSE?** She slammed the directory shut, stood up, and brewed herself a cup of tea. While she sipped her tea, she turned again to that page in the directory and quickly dialed the number.

A man answered, repeating the number she'd just dialed. "May I help you?" he asked.

"I . . . I . . . I . . ." said Maria Rosa.

"It's okay, ma'am," the nice-sounding man said. "We're a firm of private investigators. Do you need some help?"

Maria Rosa took a deep breath. "My husband . . ."

"Ah, yes," said the man. "Let me transfer you to one of our infidelity specialists."

A second later, an equally nice-sounding woman came on the line.

Maria Rosa was too rattled to absorb the woman's name. "I feel terrible calling," she said. "Stupid. I'm sure my husband isn't doing anything."

"Why don't we look into his behavior and set your mind at ease?" said the woman. "Would you like to come to the office tomorrow morning?" She said her name again, which was Sharon Knowles, and she gave Maria Rosa directions to the agency. "Bring whatever records you think will help. Phone records, charge account bills, your husband's work address, photos of him, anything."

"I feel foolish."

"Don't. You're acting very sensibly. If he's behaving himself, you won't need to worry anymore."

Basilio worked late again that night. He didn't get home until after ten. He hung his leather trench coat in the hall closet and went into the kitchen, where Maria Rosa, hearing his key in the front door, had turned on the oven to reheat his dinner.

Basilio, or Bruce, as he preferred to be called, took off his suit coat and hung it carefully over the back of a kitchen chair. He was about five-foot-nine and quite heavy. Not as heavy as his older brother, Angelo, but close. His thinning hair was combed back smoothly from his forehead forming a sort of widow's peak, a rich black that he touched up to cover the gray.

"You must be hungry, sweetheart," said Maria Rosa. "I waited for you." She felt guilty now, about her call to the infidelity specialist. "I made chicken scaloppine just for you. With fontina cheese. Your favorite." She kissed her fingers and waved them toward the stove, where the aroma of Basilio's and her late-night supper wafted toward them. "It'll take just a couple of minutes to heat up. What about pouring us a nice glass of wine while we wait?"

He loosened his tie and Maria Rosa got a whiff of unfamiliar soap. Expensive perfumed soap. "Sorry, babe. I'm too tired to eat. I gotta get up early tomorrow."

He marched upstairs without noticing the two places she'd set at the table with the good silver, the candles she'd lighted after she turned on the oven, the lace tablecloth. All to assuage her guilt. *Her* guilt?

She scowled at the departing essence of expensive soap. She turned off the oven, blew out the candles, and swiveled toward the stairs. She made a fist with her pinky and forefinger extended and pointed the fist toward her husband's disappearing footsteps in the upstairs hall.

"*Bastardo!*" she murmured.

———

Maria Rosa was in the kitchen when Basilio came down the next morning. Silently she went about her usual business of pouring his coffee, serving his toast, frying his two eggs over light.

"Something eating you?" he said, elbows on the table, chewing, with his mouth open, his toast and fried eggs. His eyes, once a clear summer-sky blue, looked tiny now, hidden as they were in folds of flesh. His belly hung over the green dollar-sign belt buckle he wore this morning.

Maria Rosa studied her spouse for the first time in a long time. How could this ugly fat man be having an affair? What woman in her right mind would want him to touch her? This was not the Basilio she'd married sixteen years ago.

Basilio took another swig of coffee. "What's the matter with you, anyway?"

"Nothing," said Maria Rosa, getting up from the table. "Will you be home late again tonight?"

"You checking up on me?" Indignant.

"Of course not," said Maria Rosa, feeling a wave of nausea as she thought about her appointment. "I wanted to know if I should hold dinner for you."

"Forget it." He forked up the last of his eggs. "You don't look so good. Maybe you should see the doc." He mopped up runny egg yolk with his toast, stuck it into his mouth, flung his napkin on the table, and got up, still chewing. "Going through the change, I suppose."

"Maybe you're right," she said, glad for an excuse to go to her appointment with the infidelity specialist.

After she'd cleared away the breakfast dishes and left a note for her daily cleaning woman, Maria Rosa drove to the shopping mall near the airport, parked at the far end, and found the building Sharon Knowles had described. She climbed up to the second floor and, somewhat out of breath, knocked on the door marked CONFIDENTIAL ENQUIRIES in gold leaf on the smoked-glass door.

A young man in jeans and a white oxford shirt, open at the neck, answered.

"I'm Mrs. Vulpone. I have an appointment . . ." Getting this much out, Maria Rosa felt faint.

"Of course. Come in. Sharon's expecting you. I'm George, her personal assistant." He led the way through an outer office with a desk, a computer, and a bank of file cabinets, into a large sunny room with an antique wooden desk, an Oriental rug, a conference table with six chairs, and two wide windows overlooking the parking lot.

A large woman with frizzled gray hair and granny glasses rose from behind the desk and extended a hand. "Sharon Knowles, Mrs. Vulpone. Have a seat."

Maria Rosa sat in one of the six chairs and Sharon sat at the end of the table, so both could view the parking lot.

"I don't know where to begin. My husband . . ."

Sharon took off her granny glasses and waited.

"I got a call from someone who said my husband . . ."

"And you'd like to prove the caller is wrong."

"Exactly," said Maria Rosa, relieved. "He's a good man, good father, good provider . . ."

"We don't want his reputation damaged if the call was unfounded."

"That's right," said Maria Rosa, lapsing into the Italian accent she'd lost years ago.

"I understand," said Sharon. "Let me have whatever paperwork you've brought with you."

Maria Rosa handed it over.

"George will make copies," Sharon said, rising. "I'll give you back your originals."

"My Basilio won't know that I've come to see you?"

"This is completely confidential, Mrs. Vulpone. We'll hope to prove Mr. Vulpone is innocent, and he never needs to know a thing. But if he's not, you'll have whatever proof I find to do what you think is right."

They finished their business and Maria Rosa gave Sharon a cash deposit. Sharon escorted her to the outer office, where George arranged for her to pick up the results at a post office box set up for clients.

"Call us in ten days," said Sharon Knowles. "We assume you don't want calls or mail from us at your home."

Maria Rosa found a detailed report when she picked up her mail at the post office box. Photos showed Basilio (Bruce) entering a motel room with a dumpy-looking female with badly dyed red hair, Basilio dining at Le Rivage with the same female, and Basilio at the departure gate at the airport with ditto. A dozen other pictures were included in the report along with a sheaf of papers—purchases on his company's credit card of jewelry, restaurant meals, and flowers Maria Rosa had never received.

Maria Rosa called Sharon Knowles. "The bastard! The cheat! The filth! To think he hoped to father my children! Disgusting! Where did you get all this terrible stuff?"

"Mr. Vulpone didn't try to hide his activities."

Maria Rosa interrupted. "So, he thought I was stupid, did he? The ugly bastard. Who's stupid, hey?"

Sharon went on. "The credit card bills you gave me were for his company's credit card as well as his own private card. You can come to my office to discuss this further, or you can pay the bill by mail, if you'd prefer."

"I'll come to your office. I want to pay cash. Who is this woman? What's her name? How did my Basilio meet her?"

"Her name is Nora Rochester and she owns a cleaning service that takes care of your husband's office and studios at night."

"Empties the trash?" asked Maria Rosa. "A cleaning woman?" A smile in her voice.

"Not exactly. She owns the company."

Maria Rosa had a sudden image of her Basilio and that woman fornicating in a Dumpster on orange peels and coffee grounds, an image that gave her some pleasure.

How could she face this, this, this slime?

One of the credit card receipts signed by her husband was for an outrageously expensive piece of jewelry bought at a store located in the same mall where she'd met with the infidelity specialist.

With the receipt in hand, she drove to the jewelry store. Behind the counter, a salesman was examining a cameo brooch in a velvet-lined box. He looked up when she entered. His silver hair and mustache matched his sleek, silvery suit. He closed the box and set it aside, then tugged down the sleeves of his suit coat and adjusted his tie. "May I help you, madam?"

"Yes, please. My husband bought this." She showed him the receipt.

He took horn-rimmed glasses out of his breast pocket, put them on, and examined the receipt. "Yes, indeed. A lovely white gold necklace set with sapphires. I remember this well. The sapphires were to match his wife's eyes. I hope you're enjoying it?"

Maria Rosa smiled. "I want a second necklace. Twice as expensive as this." She tossed the receipt onto the counter. "Platinum with emeralds. Diamonds, too. Here's his credit card number. You have the billing address. I'll pick up the necklace."

"I don't understand." He looked up into her brilliant green eyes. "Oh," he said, smiling faintly. "Perhaps I do."

When he arrived home after ten, exhausted, Basilio never noticed his wife's icy aversion to him.

Her next step was to whip herself into shape. It wasn't that long ago that she was head cheerleader at Our Lady of Notre Dame High. She'd been voted most popular girl in the senior class. Prom queen. She'd modeled in fashion shows for the women's club. Men on her brother-in-law's construction sites whistled at her.

She hired a personal trainer and a nutritionist and gave herself six months to lose thirty pounds and get back in fighting trim.

Before that six months was up, someone shot and killed Angelo Vulpone, her husband's older brother. And Bruce-Basilio was too busy, too exhausted, too involved to notice his wife's transformation into quite a nice-looking woman.

CHAPTER 28

After Orion and Finney left Dorothy's on Wednesday evening, she retrieved her phone from her purse and called Bruce at the television studio. This was an emergency and she had to talk to him immediately.

Bruce would kill her if she invited fifty people to lunch. He'd already informed her, in no uncertain terms, that she'd better ease up on the spending. No way could she deal with this auction item that Orion had set her up for.

And she absolutely, definitely could not drive the Ditch Witch drill from the Yacht Club up North Water Street in the middle of summer, when the Outstretched Palm auction was held. Bruce had warned her to keep a low, and he meant real low, profile. A pink hard hat was not low profile.

The phone rang four times before it was answered. "Triple V Cable," a young woman with a high-pitched nasal voice announced.

Dorothy snapped at the voice. "Mr. Vulpone, please." Why did girls think talking through their noses was attractive?

The voice came back on the line after a short wait. "Mr. Vulpone's left for the day."

"Did he go home?"

"He didn't say. Can anyone else help you?"

Dorothy hung up without answering and immediately pressed 2, Bruce's speed dial number. A mechanical voice told her to leave a message, and she told the recorder it was an emergency, call her immediately. Immediately, she repeated. She then punched in his home number, something she had never, ever done before.

A woman answered. "Yes?"

Dorothy disguised her voice, even though she'd never met Bruce's wife. "Mrs. Vulpone?"

"Yes? Who is this, please?"

"This is Mrs. Perry from the newspaper," Dorothy said in her new voice. "Is Mr. Vulpone home?"

"Why do you want him?" Mrs. Vulpone said.

"It has to do with advertising."

"He's not interested," Mrs. Vulpone said.

"I need to speak to him. This has to do with Vulpone's Vampire Venture's advertising campaign." Without thinking, Dorothy had let her voice return to its usual pitch.

"Why are you calling now? It's after working hours," Mrs. Vulpone said, then her voice, too, changed, both in volume and pitch. "You his girlfriend? He's not here for you," and she slammed down the phone with a crash.

"Damnation," said Dorothy, rubbing her ear, and then threw her cell phone down on the library table. The cover snapped off and the phone fell to the floor. How was she going to get out of this predicament? How could Orion have been so stupid as to set this up?

Bruce had never intended for her to get involved in the company. That was her idea. In fact, he'd specifically told her *not* to get involved. He'd pay for her cars and chauffeurs and maids, but he'd never, ever pay for a luncheon for fifty. Dorothy groaned. Potential investors in what was about to become her company. What would happen when he found out? She didn't want to think about it.

She would only need Bruce's money for a short time longer. Once Finney raised the fourteen million, she could drop Bruce. Until then, she must continue to make him believe she was merely observing Universal Fiber Optics.

She *had* to talk to Bruce, give him some plausible explanation for this, but what on earth could she tell him?

When she had that money in hand, in the bank, the money Finney was raising, she'd kiss Bruce good-bye. She shuddered at the thought of another kiss, even a good-bye one, from that slobbering lard bag.

But the timing was all wrong. Finney *had* to get that fourteen million, and fast. Orion *had* to cancel that Outreached Palm fiasco.

Victoria was slicing a banana over her Shredded Wheat the next morning. She had swallowed the very last doxycycline pill with her orange juice and felt celebratory. The phone rang. "Mrs. Trumbull?"

"This is she."

"My name is Marylou Waverley, Tris Waverley's sister."

"Yes, of course. I'm so sorry about your loss."

"Thank you, Mrs. Trumbull. Your name was given to me by a customer of ours who said he'd worked with you on Martha's Vineyard."

"Oh? Who was that?"

"His name is Emery Meyer."

"Good heavens!"

"You know the man then, Mrs. Trumbull?"

"Of course," said Victoria. "He and I have a common interest in the poetry of Robert Frost." She smiled when she thought of Emery Meyer, jewel thief and poetry lover. "It was his suggestion that you contact me?"

"Yes. He came into our store to look at some surveillance equipment, and I couldn't help him, because my brother was the one who knew . . ."

"Yes," said Victoria.

"I explained to him that my brother had been murdered on Martha's Vineyard and that's when he mentioned you."

"How can I help you?"

"I understand you do investigative work?"

"Not really," said Victoria, smiling. "I work with the police and have been able to assist a few times."

"That's what Mr. Meyer said. I told him the police don't seem to have done anything about finding my brother's killer, and he suggested that I hire you."

"I can assure you, the police are working on the case. They're terribly handicapped by lack of clues."

"I've saved up quite a bit of money, Mrs. Trumbull. I'll pay whatever you ask."

"I can't accept," said Victoria. "I'm sorry. Really, it's not a task I'm prepared to take on."

"I'm on the Island now, can I at least come and talk to you?"

Victoria sighed. How long would it take for the doxycycline to wash out of her system? She took a deep breath. "Where are you?"

"Vineyard Haven, and I'm about to get on the bus to West Tisbury."

"All right," said Victoria. "I can offer you tea and sympathy, but I can't hunt down your brother's killer."

Victoria had put away the breakfast dishes when Marylou arrived. She was a thin woman in her forties with an exhausted look about her. Even her hair, a nondescript brown, looked exhausted. She was wearing dark gray slacks and a light gray jacket over a pale yellow blouse. The jacket hung loosely on her, as though she'd recently lost weight. The yellow and gray combination seemed to drain out of her face whatever color she'd had to begin with.

"Come in," said Victoria.

Marylou settled on the captain's chair and leaned forward, her elbows resting on her thighs.

"I know you're busy, Mrs. Trumbull. I've checked up on you and I know your reputation."

Victoria started to speak, but Marylou held up a hand.

"At least hear me out, Mrs. Trumbull. I'm desperate."

Victoria could see that she was. She sat down to hear what Marylou had to say.

"Tris was involved in something underhanded. I don't know what."

"I understood that he was hired to do surveillance on the man next door."

"Yes, I knew that. He and I discussed the job at length before he took it. We're partners, you know. At least, we were. We're really just breaking into the business, Mrs. Trumbull. We have a lot to learn." Marylou reached into the large purse she'd set on the floor beside her and brought out a sheaf of papers. "There was some-thing fishy about this whole setup. He sent me checks to deposit, but they weren't from the woman who hired him. Tris didn't tell me much about what he was doing here."

"What might he have been involved in?" asked Victoria.

Marylou reached into her pocket for a tissue and blew her nose. "Sorry, I just can't get over his death."

"Why do you think he was involved in anything other than surveillance?" Victoria asked.

"After Tris came here, he got very secretive. That wasn't like him. And I started getting hang-up calls at the store. A lot of them."

"Do you have any idea as to what was bothering him?"

"None at all."

"Might he have been involved in drug dealing? Unfortunately, that's fairly common on the Island."

"He's always been squeaky clean, Mrs. Trumbull."

"Things change," said Victoria. "Was he having any financial problems? Or a drinking or gambling problem? Was he involved with a woman?"

Marylou shook her head at each question. "None of those. I'd know, at least about gambling and drinking."

"You really must talk to the police," said Victoria. "I can't trace phone calls or follow paper trails, and I don't know anything about electronics or surveillance."

"But you understand people," insisted Marylou. "That's what this is all about, I'm sure. *Cherchez les people.*"

Marylou held out the papers she'd taken from her purse. "I made copies of all the checks Tris sent. There's only one from Dorothy Roche, the one she gave him as a retainer. The rest are cashier's checks."

Victoria took the papers and looked them over. "I really don't know what to tell you, Marylou."

Marylou was silent while Victoria paged through the photo-copies. "Fifty thousand dollars," Victoria said.

"Yes," said Marylou. "The work Tris contracted to do would have been less than a quarter of that."

Victoria handed the papers back to Marylou.

"Please keep them, Mrs. Trumbull. Those are for you." Marylou reached into her purse. "I want to give you a retainer, Mrs. Trumbull."

"I can't accept it," said Victoria. "I'm working on another case that may be related to the death of your brother. If so, I'll give you any information I can."

Marylou reached into her purse. "Here's my card."

"I'm afraid you've made a trip to the Island in vain."

Marylou shook her head. "I hope you'll at least think about this. What was my brother involved in? He was a gentle guy. Why would anyone kill him?" She blotted her eyes with her tissue, looked at her watch, and stood up. "I've got to catch the bus back to the ferry."

Victoria finished the first draft of a sonnet about bees when the red Ferrari pulled up and Umberto sprang out of the driver's seat. The young woman passenger had already untangled herself from the low seat, and stood next to the car. Victoria immediately assumed this was Virginia Carroll. She was tall, but her head still only came up to Umberto's chin. Her silky black hair drifted to her shoulders and shone with blue highlights.

Victoria went to the door and greeted them. "Good afternoon, Umberto. And you must be Virginia."

"Yes, ma'am. They call me Ginny."

"Come in, both of you."

Ginny and Umberto followed Victoria into the cookroom and they sat at the table.

"I'm not used to having help," said Victoria. "I'm not quite sure what I need you to do."

"Ginny is a genius with computers," said Umberto.

"Do you have a computer with you?" asked Victoria.

"Yes, ma'am. Umberto said that's what you need." She reached into her backpack, drew out a slim black object the size of a breadboard, and powered it up to a blast of music. "When Umberto asked me to work for you I was thrilled. I've loved your poetry since I was a kid."

"Do you write poetry yourself?"

"My school newspaper published one of my poems." Ginny blushed suddenly. "I guess that's not such a big deal."

"Yes, it is. It's good to see your work in print," said Victoria. "Perhaps you'll let me read it sometime."

"You wouldn't happen to have Wi-Fi, by any chance, would you, Mrs. Trumbull?"

"I do," said Victoria. "My friend Geoffrey Parkhurst installed it for me." She opened the drawer in the table under the telephone and found a scrap of paper with a series of letters and numbers, which she gave to Ginny.

Ginny entered the long code, gave a satisfied sigh, and looked up. "Works great."

"A visitor this morning brought me copies of checks I'd like to know more about. Can you track them down on your computer?" She gave Ginny the papers Marylou Waverley had left with her. "I'd like any information you can find about the checks. Anything at all about his finances."

Ginny looked doubtful. "It's not exactly easy to find financial information." She lifted her hands from the keyboard and gazed out of the window. "Do you have a guess as to who might have given this guy the money?"

"Try Basilio or Bruce Vulpone," said Victoria.

"My uncle," said Umberto. "Your sister works for him."

"I'll need his . . ." Ginny didn't finish, but grinned suddenly and typed vigorously.

"Don't do anything illegal," said Victoria, concerned.

"They'll never catch me," said Ginny without looking up from the keyboard.

Victoria turned to Umberto. "I'm sure Tris Waverley's death is connected to your father's."

Umberto nodded.

Ginny continued to type.

A catbird called from the other side of the lilac trees. Another answered.

"Can you find out if Tris Waverley was ever in any kind of trouble, Ginny?"

"No problem," said Ginny without stopping. "I'll work on Mr. Vulpone first."

"His sister says he wasn't, but something about Tris Waverley doesn't seem right."

Ginny looked up briefly. "This financial stuff may take a while, Mrs. Trumbull."

Umberto watched Ginny with a rapt expression.

"I have to go out to the garden," said Victoria.

The fading bee balm blossoms still trembled with bees. Victoria went past and into the vegetable garden, enclosed by a ten-foot-high fence to keep deer out.

She picked Swiss chard and, kneeling down using the rake handle for support, unearthed several small potatoes. She sighed happily, eased herself up, and headed back to the house, her harvest held in the front of her shirt. She dropped her supper makings into the sink, brushed the dirt from the front of her shirt, and scrubbed her hands.

Umberto had moved his chair closer to Ginny's.

"This is taking longer than I thought, Mrs. Trumbull," Ginny said. "I have to wait until Mr. Vulpone does some banking transaction. Then, who knows?"

CHAPTER 29

While Victoria was harvesting her supper, Maria Rosa, thirty pounds lighter and wearing the emerald necklace that matched her eyes, arrived unexpectedly at the office of Sharon Knowles, private investigator.

She knocked and George, the personal assistant, greeted her. "May I help you?" he asked, then did a double take. "I didn't recognize you, Mrs. Vulpone." He stood aside. "Wow! Please come in."

"Thank you. Is Sharon available?"

"For you, of course." He rapped on the door to Sharon's office and opened it. She was on the phone and mouthed, "Right with you."

George shut the door again. "Have a seat, Mrs. Vulpone. I hope you don't mind my saying, you look great."

"Thank you," said Maria Rosa, touching her necklace.

"May I get you coffee? Or tea?"

"Nothing, thank you."

Sharon, too, did a double take when she came out of her office a few minutes later.

They sat at the conference table again.

"Whatever you're doing agrees with you," Sharon said. She indicated the necklace that matched Maria Rosa's eyes. "Is that from Mr. Vulpone?"

"In a way." Maria Rosa smiled. "I need some information, Sharon. I tried to locate Nora Rochester myself, but couldn't. Can you find her?"

"We'll try. I have some information on her already."

"Call me at home, anytime during the day."

Sharon scribbled the number on a yellow pad. "Do you need anything more than simply locating her?"

"I don't think so," said Maria Rosa.

Sharon leaned back in her chair and looked closely at Maria Rosa. "Don't do anything rash, Mrs. Vulpone."

"I wouldn't think of it," said Maria Rosa, rising.

Sharon, too, got up. "You really should keep that in a bank vault. It must be worth a fortune."

"It's meant to be worn," said Maria Rosa, stroking the emerald necklace.

Victoria won the first move at their Scrabble game the next evening. She laid down AFFABLE, using all seven of her tiles for eighty points. Five turns later Ginny attached FLAMINGO to one of the Fs in AFFABLE, using all seven of *her* tiles for seventy points. The score was close, within twenty points. Victoria leaned over the board, studying it. Then, smiling broadly, she laid down a Q on the triple word space at the bottom left-hand corner of the board, then UIX. She incorporated the last O of FLAMINGO into the word she was building and finished with TIC, the C landing on a second triple word score giving Victoria 254 points for QUIXOTIC.

"Wow!" said Ginny. "Sweet!"

"We don't often get a chance to use of all seven tiles in a move," said Victoria. "Yet we've done just that three times, and the game is young."

"And the Q and the X. Wow!"

By the time Orion came home, they were down to the last few tiles in the purple velvet Crown Royal sack. He peered at the board, then at the score, which by now totaled well over seven hundred. Victoria was ahead.

"I've got news, but it can wait until you finish the game," Orion said. "Shall I get drinks for all?"

"Cranberry juice with rum for me," said Victoria.

"Just plain juice for me, thanks," said Ginny.

By the time Orion returned with drinks, Victoria had won by

fifty points, and the two were congratulating each other on a splendid first game.

Victoria eased herself out of her chair.

"Don't get up, Victoria," said Orion.

"It's Friday night. I need to put my beans to soak."

"Ah," said Orion. "Saturday night baked beans."

When Victoria returned to the parlor, Ginny had put away the board, and Orion had folded up the card table. Victoria sat in her wing chair, Ginny perched on the stiff couch, and Orion eased himself onto the rocker.

Victoria noticed his caution. "Is your back still troubling you?"

"I'm simply being cautious. I like this chair."

"I hope your news is good."

"News, at any rate." He leaned forward. "I've set up a new company, Fiber United."

"What about UFO?" asked Victoria.

"Dorothy Roche will become president and Finney Solomon, chief financial officer. I'll remain as vice president of operations."

"You're giving up your position as president of your own company? The company you founded? That's not right."

"That doesn't sound fair to me, either," said Ginny. "Umberto told me what a great project you have." She blushed suddenly.

"Casper and I switched the project itself legally to Fiber United, the new company."

"What happens to the Ditch Witch machine?" Victoria asked.

"Since Dorothy owns the title, the new company will lease it from her, provided the terms are favorable. The old company, Universal Fiber Optics, will be responsible for payments on the drill."

"Wow," said Ginny.

"What's left of the old company?" Victoria asked.

"The name, the payments on the Ditch Witch drill, and whatever remains of the money Casper and I invested."

"Then you'll lose your investment?"

"We won't lose it unless Dorothy and Finney botch the job. The town contracts still held by Universal Fiber Optics should keep them solvent. I'm still vice president, of course, so I'll have some say." Orion grinned suddenly.

Ginny sat forward on the couch. "Umberto told me that Ms. Roche is donating a luncheon for fifty people to the Outstretched Palm auction. That's good of her."

"She also intends to drive the Ditch Witch drilling unit from the Yacht Club to her place on North Water Street."

"Wow!" said Ginny. "That will draw a huge crowd."

"I'm sure it will," said Orion.

CHAPTER 30

On Saturday morning, Victoria boiled the dried navy beans that had soaked all night and put them in the aged bean pot with an onion, salt pork, and molasses and set the bean pot in the oven on low heat.

After that, she went out to the garden to cut a bouquet of black-eyed Susans. While she was snipping carefully, avoiding the bees that were now hovering around the bright yellow flowers, Sean pulled off New Lane in his red pickup truck and parked in the west pasture. He beckoned to someone in the passenger seat. A boy.

The boy scrambled out of the truck and came slowly toward Victoria, his head down, his feet, clad in unlaced, red high-top sneakers, dragging. He was eight or nine years old, and Victoria recognized him as one of the Whitfield boys who lived down Tiah's Cove Road.

She waited to see what this was all about.

"Orion around?" Sean asked.

The boy jammed his hands in his pockets. He was a skinny freckle-faced kid with sandy-red hair. His jeans were worn through at the knees and Victoria noticed a scab on his right knee.

She set her bouquet on the nearby picnic table. "I believe Orion's in the kitchen," she said. "Would you like me to get him?"

"We'll talk to him there. C'mon, Sandy. March." Sean started toward the house with Sandy tagging reluctantly behind. Before he'd gone more than a few paces, Sean turned to Victoria. "You, too, Mrs. T. You need to hear what Sandy has to say."

Victoria looked at the boy. His face, still aimed at his feet, was hidden by his mop of tangled hair. She seemed to recall that he was the youngest of four or five children, all boys. She gathered up her bouquet, pulled off a few wilted leaves, and dropped them on the ground.

Sandy was lagging farther and farther behind. Sean reached out a long arm, grabbed his T-shirt, and pushed the boy ahead of him at a pace faster than Sandy seemed to want. The boy said nothing.

The three marched from the flower border, where Victoria had been cutting the black-eyed Susans, past the great wisteria vine, its trunk the size of a man's thigh. The three crossed the driveway, badly rutted from spring rains. Victoria reminded herself to ask David Merry to smooth out the drive with his Bobcat. They marched past the crab apple tree, across the lawn, and up the stone steps that led to the entry.

No one had said a word. Victoria wondered what on earth this boy, this child, could have done to provoke the usually impassive beekeeper.

Orion was heating water for his tea when Victoria, Sean, and the boy entered the kitchen. He looked up from the teakettle with his usual pleasant expression. "Morning, Sean. What's up?"

"Sandy, here, has something to tell you."

Victoria said, "Shall we go into the cookroom?"

"Let me fix my tea," said Orion. "Anyone else?"

"I don't think so," said Sean. He led the way down the step into the cookroom and, still holding the back of Sandy's shirt, stood behind one of the caned chairs. To Sandy, he said, "You stand there, kid, until Mrs. Trumbull is seated."

Victoria parked herself in her chair with her back to the window, Orion sat to her left, and Sean released his hold on Sandy's shirt and pushed him roughly into the seat to Orion's left.

Orion excelled at looking expressionless when he chose. He glanced now from Sandy to Sean, and back at Sandy. He stroked his mustache. He picked up his mug and sipped his tea.

"Okay, kid. Talk," said Sean.

Victoria had only seen Sean in his role as beekeeper, steady, taciturn, professional. She had never imagined him as this angry, stone-faced man. His high cheekbones shone. His eyes glittered. His mouth was a thin, straight slash above a rock-hard cleft chin. Sandy's head hung down. His hands were in his lap. He was small for his age, and his sneakered feet didn't quite reach the floor. When he moved his feet, Victoria heard the plastic tips of his shoelaces tick on the pine boards.

A crow called three notes and a second crow, some distance away, called three notes in return. Victoria was aware of her own heartbeat, of the sound of Sean's breathing, of the light gasp of Sandy's breath.

Silence.

"Talk, kid. You have some explaining to do to Mr. Nanopoulos."

Sandy looked up, his eyes full of tears he clearly was trying not to shed. "I . . . I . . . I . . ." He stopped.

"Are you about to tell me about something you did that involves me?" Orion asked softly.

The boy nodded and looked down again.

"Why don't you tell me what it was?"

"I . . ."

Silence.

"Was it something you decided to do on your own?"

The boy shook his head.

"Was it something someone suggested you do, maybe a practical joke?"

The boy nodded.

"Was it recently?"

At this, a tear, then another, and another slithered down the boy's cheeks, and he lifted the front of his grimy T-shirt and wiped his face.

"Why don't you tell me what you did," said Orion. "Did it have to do with yellow jackets?"

The boy gazed at Orion, his expression bleak.

"You put that yellow jacket nest in my car, right?"

The boy nodded.

Victoria turned her chair slightly and gazed out of the window so she wouldn't have to see either the boy's or Orion's pain.

"Now that we know what we're talking about, you can explain to me how it happened. Start at the beginning. Who thought it would be fun to put that nest in my car?"

Sandy swallowed hard, then swallowed again. "A man."

"Was it a man you know?"

"No."

"No, *sir*," snapped Sean.

"No, sir," the boy repeated.

"Where did you meet this man?"

"Up to Alley's. He bought us Klondike bars."

"Did he tell you his name?"

The boy shook his head. He glanced at Sean. "No, sir."

"Then what happened?"

"He left. We sat on Alley's porch and watched the tourists."

"Was this in the afternoon?"

"Yes." Sandy glanced at Sean, who sat, arms folded, like a chain-sawed wood figure. "Yes, sir."

"When did you see the man again?"

"Next day. I went to Alley's to pick up the mail and he was sitting on the porch."

"And?"

"He talked to me some. Asked me what my name was. Where I lived. Like that."

Orion asked quietly, "Anything else?"

Sandy shuffled his feet. "He asked what I liked to do. I told him I want to be an entomologist when I grow up."

"You like insects?"

"Yes, sir. I have an ant farm. I collect insects and have them all labeled. My mom won't let me kill anything, so I just have ones I find around, like under the porch light in the morning, you know?"

Orion nodded. "I know."

"I have a beehive, too. Like, that's how I know Mr. Sean, here. He . . ." Sandy glanced at Sean, then began again. "Mr. Sean gave it to me. He was teaching me about bees."

Sean, arms folded, looked away from the boy.

"So you know how to collect a yellow jacket nest."

The boy's enthusiasm faded. "Yes, sir. It was on the side of the barn, up near the eaves."

"What did this man look like?"

The boy shrugged. "He was just a man."

"Fat? Skinny? Tall? Short?"

"He wasn't fat."

"Young? Old?"

"Not old."

"C'mon, kid." Sean turned to the boy. "Speak up."

"He was just a man," said Sandy to Sean.

"Did the man pay you to put the nest in my car?"

"No, sir. He said you was, were, I mean, a friend of his and he said he wanted to play a joke on you, and you'd think it was funny, and he gave me a sheet of postage stamps. Thirty-three-cent postage stamps with beetles and katydids and spiders and ants and like that. I don't want to use the stamps because they've got descriptions on the back, you know?"

Orion stroked his mustache. "You know, don't you, what happened when I opened my car door?"

"Yes, sir." The boy looked down again. "I almost killed you."

"What do you think I should do about this?"

"I don't know," said the boy, his eyes still averted.

"You know you've got to take your punishment?"

"Yes, sir." Sandy looked up briefly. "I'm awful sorry, sir. I didn't think they'd sting you like that."

Sean grunted.

Victoria, still gazing out the window, saw a cardinal and a blue jay picking up seeds that had fallen on the grass from the bird feeder. Bright red and lavender blue.

Orion said, "What do you think would be a fitting punishment?"

"Taking away my insects and my ant farm and my beehive." The boy was staring at his hands, which were folded in his lap. "Sir," he added.

"I don't think that would be appropriate," said Orion. "Any other ideas?"

"Take my allowance for the rest of my life."

"No, that wouldn't begin to do." Orion turned to Sean. "Do you need help in cleaning out the hives and scrubbing floors in your bottling room?"

Sean turned his head toward the boy, so stiffly it seemed to squeak. "Yeah."

Victoria turned back to the two men and the boy. No one paid any attention to her.

Orion asked, "Is Sandy responsible enough to work for you, Sean?"

A long silence. Sandy glanced from Orion to Sean, then back down to his hands.

"I've got one hell of a lot of dirty work I need done, real dirty work that a kid can't mess up."

Orion turned to Sandy. "What about that? Cleaning hives, cleaning glassware, sweeping and mopping floors? An apprentice. Whatever work Sean needs done?"

"Yes, sir," said Sandy. "I can do that. I can."

Orion addressed Sean. "Would two mornings a week for the next year be any help to you?"

Sean, arms still folded, said nothing.

Orion turned back to Sandy. "Look at me."

Sandy looked up.

"That's only part of the punishment," said Orion.

Sandy nodded.

"You're to write a report on the differences among bees, hornets, and wasps. Include what happens to someone who's allergic to insects and gets stung and how you treat them. The report's to be at least five hundred words, it's to be in your own writing—don't copy someone else's words—and I want it by next Sunday. Understand?"

"Yes, sir."

"Go to the library and look up books on insects. You're not to use your computer."

"I don't have a computer," said the boy.

"List the library books you look at. Can you do that?"

"Yes, sir."

"Do your parents know about the practical joke?"

Sean unfolded his arms and dropped his hands to his lap. "I told them," he said. "His old man whipped him."

Victoria got up from the table. "I believe we can all use a glass of lemonade."

CHAPTER 31

Maria Rosa answered the kitchen phone. "Yes?"

"Sharon Knowles, Mrs. Vulpone. I have information."

"Yes, please."

"Nora Rochester, the woman your husband—"

"Yes, yes, I know." She moved a chair closer to the phone and sat down.

"Nora Rochester is on Martha's Vineyard and is going by the name 'Dorothy Roche.'"

"Dorothy Roche? She's just a girl, an actress who works for my husband."

"Your husband's friend is using her name then."

Maria Rosa made a clucking sound with her tongue. "So my husband set that fake Dorothy Roche up in a love nest?"

"It looks that way."

"Where?" Maria Rosa reached for a scratch pad and pen.

"It's an island off the coast of . . ."

"Yes, yes. I know all about Martha's Vineyard. Where is this love nest?"

"I'm not sure Martha's Vineyard houses have numbers. She's staying in a place in Edgartown, North Water Street."

"That's a high-price neighborhood."

"The house is midway between Main Street and the Harbor View Hotel." Sharon gave her a few details about the fake Dorothy Roche including the fact that Dorothy was donating an item to the Outstretched Palm auction that was already creating quite a buzz on the Island.

"What's this auction for?"

"To raise money for Island charities. Celebrities donate items and wealthy people bid on them."

"She's a celebrity?" Maria Rosa sketched a row of daggers on her scratch pad.

"She must think she is. She's driving a Ditch Witch drill rig from the Yacht Club to her place."

Maria Rosa laughed. " 'Ditch Witch'? What's a Ditch Witch drill rig?" She laughed again and added drops of blood to the points of the daggers.

"It's a drilling machine she owns. The company she's with uses it to install some kind of special cable."

"Her cleaning company owns a drilling machine?"

"No, this company is installing a fiber-optic cable on the Island."

"Ah," said Maria Rosa. "I think I'm beginning to understand something. Go on, you were saying?"

"The high bidder gets to ride on the Ditch Witch rig and also wins luncheon for fifty friends."

"*Fifty* people! Who's paying for this?" She drew a line under the drops to represent a pool of blood. "Never mind," she said quickly. "I think I know. When's this auction?"

"A week from tomorrow."

"Thank you very much," said Maria Rosa, and hung up. She tore off the top sheet of the scratch pad, crumpled it up, and hurled it into the kitchen trash along with the orange peels and coffee grounds.

After Sean left with Sandy tagging after him, Victoria cleared away the lemonade glasses. Orion stashed them in the dishwasher, then he and Victoria sat down again.

"Orion," said Victoria, "you handled that well."

"Poor kid," said Orion.

"Sandy answered one question, but that leaves us with a few others. Who was the man who convinced him to play that trick on you?"

"I can't imagine."

"Who would want to harm you? That makes no sense whatsoever." Victoria watched a bright red cardinal forage for seeds on the ground under the feeder. "It can't be someone protesting the fiber-optic cable. For the first time in history, it's a project no one opposes."

"I don't know, Victoria. I just don't know."

Dorothy paced back and forth in her North Water Street house, waiting for Bruce to call. Cell phone reception here was unreliable, and she didn't dare leave the house.

The phone rang.

"Hello?" Dorothy answered.

"What in goddamn hell do you think you're doing?"

Surely he hadn't heard this quickly about the auction item. "Bruce, darling . . ." she began.

"Don't you goddamn 'darling' me, bitch."

"What's the matter, Bruce?"

"You know goddamned well what. I'm not paying for some luncheon for fifty people. Are you out of your mind?"

"I can explain," said Dorothy, thinking fast.

"You can explain it to me, all right. Pick me up at the airport in a half-hour."

Dorothy heard the unmistakable whine of an airplane engine before Bruce disconnected. She slammed down the phone and checked her watch. The plane was due to land at three-thirty. She'd have to leave for the airport in ten minutes. She'd get Courtney to fix something special for supper, lobster salad and that white Burgundy.

How could Orion have been so stupid? Everyone on the Island seemed to know about that auction item. How, she had no idea. What was she going to tell Bruce?

And when was Finney going to come up with the money? Bruce and Finney knew nothing about each other. Immediate action was critical now that Bruce was nosing around.

———

Finney felt a resurgence of confidence. People who would bid at the Outstretched Palm auction a week from tomorrow were probably on Island already, and he intended to shake hands with everyone he could.

First, he'd contact Victoria Trumbull, give her the opportunity to invest her millions. That would shame Dorothy into putting in a couple million of her own. After that, he'd personally shake hands with every one of the wealthy auction goers.

In his wallet he had the new credit card but not much cash. Even with considerably cheaper accommodations, his budget was stretched.

The room he was renting, within walking distance of Victoria Trumbull's, was clean and comfortable. He looked out the window at a tailless cat making its way through the underbrush, stalking something.

The wealthy seldom quibbled over big expenditures, he told himself. It was the small stuff that seemed important. That explained why Mrs. Trumbull rented rooms. Small stuff. Three or four million would seem like nothing to her.

He dialed the phone in the downstairs hall.

Victoria answered.

"Finney Solomon, Mrs. Trumbull. I don't know if you remember me, but I came by a few days ago and you were kind enough to look at my resume."

"Certainly I remember you."

"Well," said Finney, suddenly feeling awkward, "I'm staying here in West Tisbury."

Victoria said nothing.

"Would you mind if I called on you again? I'm just down the road."

"You're welcome to stop by," said Victoria.

"Thanks, Mrs. Trumbull. I'll be there in ten minutes."

"Make it later, around four," said Victoria. "I'm in the midst of something right now."

"Thanks, Mrs. Trumbull," said Finney, and set the phone down.

CHAPTER 32

Dorothy checked her watch. Only a few minutes before she had to leave for the airport to pick up Bruce. Why hadn't he given her more warning? She applied her makeup carefully and checked her hair in the powder room mirror. Her roots showed. She rummaged around in her dresser and found a green velvet hat. That would have to do. She found matching green slacks and a light-hearted floral-print blouse. She mustn't arrive late at the airport. Bruce had sounded in a horrible temper.

How was she going to explain this strange idea of Orion's to him? She'd think about that on the way to the airport.

Victoria had been going through financial information that Ginny had found on the Internet when Finney called. She was sitting at the cookroom table, where Ginny had set up her laptop and printer.

Tris Waverley seemed to be a legitimate businessman trying to make a modest living running an electronics store. He'd deposited a cashier's check for a thousand dollars around the time the false Dorothy Roche had given him a retainer. However, the week before he was killed, he'd sent a series of cashier's checks to his sister. The checks totaled more than fifty thousand dollars.

Victoria set the pages aside. "Have you found anything on Basilio Vulpone?"

"I've tapped into his computer, but now I have to wait until he does an online bank transaction. Then we're in."

"Are you sure this is legal?"

"You don't want to know, Mrs. Trumbull."

Dorothy arrived at the airport as the plane pulled up to the chain-link fence. A slim, tanned young woman in shorts, a sleeveless blouse, and boating shoes waited by the gate. She smiled at Dorothy, who suddenly felt hot and overdressed in her velvet hat and green slacks.

"Are you waiting for your husband?" the woman asked.

"Just a friend," said Dorothy, and turned slightly so she wouldn't have to converse.

The propellers slowed and stopped; the pilot climbed down and opened the baggage compartment in the wing.

Dorothy wet her finger and smoothed her eyebrows, pressed her lips together to redistribute the lip gloss she'd applied hastily, and stood with what she hoped was a disarming attitude.

Two passengers disembarked, a nice-looking man dressed in khaki pants, a blazer, and an open-necked shirt, and Bruce.

Dorothy always felt embarrassed when she saw him after a separation. He was soft and doughy, and his eyes looked small in his fleshy face. He wore a rumpled, double-breasted, pin-striped suit with a white shirt and yellow tie.

The ground crew opened the gate.

Bruce put on his sunglasses, hiding his eyes, and glanced toward his fellow passenger, who was grinning and heading toward the young woman in shorts.

Dorothy waved her arm to get Bruce's attention. He lumbered toward her. The couple had left.

"Just what in hell . . ." he began.

"Darling, I have so much to tell you! All sorts of exciting things are happening. You'll be so proud of me." She took his arm.

He shrugged her off. "Gotta pick up my suitcase."

"I'm so glad you're planning to stay." She followed him inside the building. He lifted his suitcase off the rack and pulled up the handle.

"I'm dying to tell you about the work I've done." She turned coyly to him. "Would you like to drive?"

"Where's that driver you hired?"

"I wanted it to be just the two of us, darling."

Bruce grunted. "You drive. You've got one hell of a lot of explaining to do."

He stowed his bag in the back of the car and went around to the passenger side. Dorothy was already in the driver's seat, adjusting her hat, which kept slipping down on her forehead. She felt sweat trickling down behind her ears. She'd have to get to the hairdresser's right away, before Bruce noticed the roots.

She pouted prettily. "I have an appointment at the hair salon I simply can't break. Bad boy, you should have warned me that you were coming." She backed smoothly out of the parking space and headed away from the airport.

"Cut the shit, Dorothy. What in hell were you thinking, lunch for fifty people? You crazy?"

On the way to the airport, Dorothy had decided on innocence, pure girlish innocence. She couldn't see Bruce's eyes behind the dark glasses. On the straight road she turned, just long enough for him to see her eyes brimming with tears. "I thought you'd be so proud of me. I wanted to surprise you."

"Surprise me? Hell, everyone on the Island, everyone on the East Coast knows that some dame called Dorothy Roche is auctioning off a ride on a drill rig and lunch for fifty. Some surprise. I told you . . ."

Dorothy turned quickly to him again, the tears oozing down her cheeks now. "I know you wanted me to keep a low profile, but darling," she looked back at the road. "This was such a wonderful opportunity for you. I know you're interested in this company of Mr. Nanopoulos's, and I thought you'd be pleased with me, finding out all I could about it?" She looked at him again.

"Watch it!" said Bruce, bracing his hands on the dashboard. There was a squeal of tires and the crunch of metal as Dorothy plowed into the back of a red Volvo station wagon driven sedately at exactly the speed limit by an elderly woman.

While they waited for activity on Bruce's computer, Victoria was getting to know her assistant.

"Tell me about your sister," Victoria said, moving the stack of

217

printed pages to one side. "Your last name is Carroll and hers is Roche."

"She's actually my half-sister," said Ginny. "Two years older. We have the same mother, different dads. Her dad was in the army. He died jumping out of an airplane."

"I'm so sorry," said Victoria. "Was he a paratrooper?"

"It was a friend's airplane and he did it on a dare."

"Good heavens. Did his parachute fail to open?"

"My mom told me he wasn't wearing a parachute. That was a couple of months before Dorothy was born."

Victoria didn't know what to say.

"A year later, my mom married my dad, and here I am. He adopted Dorothy. He's the only dad she's ever known."

"But she kept her biological father's name?"

"Just as her stage name. She's really Dorothy Carroll. She thinks her dad was a hero, you know? She honors him by being, like, a TV vampire?" Ginny shrugged. "Go figure." She went back to her computer. "While we wait to see if Mr. Vulpone does an end-of-day bank deposit, I'll track down that woman using my sister's name." Ginny tapped industriously then stopped. "Do you have any clues about her? I'm only coming up with stuff on my sister."

Victoria thought a moment. "She claims to have had a limousine service and a cleaning service. She may have had a contract to clean the television studio."

"That should do it." Ginny went back to the keyboard.

Victoria busied herself in the kitchen, not wanting to stray too far from the magic of the Internet. A few minutes later, Ginny called out, "Hey, Mrs. Trumbull! Got it!"

Victoria draped the dish towel she'd been using over the towel rack and stepped down into the cookroom. "Triple V," Ginny looked up, "the vampire TV studio my sister works for? They contracted with Ride-A-Broom Services to clean the studio. Nora Rochester heads the company."

"Good job," said Victoria. "Can you find out anything about Nora Rochester?"

"Sure. No problem."

At the end of another half-hour, Victoria had a computer print-out of Nora Rochester, a.k.a. the False Dorothy Roche, everything from date of birth fifty-seven years earlier, through three marriages that apparently yielded the money to finance the start-up of her cleaning and limousine services. Before four o'clock, when Finney was due to arrive, Ginny called out again to Victoria, who was sorting brown paper bags she'd saved from her Cronig's shopping. "He's made a deposit, Mrs. Trumbull. We're in!"

"I don't understand how that helps," said Victoria, tucking the bags into a carrier bag.

Ginny tapped away. "You know the copies of cashier's checks that woman whose brother was murdered gave you?"

"Right. Marylou Waverley."

"Maybe Mr. Vulpone withdrew the same amounts near those same dates, know what I mean?"

"I think so." Victoria stashed the bag of bags in the closet under the stairs and joined Ginny, who gave her another stack of print-outs. A short time later, Ginny printed out still more.

"Wait until you see this, Mrs. Trumbull!" She handed several sheets to Victoria, who looked them over.

"This is wonderful," said Victoria. "It confirms what I suspected. Bruce Vulpone is signing the expense account for Dorothy Roche that has her renting a large house on Martha's Vineyard, cars, chauffeurs, gourmet food." She looked up from the papers. "I gather your sister Dorothy isn't renting that house on North Water Street?"

"You mean, set up by that big fat slob?" Ginny laughed. "No way, Mrs. Trumbull."

"And he withdrew fifty thousand dollars from his account shortly before Tris Waverley deposited fifty thousand dollars. Good job, Ginny!"

A short distance from the airport, echoes of the crash of the Mercedes into the red Volvo faded away into the scrub oak alongside the West Tisbury–Edgartown Road along with the tinkle of broken glass dropping piece by piece onto the road.

The airbags had deployed. The car was full of a nasty white powder and stank of something worrisome. The plastic cover on the steering wheel had flown up into Dorothy's face and smacked her in the nose, which was bleeding.

"I hope you kept the insurance up," Basilio snapped.

"Yes, yes." Dorothy was badly shaken and bleeding, yet the bastard hadn't even asked if she was all right.

He unbuckled his seat belt, brushed himself off, slithered out of his seat, and limped between the two cars, which had rebounded two feet apart. He kicked aside broken glass from the Volvo's red taillight and the Mercedes's clear headlight.

"What in hell did you think you were doing, lady?" he yelled at the elderly driver. "You could've got us killed."

The woman opened her car door. No airbag, apparently. She unfolded like a carpenter's rule until she stood, a good four inches taller than Basilio. She loomed over him. She hadn't uttered a word until now.

"What are you talking about, you foolish little man? Are you in-toxicated? The top speed limit on this Island is forty-five miles per hour. Your car was going at least sixty." She folded her long arms over her narrow chest. She was wearing a gray blazer and a sharply pleated gray-and-pink plaid skirt that hung below her knees. "I'm calling the police to insist they issue you a speeding ticket." She started back to the open door of her car, reached in, and brought out a large leather purse.

Dorothy continued to sit, waiting for Bruce to realize how se-verely injured she was. She'd used three tissues to sop up the blood from her damaged nose. Perhaps broken. If so, she would sue someone. Blood had dripped on her beige silk blouse. What were the symptoms of shock?

"Check the damage," Basilio said to the tall woman.

"Give me your name and phone number," she replied, extracting a notebook and pen and cell phone from the purse. "I'm on the staff of the *Island Enquirer*. We're waging a campaign against speeders." She looked down at him, notebook and phone in one hand, pen poised in the other. "Your name?"

"My name . . . ?" He was beginning to sweat. "Oh, hell." Basilio gave her his name.

"Address?"

"Damn!" He gave her that.

"May I ask what the hurry is? Or was," she added.

"My friend . . . associate . . . was distracted."

"Obviously. I suppose you weren't wearing seat belts." The woman checked the Mercedes license plate, jotted it down, and flipped open her cell phone.

"Wait," said Basilio. "Why don't I give you a check? That should cover everything."

"You're bribing me? What on earth are you thinking?" She punched in a number.

Basilio snatched the phone out of her hand and snapped it shut. "Let's talk. If there's no serious damage, no problem. No need for the police. You don't want a check, I won't give you a check."

"My phone." She held out her hand.

"Let's be reasonable. I'll pay for the broken taillight. My friend learned her lesson. No more speeding."

She continued to hold out her hand.

"No police. Think of the paperwork, wasted time. This Island is a friendly place." After a long stretch of silence, he handed the cell phone back to her.

She took a deep breath. "We'll see what other damage has been done." Before she moved she peered through the fogged-up windshield of the Mercedes. "Your friend seems to be injured."

Dorothy closed her eyes.

"She'll live," said Basilio, checking the front fender. "Seems to be okay. Only a small dent and the broken headlight." He looked at the Volvo's rear. "Taillight and some dents. Can't tell what's new."

The woman's mouth was a tight line. "Do you have any comment for the paper?"

"No comment," he said. "What are you writing?"

"I write the garden column." She folded herself back into the driver's seat and drove off sedately.

Basilio got back into the passenger seat. "Bitch," he said. "I never gave her that check. Let's go."

Dorothy moaned.

He turned to her. "What in hell's your problem?"

Victoria was in the kitchen when Finney arrived.

"Where's your driver?" she asked.

"I'm staying at a place down the road. I walked."

Victoria introduced him to her assistant.

Ginny got up from her computer. Victoria, who'd accepted her assistant as a personable-appearing young woman, hadn't paid much attention to her looks. Now, she had a moment of seeing this young woman through the eyes of a young man, and was struck by how lovely she was.

Ginny was almost as tall as Victoria and had a trim, athletic figure. Her lustrous blue-black hair was pulled back from her face and held with a silver flower pin. Her eyes, dark brown and slightly almond shaped, were framed by thick, long lashes. No wonder Finney was staring at her, his mouth open, his face flushed.

Ginny held out her hand and Finney took it in his.

"You look familiar," said Ginny. "Have I seen you before someplace?"

"I don't think so."

"I'm sure I have. Where are you from?"

"The New York area," said Finney.

"Jersey City. That's where I've seen you."

Finney cleared his throat.

Victoria sensed an awkwardness she couldn't quite place. "Would either of you care for a glass of wine?"

Finney stared at the floor.

Victoria said, "Ginny?"

"No, thank you, Mrs. Trumbull. Back to work." She indicated the computer with its screen saver of colorful swimming fishes, and sat, her back to Finney.

Victoria turned to Finney, who was staring at Ginny's back. "Wine, Finney?"

"Oh, sorry. Thanks."

"Let's go into the parlor." She led the way and sat in her wing chair. Finney perched on the stiff couch. Victoria poured the wine.

"You wanted to talk to me."

"Right, Mrs. Trumbull." The flush faded from his face and his look of assurance returned. "I thought you might be able to help me."

Victoria frowned. "Why me?"

Finney smiled. "I know you're well connected."

"What are you talking about?" said Victoria.

Finney sat forward on the sofa and twisted his wineglass around and around on the coffee table. "You know the movers and shakers on the Island."

Victoria's connections were to the Island's poets and writers, sheep farmers, fishermen, and artists. She didn't think those were the movers and shakers Finney meant.

"People who get things done, Mrs. Trumbull. People who contribute financially to Island causes. You know."

"I don't believe I do." Victoria felt a growing distaste for this young man. The other day, when she'd pointed out that the positions he'd overstated were no more than clerical jobs, she'd assumed she'd put him in his place. Apparently not.

"It's a great opportunity for you, Mrs. Trumbull. And the Island, of course."

"What opportunity are you talking about?"

"We've embarked on an optical-fiber-cable project that will revolutionize the Island and its way of communicating. I'm sure you've heard about it."

Victoria, who'd listened to hours of Orion's lectures on fiber optics, said nothing. She sipped her wine.

"It's not a technology many people understand, Mrs. Trumbull. But for those who invest in our company, the yield will be astronomical."

At that, Victoria curled her toes and her sore toe bumped the edge of the hole Elizabeth had cut in her shoe. She gasped in pain.

Finney didn't seem to notice, because he went on. "You may

223

have heard of Dorothy Roche, a wealthy woman who's been on the Island only a few months."

Victoria wondered if taking her shoe off would relieve the pain or make it worse. She sat up straight.

"I'm sure you'll be seeing her at the Outstretched Palm auction." He looked with great sincerity at Victoria. "She's offered a ride on our drill rig and will host a luncheon for fifty friends of the top bidder."

"I don't go to the auction," Victoria said primly.

"Oh," said Finney, taking a gulp of wine.

Neither spoke for an uncomfortably long time. Finally Finney said, "Dorothy and I hope you'll invest in UFO."

Victoria looked puzzled. "Invest?"

"The return on your investment would enable your grandchildren to live quite comfortably."

"What are you talking about?"

"Three million would give you an excellent return."

"Three million? Dollars?" Her toe throbbed.

"It's a great opportunity." Finney sat back, having said what he'd intended. "I'll be glad to handle the paperwork."

Victoria was speechless. She stared at this very young man, her eyes wide open, her nose lifted.

"We'll discuss this with your financial advisor if you'd prefer," Finney said. "Perhaps you'd feel more comfortable dealing with him." Victoria was still staring at him. "Or her, of course," he added.

Victoria rose from her seat. "Young man," she said in her deep, firm voice. "I think it's time for you to leave."

It was Finney's turn to look puzzled. "But Mrs. Trumbull, we've hardly spoken."

"Let me show you out," said Victoria, wincing with pain as she stood up.

After Finney left, Victoria stormed into the cookroom, pulled out her chair, and sat down with a thump. Ginny lifted her hands from the keyboard.

"The idea. The very idea," said Victoria. "You seemed to know him."

"He's an arrogant creep, Mrs. Trumbull. Besides that, he's stupid. I suppose he can't help being stupid."

"How do you know him?"

"He went to the community college my sister attended."

"In Jersey City?"

She nodded. "He studied business and didn't do all that well. He kept hitting on the women students and wouldn't take no for an answer. Real asshole. Excuse me, Mrs. Trumbull."

"Understandable," said Victoria, and began to unlace her shoe.

CHAPTER 33

———

Back in his room, Finney crossed Mrs. Trumbull off his list of investors. She had almost literally thrown him out of her house. Eccentric was a good description. Here she was, with a chauffeured Bentley, yet she dressed like a bag lady and lived in that shabby old house.

Finney looked at his watch and decided he'd have to talk to Dorothy. He hiked the quarter-mile up New Lane from his bed-and-breakfast to Edgartown Road and the bus route. Doane's newly hayed pasture was on his left; Mrs. Trumbull's overgrown meadow was on his right. A kid sailed past him on a bicycle. The bus was due in about ten minutes. While he waited, he went through his wallet to see how much money he had. He pulled out his bus pass. That was a wise investment. He smiled when he thought of a bus pass as an investment compared to the fourteen million he had in mind. When the bus showed up he climbed aboard.

"Nice day," said the driver, a pleasant woman.

"Right," said Finney, who didn't feel as though it was a nice day at all. He sat in the back of the bus. At the last stop on Church Street, he left the bus and walked over to North Water Street. Dorothy's Mercedes was parked in the space next to her house, and she was sitting in it. The windows looked as though they were steamed up.

Was he intruding on something? Was Dorothy reliving some past adventure in the back seat of a car?

Then he realized the steam was actually white powder. He could barely make out a second figure in the passenger seat. He rapped on the driver's side window. Dorothy lowered it.

Finney took one look at her. "What happened?" The inside of the car was chaos. White powder, blood, and a smell like that of a rutting goat, although he'd never smelled a rutting goat. "My God! I'm not intruding, am I?"

"Oh for Christ's sake," said the male passenger. "She hit a Volvo, the air bag went off, and she wasn't wearing a seat belt."

Dorothy's face was swollen. Both eyes were black, her nose was mashed in, and dried blood streaked her face and stained her silk shirt.

"You've got to see a doctor. You look terrible."

"Mind your own business, sonny." The passenger got out of the car. He was a stocky guy, much shorter than Finney. He hitched up his pants. "Who in hell are you?"

Finney stood up straight and assumed his financier expression, nose raised, mouth turned down. "I'm Finney Solomon, Ms. Roche's partner." He held out a hand for the guy to shake, but the guy ignored it. "And you, sir?"

"Partner!" The man bent down to look at Dorothy, who was slumped over the wheel. "Doing just what?"

"Our company is installing an optical-fiber cable throughout the Island."

"Is that right?" said the man.

"You haven't told me your name, sir."

"None of your goddamned business." To Dorothy, "Get out."

"I'm not sure I—" Dorothy whimpered.

"Get out!"

"She's injured. Can't you see?" said Finney. "I'll take her to the emergency room."

"You'll do no such thing." To Dorothy, "You getting out on your own, or am I yanking you out?"

"Sir!" said Finney.

"Shut up," said the man.

Dorothy slowly opened the door, slowly swung her legs around, slowly eased herself out of the car, and slowly walked past Finney without looking at him and into her house on North Water Street.

The man came around the front of the car, hands balled up into fists, and glared up at Finney. "Partner, hey? In a fiber-optics company, hey? What the hell are you?"

"I'm chief financial officer."

"Chief financial officer." The man laughed.

Finney lifted his chin and gazed down at the man. "May I ask what your interest is in this?" With that, the man laughed again, a loud nasty laugh.

"Who are you?" asked Finney.

"Let's hear who you are, first. Chief financial officer. What do you do as chief financial officer?"

"I raise money through venture capitalists, sir."

"Yeah? Where'd you learn about that, in play school?"

Finney flushed. "I was mentored by the best. None other than Angelo Vulpone."

"Is that right?" the man said again. "The great Angelo Vulpone?"

"Yes, sir," said Finney. "Will you tell me who you are, now?"

"Sure," said the man, shoving his hands into his pants pockets. "My name's Basilio Vulpone. Tell you anything?"

Finney swallowed.

"Angelo Vulpone's kid brother, that's me. Better crawl out from under that rock and get outta here before I remember some more of who I am."

Finney couldn't think of what to say. "Ms. Roche needs to see a doctor."

"Hell she does," said Basilio Vulpone. "I go in there, I'm beating the shit outta her. Understand?" With that, he turned away from Finney, limped up the front steps, wrenched the door open, and slammed it shut behind him.

Ginny worked on her computer after Finney left, and Victoria soaked her sore toe in Epsom salts. When she could, she slipped her shoe back on and went out to the garden to deadhead the bee balm. She carefully snipped those that no longer held interest for the bees. A few hovered around the last of the blossoms, but most had moved on to the black-eyed Susans.

She was raking up the spent blossoms when Sean's truck turned off New Lane into her pasture and stopped. He got out and slammed the door.

Victoria propped her rake against the screening of the vegetable garden and waited.

Sean stuck his head through the open truck window. "Get out, kid."

Sandy Whitfield, the boy who'd put the yellow jackets in Orion's car, slipped out of the passenger side and came around the front of the truck, head down, feet scuffing the short pasture grass, shoelaces undone.

"Thought you should hear this, Mrs. Trumbull," said Sean. He turned to Sandy. "Go ahead."

Sandy stopped in front of Victoria and looked up at her. "The man who told me to play that trick . . . ?"

"The yellow jacket nest."

"Yes, ma'am. Well, I seen him . . ."

"Saw him," said Sean, who was leaning against the side of his truck, arms folded, feet crossed.

Sandy glanced at him. "I *saw* him walking up New Lane."

"Go on, kid," said Sean.

"Was it today you saw this man?" asked Victoria.

"Yes, ma'am. Walking up New Lane."

"How long ago was that?"

"I went home for lunch and after lunch I went fishin' and I seen him when I was coming home."

"What did he look like?" asked Victoria.

Sandy looked over at Sean and shrugged.

"Was he Sean's age?" asked Victoria. She wanted to sit down, or at least prop herself up with something. She reached for the rake and folded her hands on top of the handle and rested some of her weight on it.

"He wasn't *that* old," said Sandy, implying that Sean was elderly.

"What color hair did he have?"

"It was short. Brown, I guess? Not real dark brown."

"Was he fat or thin?"

Sandy looked down at his toes. "Thin."

"What was he wearing?"

Sandy shrugged.

"Jeans?"

"No, ma'am. Tan pants."

"A jacket?"

"I guess. Dark, like black?"

"He was on New Lane. Where were you?"

"I was riding my bike."

Victoria set the rake against the deer screening again. "How old are you, Sandy?"

He stood up straight. "Almost nine."

"You've been most helpful. Thank you."

"Sandy's almost finished the report for Mr. Nanopoulos," said Sean. "It's not bad."

Sandy thrust his hands into his pockets and looked down at his sneakers with the trace of a smile.

"You know who the guy is, Mrs. T?" Sean asked, pushing himself upright from the side of the truck.

"I believe I do," said Victoria.

In the downstairs bathroom, Dorothy removed her bloodied silk shirt and dropped it into the wastebasket, washed her face carefully, examined her poor sore nose and black eyes, and after deciding between two robes hanging on the door, chose the simple white terry cloth rather than the leopard print. As she was combing her hair back in a plain girlish style, the front door slammed shut.

She checked her reflection in the mirror to make sure her expression was a suitable combination of innocence and penitence and decided a subtle limp would be appropriate.

"Bruce," she cried, clasping her hands under her chin. "Thank God *you* weren't hurt!"

His expression was murderous. At this moment, she could

picture him killing her. He advanced toward her, and she pulled the robe around her throat.

"Follow me," he said in a low growl she had never heard before, and she followed him into the library.

"Sit," he said, pointing to the very chair she'd sat in when Orion announced the donation she was to make to the Outstretched Palm auction.

She sat.

Perhaps it was about the auction, not her takeover of the company. That auction item wasn't her fault. It was Orion's publicity stunt. She hoped Orion would realize her death had been his fault.

Bruce sat in the chair facing her and crossed his arms. He stared at her. She looked away. Was he feeling sorry for how badly injured she was? Did her black eyes make her look forlorn and pathetic?

"So. You're the CEO of Universal Fiber Optics."

"Ah . . . ah . . . ah . . ." This was not what she expected.

"That kid out there, that Finney something or other, he's your chief financial officer?"

Dorothy clutched the robe around her throat. "He's just the person you need. He can manage the finances of your company when you take over. Your own brother mentored him. He's raising fourteen million for you."

"What in hell are you blathering on about?"

"I've been working, the way you wanted me to, undercover, finding out about—"

"Shut up, will you!" He crossed his ankle over his knee and his pants leg rode up. Pale elastic threads from the top of his sock were tangled in the black hair of his leg. She stared with fascination. "I've seen rotten actresses, and you take the cake. Whose idea was that?"

"Idea?"

"You driving the drill rig up Main Street."

"North Water Street," Dorothy corrected. "Orion Nanopoulos. That was his idea."

"And the luncheon for fifty people? You expect me to pay for that?"

"The guests can be anyone the winner wants to invite," said Dorothy, not answering his question. "Potential investors, the people you want."

Basilio uncrossed his arms and slammed his fists on the chair arms. "I don't want a thing, understand? No people, no publicity, no fancy lunches, no broad riding a drill rig up Main Street. You know goddamned well Angelo never had a thing to do with that snot-nosed kid."

Dorothy relaxed slightly and tightened her belt.

His voice, low up until now, rose. "I told you to look into this company on the strict QT. Not take it over."

Dorothy clutched her throat. "I did it for you."

"You're a pretty slow learner." He jabbed a thick finger at her. "You should know by now what happens to people who double-cross a Vulpone."

Dorothy paled.

He laughed. "You hire this phony kid . . ."

"He's wealthy."

"That punk? He doesn't have two cents to his name."

Dorothy dropped her hands from the collar.

"It's over," he growled. "Not the first time someone threw you out of his house, is it?"

"What about our business?"

"You think I'd ever trust you again?"

"The auction . . . ?"

"Yeah, the auction," he repeated. He stood up. "You go ahead with that luncheon."

"Thank you, Bruce."

"Your dime."

Dorothy was aghast. "*I* pay?"

"You expect me to pay? When you finish washing the luncheon dishes, pack up and get the hell outta my house and my life." He folded his arms over his thick chest. "And give me back that sapphire necklace."

"But . . . ?"

Basilio's face turned an unhealthy bright red. "I feel like squashing you like a cockroach." He clapped his hands together with a loud splat. "An insect. Want to argue with me? You better shut your goddamned fat mouth and thank the good Lord you can still walk outta here."

CHAPTER 34

After Sean and Sandy left, Victoria called Casey with the news that she knew the identity of the would-be yellow jacket killer.

"Put the coffee on. I'll be right over."

Five minutes later, Casey was in Victoria's kitchen stirring milk and sugar into her coffee.

"You knew Sandy Whitfield admitted to putting the yellow jacket nest in Orion's car."

Casey nodded.

"Sandy recognized a man walking up New Lane as the one who'd put him up to the trick."

Casey set her mug on the table. "Who was it?"

"Finney Solomon. He's staying at that place on New Lane, and was coming to talk me into investing three million dollars in his project."

"Three million? In his project?"

"He believes I'm a rich eccentric."

Casey laughed. "Maybe he's half-right."

Victoria ignored the slur and sipped her coffee.

"What project is this?"

"He and the false Dorothy Roche plan to take over Orion's fiber-optics company. Or they've already done so."

"Nice pair. I'll call Smalley and see how he wants to handle this."

A minute or so later, Casey hung the phone back in its wall cradle. "Smalley says to keep him informed, but since it happened in West Tisbury and since no one was killed, for us to go ahead with our investigation."

"What about their investigation into the two deaths?"

Casey shook her head. "Smalley said they were tied up. Didn't say with what. But the murders are top priority."

"Assuming Finney admits to the yellow jacket plot, what can we do to him?"

Casey sighed. "Not much, I'm afraid, Victoria. He can act contrite, say it was a practical joke gone wrong, and he'll get a slap on the wrist."

"It was attempted murder." Victoria pushed her chair away from the table and stood up. "He can't get away with that. That's not right."

"You have some thoughts on how to deal with him?"

"Orion will," said Victoria, and she smiled.

Orion returned on Monday after a couple days off Island. Victoria was in the garden, as usual. She gathered up her basket of tools and headed toward his car. His window was down and he was listening to *All Things Considered* on public radio. He was turned away from her and hadn't seen her approach.

She rapped on the side of the car. "Do you have a few minutes to talk? I have news for you."

He switched off the radio. "Always have time for you."

"Finney Solomon stopped by on Saturday urging me to to invest three million dollars in his fiber-optics company."

Orion laughed.

"And I've identified the yellow jacket jokester."

"Jokester, hey?" Orion closed his car window, got out, and stretched his arms over his head.

"I'll make a pot of tea and we can sit out by the fishpond." She headed to the house.

"I'll make the tea," Orion called to her back. "You put your gardening things away."

Ten minutes later, Orion and Victoria, the dirt scrubbed out from under her fingernails, were seated on the moss-covered benches overlooking the fishpond with the teapot on a small table between them. Victoria poured and passed a mug to him.

"Start with the yellow jacket jokester," said Orion, taking the mug.

She told him how Sandy had recognized the man.

"Let me guess," said Orion. "Finney Solomon."

"Sergeant Smalley told Casey there's nothing he can do. I thought you might have some ideas."

Orion grinned.

"Do I dare ask what you have in mind?"

"You can ask," said Orion, smiling.

Victoria turned her attention to the goldfish, which had multiplied during the early part of summer. In the low afternoon sunlight the pond sparkled with gold glints as the fish turned and darted in unison.

"It's been over four weeks since Angelo Vulpone's murder," Victoria said. "Now, Tris Waverley has been killed and Finney tried to kill you. Did he kill Angelo and Tris?"

Orion bent down, pulled up a grass stem, and stuck it in his mouth. "I doubt it."

"The state police are still convinced that Angelo's death is connected to the mob, despite his sons' opinion that the mob would have chosen a restaurant or the front steps of a victim's house, a public place in their own territory to show they can kill with impunity."

Orion tossed the grass stem aside and laid his arm on the back of the bench.

Victoria said, "Why was Angelo murdered and why here? And why Tris Waverley?" she leaned forward, and the approaching school of fish swerved with a bright flash. "You talked with Roger Paulson. What did you think of him?"

"Paulson is interested in more power."

"You said he'd worked with Angelo Vulpone in the past. Did you learn any more about that relationship?"

"When Casper went to see him, Paulson claimed his wife committed suicide because of Angelo."

"Good heavens!"

"When I talked to Paulson, I didn't get beyond saying, 'I

understood Angelo was responsible for your wife's—' and he cut me off, furious."

"I have a feeling our Dorothy was Angelo's mistress before Basilio took over. Do you suppose Angelo had an affair with Paulson's wife?"

"We'll never know."

"Perhaps she was pregnant by him."

Orion shrugged. "Paulson's only comment when I was leaving was that he'd be an easier partner to work with than Angelo."

"I'll see what Ginny can find out about the two men." Victoria watched the fish. "Then there's Basilio. Angelo objected to his younger brother dropping his Italian name and calling himself Bruce. A terrible insult to the family. Basilio was insanely jealous of his older brother. He tried in every way to outdo him. The final insult was that Angelo had two sons while Basilio had no children."

Orion nodded.

"And then there's Finney Solomon. Why should he attempt to kill you?"

"A good way to get rid of me."

"Finney claims Angelo Vulpone mentored him, but Angelo's sons never heard of Finney Solomon. They say their father never mentored anyone."

Orion pulled up another grass stem, picked it apart, and tossed the pieces into the fishpond.

"Finney convinced Dorothy the false that he's wealthy. I don't think so. Ginny says he's living on credit cards he gets in the mail. For his part, Finney is convinced that Dorothy is wealthy, and yet she hasn't a cent of her own. It's all Basilio's. What is the relationship between Basilio and the false Dorothy? Something's going on besides this much-too-obvious love nest."

"Do you know anything about Basilio's wife?"

"Her name is Maria Rosa," said Victoria. "Her nephews say she won't confront her husband about the other woman."

"The other woman being our false Dorothy Roche," said Orion. "Passive types can turn into savage killers."

The sun had gone down behind the house and the evening air was chilly. Victoria got slowly to her feet.

"We have a number of avenues to explore," Victoria said. "Roger Paulson's relationship to Angelo. And Finney's and Basilio's." She thought a moment. "And the false Dorothy's. How well did she know Angelo?"

Orion took the tray. "I'll carry this in."

Victoria shivered in the sudden chill and rubbed her arms. "It's nippy this evening."

As he held the door for her, he said, "Are you going to the auction? It's less than a week from now."

"Hardly," said Victoria. "I don't have the time, money, or inclination to bid on items I don't need."

"It's for a good cause."

"Of course." Victoria softened. "But a hundred dollars is too much to pay for the privilege of not bidding on a luncheon I could prepare better myself."

"I have a proposal to make, Victoria." He set the tray on the kitchen counter. "This auction will be special. I'd like you to go with me as my guest."

"At a hundred dollars?"

"It will be well worth it, Victoria. Guaranteed."

Maria Rosa, newly svelte, freshly coifed, wearing the emerald necklace that matched her eyes, and looking anything but passive, booked herself a first-class flight for Friday, August 10th, out of Newark to Boston, a flight that connected with a Cape Air flight to Martha's Vineyard. She charged the airfare to Basilio's American Express Platinum card, as she had charged her necklace.

After a good night's sleep, Victoria came down the next morning to find Ginny already at work. Ginny looked up from her computer with a broad smile.

"I found what you wanted, Mrs. Trumbull."

"Roger Paulson's connection to Angelo Vulpone?"

"Yes, ma'am. I'll print it out for you." She tapped keys and the

239

printer whirred into action. "Seems like Mr. Vulpone screwed Mr. Paulson out of several million."

"Good heavens!" Victoria sat down at the table.

Ginny removed the pages the printer had spewed out. "It's all here. Paulson and Vulpone were partners way back when, in their twenties. They started a construction company with Paulson's family money and Vulpone's business knowledge."

"I suppose the relationship went sour?"

"To put it mildly. Ten years later, the company was one of the top construction companies in the world." She glanced at Victoria. "Then Vulpone cut Paulson out. He's locked up everything, legally. Paulson lost everything. The family money and any share in the huge profits." She handed the pages to Victoria, who skimmed through them.

Ginny continued, "Paulson told the *Financial Journal*, well, you can see for yourself, Mrs. Trumbull." She pointed to the pages Victoria was shuffling through.

"Yes, I've found the place." She read, then looked away. "Mr. Paulson sounds quite intemperate."

"To say the least."

"This explains part of his antagonism." Victoria set the pages aside. "Can you find anything about Roger Paulson's wife's suicide?"

CHAPTER 35

"I dug deeper into Finney Solomon's background, Mrs. Trumbull," said Ginny later the next morning. She'd been working steadily and refused to stop for a break. "I found out a lot more stuff about him."

Victoria was at the kitchen sink arranging black-eyed Susans in the blue vase.

"He's a lot older than he looks, for one thing."

"That would explain all the jobs he's held," said Victoria, trimming the flower stems. "Anything else?"

"He's got a record."

Victoria dropped the flowers in the sink and went to the cookroom door. "A record?"

"He beat up a girlfriend. But she withdrew her complaint when she got out of the hospital."

"Really!"

Ginny scrolled down the computer screen. "A company called Blake and Brown filed charges of embezzlement against him for stealing fifteen hundred dollars. He paid the money back, they dropped the charges and fired him."

"Interesting." Victoria sat down across from Ginny.

Ginny scrolled down. "Looks like he was arrested for possession of drugs, but I can't find any details."

"Any clue as to his relationship to Angelo Vulpone?"

"I was saving this one till last, Mrs. Trumbull. He was stalking Angelo Vulpone and Mr. Vulpone took out a restraining order against him."

Victoria sighed. "And here I thought he was nothing more than an unusually obnoxious and naive young man."

Victoria was absorbing Ginny's latest report on Finney Solomon when Casey stopped by.

"I don't believe you've met my personal assistant."

Ginny looked up. "Good morning, ma'am."

Casey nodded. "Personal assistant?"

"Yes, ma'am. I'm helping Mrs.Trumbull with her murder investigation."

Casey scowled.

Ginny rose. "I'll step outside."

"Sit down, Ginny." Victoria turned to Casey. "Well?"

"Sergeant Smalley wants to talk to you. I'm here to take you to the police barracks."

On the way there, Victoria told her what she'd learned from Ginny's Internet search. About Angelo Vulpone and Roger Paulson, and about Finney Solomon's record.

She finished by saying, "We've concentrated on Angelo Vulpone's death so much we've overlooked Tris Waverley's."

"Not much to go on," said Casey.

"Tris Waverley deposited fifty thousand dollars into his sister's and his account shortly before he was killed. According to her, it had no connection to their business."

"Sounds like a drug transaction," said Casey.

They turned in at the state police barracks, a tidy restored Victorian house, light blue with white trim, not far from the hospital. Casey parked behind the building and they went in the side entrance. Sergeant Smalley led them into the conference room.

In the past, Victoria had had other dealings with Smalley, and liked the big, rugged officer. The three sat around the table. Smalley set a yellow legal pad in front of him. "I'm sure Chief O'Neill told you we're following every lead possible in the deaths of Angelo Vulpone and Tris Waverley." He clicked his mechanical pencil to expose more lead and looked down at the writing pad. "We know you've made contacts that we haven't." He drew an elaborate swirl that looked like the tendril on a grapevine.

Victoria said, "Would you like us to give you copies of all the information we've uncovered? I'm not sure all of our investigation has been done legally."

Casey cleared her throat and glanced out the window to where she'd parked the Bronco.

"That's what I was afraid of." Smalley tossed his pencil down. "That girl who's helping you is probably a genius at illegally breaking into computers."

"Shall we stop this discussion now?"

He stroked his chin with a burly hand, picked up his pencil, and drew a bunch of grapes under the tendrils. "I didn't hear you talk about anything illegal, Mrs. Trumbull." He drew a leaf sprouting from the tendril. "I don't need to know how you obtain your information. You've had a great deal of experience and can make educated guesses most of us can't, you understand?" He met her eyes.

"I understand. I'll be happy to give you my guesses based on long experience."

Then she told him she had a hunch that Basilio had withdrawn fifty thousand dollars shortly before Tris Waverley deposited fifty thousand dollars.

Smalley nodded, writing notes under the heading of an elaborate grapevine bearing fruit.

She told him she guessed that Finney Solomon was not a disciple of Angelo Vulpone's; in fact, she'd had a vision of Angelo taking out a restraining order against Finney.

Smalley grunted, "Keep it simple, Mrs. Trumbull."

"I suspected, then, that years ago Roger Paulson might have had a bitter feud with Angelo involving millions of dollars. All guesses, of course. Am I going too fast?"

Smalley cracked a weak smile and kept writing.

"The Dorothy Roche renting the house on North Water Street is actually Nora Rochester, the owner of a small cleaning firm in

Secaucus, New Jersey. She's taken the name of the vampire actress, Dorothy Roche, because her lover, Basilio Vulpone—"

"What!" Smalley stopped writing. "Vulpone?"

"Angelo's younger brother."

"Go on."

"Basilio Vulpone owns a television studio that produces vampire films, and the real Dorothy Roche, who's about twenty years old, acts in them. Dorothy Roche is her stage name. Her real name is Dorothy Carroll."

Smalley tossed his pencil to one side.

"My personal assistant is the real Dorothy Roche's sister," said Victoria.

"Good Lord!" said Smalley. He picked up his pencil again. "Where were we going with this line?"

"Back to my educated guesses. Basilio set up the false Dorothy Roche in the North Water Street house ostensibly to gather information on Orion Nanopoulos's project. Might this be a cover-up for drug smuggling?"

"Good thought."

"Maybe the false Dorothy Roche double-crossed him by attempting to take over the fiber-optics company using his money." Victoria sat back. "If they're dealing with drugs, Basilio must be quite upset about any publicity."

"You've been busy, Mrs. Trumbull. Can you guess as to who the killer might be?"

"Basilio was insanely jealous of his brother. I think he prided himself in taking over Angelo's mistress."

Smalley drew a trellis around his grapevine.

"Roger Paulson was financially ruined years ago when Angelo cheated him. Paulson's wife committed suicide, and he blames Angelo."

Smalley flipped to a new page on his yellow pad.

"Finney Solomon, who presented himself as a wealthy financier, is nothing but an impecunious, petty chiseler who pretended to be a disciple of Angelo Vulpone's to induce investors to give him the money."

"And his motive?"

"Angelo had taken out a restraining order on Finney and may have threatened to eliminate him."

"That was an educated guess, I believe," said Smalley, writing on the clean sheet.

"Then there's the fake Dorothy Roche."

"Right."

"If she was Angelo's former mistress, and I'm pretty sure she was, his wife may have found out and given him an ultimatum. I heard that he'd had a mistress he dumped."

Casey had said nothing during the interview. She sat quietly, hands in her lap.

Smalley folded his hands on top of his yellow pad. "What about Waverley?"

Victoria shrugged. "I have no idea how that fits in. Tris Waverley clearly got fifty thousand dollars from Basilio Vulpone, but why? It would fit in with a drug business. Or perhaps blackmail."

Smalley said, "Mrs. Trumbull, we appreciate everything you and your assistant have done. We'll follow up your educated guesses legally."

They all rose and shook hands.

"Thanks for bringing Mrs. Trumbull, Chief," he said to Casey. "Mrs. Trumbull, if you have any other educated guesses to share, we're wide open. Tell your assistant we can't condone her hacking, we won't even acknowledge it, but if I could, I would give her my thanks."

"Of course."

CHAPTER 36

On Friday, Maria Rosa took a cab to Newark Airport. Basilio, as usual, was away on a long trip.

When her flight was announced, she boarded with the other first-class passengers, and found her seat number on the right side of the aircraft. A nice-looking man stepped into the aisle from his seat next to hers and lifted her travel case into the overhead compartment.

"Thank you so much." She fluttered her eyelashes the way she'd almost forgotten, and settled into the seat next to the window. She smiled at the man and selected the catalog of delightful objects she didn't need from the seat pocket in front of her and opened it at random.

"Going far?" asked the man.

Maria Rosa glanced at him. He looked familiar and was even nicer looking than she'd first thought. Had she seen him someplace? A movie star? Or a TV anchor? She smiled and fingered her necklace. "I'm going to Martha's Vineyard."

"What a coincidence, so am I. You have a place there?"

"I'm staying at a hotel in Edgartown." She closed the catalog, hoping this was the beginning of a pleasant conversation. "And you?"

He nodded. "I'm staying at the Harbor View."

Maria Rosa let out a refined squeak. "That's where I'm staying."

"A wonderful hotel. You're flying Cape Air?"

Maria Rosa nodded. Before she left home she'd experimented with mascara, and her eyelashes were exceedingly long and lush. She'd touched her upper lids with green, a shade that emphasized the color of her eyes.

"Do you fly to the Vineyard often?" he asked.

"This is my first visit."

"I hope small planes don't bother you."

Maria Rosa was not afraid of anything. However, she allowed her voice to quaver slightly. "Small planes?" She looked up, wide-eyed.

"We may be the only passengers," he said reassuringly. "Is your trip business? Or pleasure?"

The flight attendant came through, checking to see that seat belts were securely fastened, that overhead compartments were safely shut.

"A little of each," said Maria Rosa. "I'm attending the Outstretched Palm auction."

"Another coincidence. I'm one of the auction items," he said modestly.

"Really!" Maria Rosa smiled, knowing her smile was her second best feature after her eyes. "You, yourself are the item? And who are you, by the way?"

"Sorry," said the man, and flushed slightly. "I'm afraid I'm used to being recognized." He extracted his slim leather wallet from his back pocket and removed a card. "I'm Bill Williams."

Maria Rosa tried to look delighted, but had no idea who Bill Williams was.

He, in turn, looked disappointed. "Sports announcer. As an auction item, I'm offering a seat next to me in the broadcast booth for a Giants game, plus lunch with the sports news reporting gang."

"Of course," said Maria Rosa, still mystified. "I'm sure I've seen you."

The safety announcement came on and Maria Rosa dutifully watched and listened to instructions about what to do in the unlikely event of a water landing.

"And you, beautiful lady, are . . . ?"

"I'm Maria Rosa Vulpone." She tugged on the strap of her seat belt to tighten it.

The plane started to move, and Maria Rosa suddenly felt nervous, an alien emotion. She hadn't flown in an airplane for a long, long time.

"Vulpone," Bill Williams repeated. "Any relation to the Triple V TV channel?"

She nodded, feeling slightly embarrassed. "The same. My husband, Basilio. Bruce."

"Great programming," said Bill Williams. "I love vampires. I know it's for kids, but, well . . ."

The plane turned onto the runway, the engines roared, they started to move down the runway. Maria Rosa felt faint. The airplane tilted up suddenly, machinery somewhere beneath her made a horrible grinding noise, a section of the fragile wings opened and she could see the vanishing ground through the crack, which then closed. She clutched Bill William's hand in hers.

"It's okay, Maria Rosa. Don't you worry about a thing." He put his left hand, a large, strong, muscular, comforting hand, on top of her trembling one. "I won't let anything happen to you."

The plane leveled off. Maria Rosa removed her hand from his, and looked suitably ashamed of herself.

"I'm so sorry," she murmured over the roar of engines.

"Quite understandable." He patted his chest. "I'm honored to be of assistance."

She turned to the window and looked down at the tiny houses below, the green trees, the bright golf courses with patches of white sand, the turquoise swimming pools.

He cleared his throat and she looked away from Earth so far below. "I hope you'll excuse me for a few minutes. I have to text my office."

Maria Rosa looked out again. They were flying through an insubstantial cloud that blocked her view.

Bill Williams extracted an iPhone from his sports coat pocket, unlocked it, and began texting.

Five minutes later they were above the clouds, solid puffs of whipped cream that reflected dazzling sunlight.

The flight attendant wheeled a cart down the aisle with complimentary beverages. Bill requested champagne.

"I really shouldn't," said Maria Rosa, accepting the long slender glass the flight attendant poured.

When the cart was wheeled away he asked, "Will your husband be picking you up?"

Maria Rosa took a sip of her champagne, decided she liked it, and took another small sip before she answered. "He doesn't know I'm going to Martha's Vineyard."

"Ah!" said Bill Williams. "Perhaps I can give you a ride to our hotel, then?" He emphasized the word "our."

"I don't want to trouble you."

"No trouble at all. A volunteer from the auction committee is picking me up. I'm sure there'll be room for both of us. What made you decide to attend the auction?"

"Some woman," Maria Rosa permitted herself a small smile, "is donating a ride on a drill rig plus luncheon."

"I heard about that. It's made the national news. And you intend to bid on it?"

"I intend to win it."

He examined her with respect—the emerald necklace, the eyes, the smile—and lifted his empty glass in a toast to her. "Good luck."

The flight attendant came back down the aisle sans cart, carrying the champagne bottle swathed in white linen. "More champagne, sir? Ma'am?"

"Why not," said Bill, handing over both glasses.

"Do you have dinner plans?" he asked when they'd clinked their glasses together for the second time.

Maria Rosa, now fully accustomed to being airborne, soothed by drink, and positive that she *would* win that bid, said, the way she might have back at Notre Dame High, "If you're inviting me to dinner, sir, I'd be delighted."

The next morning, the day before the auction, Maria Rosa walked slowly down North Water Street admiring the elegant captains' houses on her right. It was a bright, clear day, cool enough for a sweater. After dinner the evening before, she and Bill Williams had hiked down the path from the hotel to the lighthouse, then strolled along the beach, talking until the evening chill set in.

Somewhere along here on North Water Street, between the Harbor View and Main Street, the bogus Dorothy Roche was staying, Maria Rosa mused. Courtesy of *her* Basilio, the cheat. The liar. The fat fool.

Such a difference. Bill Williams would never have chewed with his mouth open, or put his elbows on the table. He was so courteous. Would Basilio have walked with her? Never. He was fat and lazy. Bill Williams was slim and tall and fit. Would Basilio think of strolling along the beach, picking up shells, talking, laughing? Never.

She sighed.

As she approached one of the big houses on her right, she saw a familiar car, a Mercedes like Basilio's. Except for a small patch on the driver's side that had been wiped clear, the windows were dusted with white powder that kept her from seeing inside. Before she had time to think about what the white powder meant, the front door of the house opened. She heard a woman's voice, a man's growl.

She crossed the road and stood half-hidden behind a large lilac bush, its heart-shaped leaves concealing the dry remembrance of flowers.

Basilio emerged from the house, climbed down the front steps, turned right, and lumbered toward Main Street without even glancing in her direction.

Maria Rosa headed back toward the Harbor View, the white houses now on her left, the harbor on her right. She felt curiously light and quite pleased with herself.

The Ferrari skidded to a stop in the drive. Primo escorted a young woman, who bore a strong resemblance to Ginny, into the kitchen. Ginny got up from her seat with a squeal of delight and threw her arms around her sister.

Primo stood by with a smile.

Victoria said, "You must be the true Dorothy Roche."

The young woman, girl, really, turned immediately. "How rude of me! I'm so sorry!" She then embraced Victoria.

"I didn't think you could break away from that awful boss of yours," said Ginny.

"He's out of town. Primo," she blushed prettily, "made a flight reservation for me and, well, here I am."

"Wonderful timing," said Victoria. "I hope you're planning to take both girls to the auction tomorrow?"

Primo hesitated. "As your chauffeur . . ."

"I have a date," said Victoria. "He'll be driving me."

CHAPTER 37

The day of the Outstretched Palm auction was clear, bright, cool, and dry. A perfect day for the event.

Victoria dressed in her green plaid suit and white blouse with a soft bow at the neck. She clipped on the earrings that went with her suit, found her leather purse, and she was almost ready to go.

She located her police hat in the black bowl under some papers, and tucked it into her purse. She then decided to take her lilac-wood walking stick. Not only would it be good camouflage, making her seem frail, it would also serve as a weapon, in case she needed such a thing.

Orion had promised to get her to the auction well ahead of time. He came directly from his office, wearing jeans, boots, and an olive green cotton shirt.

They arrived almost an hour early and the mown hayfield parking area was already half-full. Volunteers in orange vests directed them to a spot and Orion and Victoria walked to a gate in a tall freshly clipped privet hedge, where volunteers took their tickets. The gate led to the enclosed lawn behind the hotel.

The volunteer said, "Thank you sir, madam," and turned to the next person in line. "May I help you, sir?"

A hundred or more white folding chairs were set up on the ultra-green grass under a large tent. Edging the lawn, between it and the enclosing hedge, was a wide flower bed in a palette of colors and sizes that ranged from pale blue lobelia to sunflowers as tall as small trees.

"You could hide in there," Victoria said, "surrounded by scents and color. What a paradise for children!"

A gray-haired volunteer in a filmy white dress greeted them. "Mrs. Trumbull! We were so glad to hear you were coming. We have two seats for you on row three, right on the aisle. And, Mr. Nanopoulis, there's a cash bar, if you'd like a bit of refreshment before the event."

Victoria wanted to browse on her own. "I'll see you back at our seats," she told Orion.

Orion, too, wanted to browse. After a few minutes of strolling through the crowd, looking and greeting, he spotted Finney Solomon talking with great sincerity to a prosperous-looking elderly couple.

"Finney," Orion interrupted. "Great to see you." He turned to the couple. "Wonderful event. My name's Nanopoulos. Orion Nanopoulos." He held out a hand to the man and they shook.

"Matthew and Martha Lodge. Your name is certainly familiar, Mr. Nanopoulos. Horses, right?"

"A long time ago," said Orion.

Finney cleared his throat.

"I see you've met my friend, Finney Solomon." He turned to Finney. "You must be relieved to have that Blake and Brown matter cleared up."

Finney paled.

"Blake and Brown?" asked Matthew Lodge. "Blake is a good friend. Fine man. Had a problem with an embezzler a few years back. Did you have some dealings with the firm?"

"I . . . I . . ." said Finney. "Some time ago."

"Couldn't have been too long ago, young man," said Matthew Lodge with a hearty laugh. "Finney Solomon. I'll tell Blake I ran into you on the Vineyard. You're, what, chief financial officer of a fiber-optics firm?"

Finney glanced around. "I see someone I've got to say hello to. Good to meet you."

"Nice fellow," said Matthew Lodge.

Orion smiled and watched where Finney was heading.

Victoria rolled up her program and took it with her. She strolled down the center aisle, appreciating the feel of soft grass under her feet. She greeted a dozen people who knew her, and kept walking and looking. She reached the last row of chairs and left the shelter of the tent. The sunlight was dazzling, and it took her eyes a moment to adjust. She shaded her face with her rolled-up program.

Finney Solomon appeared out of the bright light, glancing nervously over his shoulder. He was wearing his navy blazer, an open-collared white shirt, and khaki slacks, and looked quite collegiate except for his expression, which was one of extreme distress.

"Oh, Mrs. Trumbull."

"Are you all right?" Victoria asked.

"Fine, fine." He ran a hand over his crisply cut hair.

"Here's Orion," said Victoria.

"Gotta say hello to someone," said Finney, leaving.

Before he moved off, Victoria asked, "Have you seen Dorothy Roche?"

"She's around somewhere," he said, and dodged away.

Orion sauntered after him.

Victoria passed a familiar-looking man, short with black hair and bright blue eyes. After she'd gone a few steps she recalled who he was. Roger Paulson, the automobile man from Chappaquiddick. She turned back.

"Mr. Paulson? Victoria Trumbull."

He started as though he'd been thinking about something entirely different from the scene around him. "Yes, of course, Mrs. Trumbull. I know your name, certainly, and your reputation. Nice to meet you."

"You, too, Mr. Paulson."

"Please, Roger." He was squinting up at her, facing directly into the sun. Victoria moved to one side so he was partly shaded.

"Some interesting items," she said, tapping her program on her palm. "Will you be bidding on any of them?"

"Probably." He thrust his hands into his pockets and rocked onto the toes of his boots, making him, for a moment, an inch taller. "I like to support the auction."

"That drill rig item must be of special interest to you." Victoria leaned on her stick to make herself a bit closer to his height.

He frowned. "What makes you say that?"

"Weren't you an associate of Angelo Vulpone's?"

His frown deepened. "What are you talking about?"

"The Ditch Witch drill seems to be a key to the success of the fiber-optics project Angelo planned to invest in."

"I don't see what that has to do with me." He rocked back onto his toes again.

"Don't you plan to invest in the project?"

"Rumor. Pure rumor, Mrs. Trumbull."

"I understood you and Angelo were partners."

"I've had nothing to do with that man for years, Mrs. Trumbull. He's dead now. Can't say I'm sorry." He glanced in the direction he'd been looking when Victoria first saw him. "I see someone I need to talk to. Nice to meet you, Mrs. Trumbull." With that, he moved on, and Victoria watched him disappear into the crowd.

"Mrs. Trumbull! Victoria!"

Victoria recognized the scent and turned, and there was the object of her search, Dorothy Roche, weaving toward her. If Dorothy hadn't called out, Victoria would not have recognized her. Her face was partly hidden by a wide-brimmed garden party hat wreathed with purple and blue artificial flowers. Below the hat, her face was almost totally hidden by large sunglasses. Victoria could see that Dorothy's nose was swollen. Her skin below the glasses was a patchy black, edged in greenish yellow. A coating of pink paste, instead of hiding the damage, emphasized it.

Victoria couldn't help asking, "What happened?"

"The air bag in my car went off when I bumped into something, really just a gentle bump." When Dorothy spoke Victoria got the strong impression that Dorothy had been drinking. "They're terribly dangerous. Air bags."

"I'm so sorry." Victoria turned away from the ruined face and smell of perfume mixed with semimetabolized liquor. "Such an imaginative item you've contributed. That's bound to be a big moneymaker for the auction."

"I didn't offer it. I want to keep a low profile, and then that foolish naive Orion Nanopoulos came up with the bright idea. I can't go through with it. I can't!"

"It means a great deal to the Outstretched Palm Fund."

Dorothy smiled unconvincingly and looked away from Victoria, off to her right. She put her hands up to her face, gasped, and turned away. "Sorry, I've got to see someone." She hurried off in the opposite direction from whatever it was that had startled her.

Victoria leaned on her stick again and looked around to see who or what had upset Dorothy. A heavyset man wearing a rumpled, pin-striped blue suit was mopping his forehead with a handkerchief while he argued with an attractive woman who was quite a bit taller than he was. The woman was probably in her early fifties with a trim figure. Her dark hair was streaked with wings of white that no beautician could have conjured up, and she wore it pulled back in a chignon that looked quite stylish. She wore a simple white linen dress, as yet unwrinkled, and an extraordinary necklace set with green stones.

Victoria casually strolled over to the couple. "Lovely afternoon for the auction, isn't it." She interrupted the man's angry flow of words.

The woman turned away from the man, and smiled. "Delightful. Have you attended this auction before?"

"This is my first time," said Victoria.

The man scowled. He stuffed his handkerchief into his suit coat pocket and smoothed his tie.

"My first time, too," said the woman. "In fact, this is my first visit to Martha's Vineyard. Have you spent much time on the Island?"

"I live here," said Victoria. "I was born here."

"How fortunate you are." The woman extended a slim hand. "My name is Maria Rosa Vulpone."

The man coughed, covering his mouth with a fist, then stuck both hands in his suit coat pockets.

Victoria took the woman's delicate hand in hers. "I'm Victoria Trumbull."

"Mrs. Trumbull! Just this morning I was reading your column in the newspaper. What a pleasure to meet you." She turned to the man. "This is my husband, Basilio."

The man removed a hand from one pocket and offered it to Victoria, a fat, soft, white hand.

"Your name, Vulpone, is familiar to me," Victoria said to Basilio. "Was it your brother, Angelo . . . ?"

Basilio crossed himself with his free hand and glanced heavenward. "My older brother, bless him."

"My condolences. This must be a difficult time for you. It's been, what, five weeks?"

Maria Rosa said, "Basilio needed distraction from the tragedy of his loss."

Basilio pursed his lips.

"Quite understandable," said Victoria. "What brings you to the Island?" She addressed both of the Vulpones. "Besides the auction, that is."

Basilio fished a pair of designer sunglasses from his breast pocket and covered his eyes with them.

Maria Rosa answered with an elegant touch of her Italian accent. "My husband is here on business, aren't you, Basilio?"

Basilio grunted. Victoria couldn't see his eyes. "Do I understand you're in the television business, Mr. Vulpone?"

Again, Maria Rosa answered. "My husband is the director of Triple V Cable."

"Do you have plans for a television show on Martha's Vineyard?"

Basilio said, "Could be." He took his wife's arm. " 'Scuse us, Mrs. Trumbull."

With that, he led his smiling wife away.

Victoria felt someone behind her and turned to see Orion. "Shall we take our seats, Victoria?"

"I gather you've found a way to deal with Finney."

"A start," said Orion.

As they ducked back under the tent flap and strolled down the center aisle toward their seats, Orion asked, "Who were those two?"

"None other than Basilio and Maria Rosa Vulpone."

"The wife?"

Victoria smiled. "I believe she's shaped up."

"I guess so."

They greeted people around them and took their seats.

Trip Barnes, the auctioneer, started off with banter that warmed up the crowd and led to spirited bidding. The more outrageous Trip's comments, the higher the bids went. A watercolor by a well-known Island artist started at five hundred dollars and sold for five thousand. A day of fishing with a local boater went for three thousand. Breakfast for eight prepared by a local celebrity vocalist and accompanied by her singing went for eleven thousand.

Bill Williams's offer of a seat in the press box at a Giants game went, to Maria Rosa, for six thousand.

Small items such as autographed books, costume jewelry, a weekend at a bed-and-breakfast, and a floral arrangement went for vast sums of money.

By four o'clock the auction had raised more than three hundred thousand dollars, and the ride on the Ditch Witch drill rig was next, the last item to be offered.

Trip beckoned to a high school student dressed in the purple uniform of the Regional High School band and he climbed the several steps to the stage. The kid, lanky, with his spiky hair dyed purple to match his uniform, carried a snare drum on a harness around his shoulders and waist. At Trip's signal he began a drum-roll that went on for a full minute.

Once he had the attention of the crowd, Trip held up both arms. The kid lifted his drumsticks.

"Our final item, ladies and gentlemen, the item you've been waiting for, the item that may never again be offered to the public, the item that, if you win, your grandchildren will tell their grand-children about is . . ." He lowered his arms and the drumroll started up again for a few seconds and stopped.

". . . fabulous, unique. A ride from the Yacht Club up North Water Street aboard a Ditch Witch horizontal directional drilling unit, a fantastic machine, to a fabled captain's house where you will play host to a luncheon for fifty—did I say fifty? Yes, ladies and gentlemen—fifty people of your choice. Friends, business associates, people you want to impress, people you can't stand . . ."

Laughter.

"And the name of the drill rig, alone, ladies and gentlemen, is worth emptying your bank accounts for. We begin the bid at five thousand. Do I hear five thousand, five thousand?" He pointed. "Six thousand, six thousand?" He pointed. "Seven, give me a seven." He pointed.

Roger Paulson nodded.

"Eight thousand, eight?"

The bidding went on up until only three people were bidding, up to ten, twelve, and slowed. Paulson dropped out. Two people were still bidding.

"Thirteen thousand, ladies and gentlemen. The gentleman in the blue suit, do I hear thirteen? Yes. The lady with the emerald necklace, want to go for fourteen? Yes." He pointed. "Sir, fifteen? Yes. Ma'am, sixteen? Yes, thank you, ma'am. Sir, you can't let some young slip of a thing outbid you, do I hear seventeen? Yes." Pointing. "Ma'am, you don't want that fat slob to outbid you."

Laughter.

"Eighteen, do I hear eighteen, ma'am? Stand up for your rights. Eighteen, eighteen. Thank you."

"Nineteen!" shouted Basilio.

"Twenty!" cried Maria Rosa.

"Twenty-one, you bitch!" shouted Basilio.

"Sir, sir, please!" called out Trip.

"Twenty-two," cried Maria Rosa.

"Twenty-three," shouted Basilio.

Trip looked from one to the other and shrugged at the audience.

The high school drummer waited with drumsticks lifted.

"Twenty-four!"

"Twenty-five!"

Trip called out, "You sure the check won't bounce?"

Laughter.

"Twenty-six!" cried out Maria Rosa. "Twenty-six!"

"Sir?" asked Trip.

"Bitch," said Basilio.

"Twenty-six thousand?" said Trip. "Sir?"

Basilio growled.

"Going," said Trip. "Going, going, going, gone! For twenty-six thousand dollars to the angel in the emerald necklace!"

The drummer drummed. The audience applauded, a standing ovation. Victoria turned to Orion. "What do you suppose that was all about?"

Orion grinned. "I can only guess."

"I wonder where Dorothy is."

It was some time before things quieted down enough for Trip to announce that tea, meaning champagne and gourmet cakes and sandwiches, was served, and that winning bidders should take their checks to the volunteer at the table to his right.

Matt Pease, the photographer for the *Island Enquirer,* came by. "Mrs. Trumbull, have you seen the woman who contributed the Ditch Witch item? Great story."

"Dorothy Roche," said Victoria. "I saw her before the event. She was in a minor accident, so she may be shy about being photographed."

"I'll keep looking for her. She hasn't left, according to the gatekeepers."

"She's probably hiding," said Orion. "She's a mess with black eyes and a broken nose."

"Hiding where, though?" Victoria shook her head. "Something's not right."

Trip held up his hands. "Thank you all, ladies and gentlemen, for the most successful auction in the history of the Outstretched Palm Fund. We've topped four hundred thousand dollars."

CHAPTER 38

People rose from their seats with a rustle of clothing, the scrape of chairs being folded, laughter, congratulations, greetings. Voices resounded under the canvas of the tent.

"Wait here, Victoria. I'll get you a glass of champagne and a plate of food," said Orion, and moved along with the crowd away from the tent.

As soon as he turned his back, Victoria headed toward the stage, where Trip was gathering papers together.

"Afternoon, Mrs. Trumbull." Trip snapped an elastic around the papers and stowed them in an inner pocket of his vest. "Some action, all right."

"Wonderful job, Trip. Have you seen Dorothy Roche?"

"Not since before the bidding started. I'm surprised she wasn't here to accept congratulations. Twenty-six thousand is an all-time record. Press was looking for her."

"I've got to find her."

"When you do, tell her how much we appreciate what she's done for the community. I've got to uncork champagne. Anything I can do for you before I leave?"

"No, thank you. I'll look for Dorothy."

The stage was set up in front of the wide flower border backed by the tall privet hedge. Victoria climbed down the back steps of the stage, holding the railing tightly. Dorothy had been drinking. She'd probably decided to keep out of sight of the crowd. She did look ghastly.

The noise of the crowd had faded to the far corner of the area.

Victoria heard crickets and the creak and snap of stage boards adjusting to whatever boards adjusted to.

The platform was about three and a half feet above the soft grass. Dorothy was so obviously drunk, perhaps she'd crawled under the stage where it was cool, like a stray pup. When Victoria had caught her breath, she leaned down, bracing herself with her stick. It took a few moments for her eyes to adjust to the dim light underneath.

The smells under the stage were a mixture of mown grass, the slightly vanilla-like fragrance of the sun-washed wooden stage, and moist rich earth.

No scent of Dorothy.

Victoria was somewhat relieved. The flower border was an ideal hiding place. Dorothy might have settled in there.

Victoria walked along the border, parting the lush growth with her stick and calling Dorothy's name. She hadn't realized how wide the border was. There was room for a card table and four bridge players to hide. The fragrance of the flowers was overwhelming, now she was close to them, and bruising the blossoms as she probed with her stick.

Then she spotted a crushed path into the flowers and her nose picked up the scent of Dorothy's perfume. She pushed the dense growth aside with a feeling of dread.

Orion returned with two plates of food and two flutes of champagne. Most of the chairs had been moved closer to the food, and he stood at the seats he and Victoria had occupied. He assumed Victoria would be in the shelter of the tent, out of the sun, but he didn't see her.

As he was puzzling over his next move, Victoria appeared from the back of the stage. Her face was flushed and she was clearly upset. When she saw him, she hurried across the stage, and he met her at the steps the drummer boy had used earlier.

"What is it, Victoria?"

"I found Dorothy. Do you have your phone with you?"

"Is she all right?"

"We need an ambulance."

"She's not dead, is she?"

"She's still breathing."

He pulled his phone out of his pocket and dialed 911.

"Ask them not to upset the crowd," said Victoria as Orion spoke to the communications center.

He put his hand over the mouthpiece. "The police?"

"Tell them to let Casey know. This isn't our jurisdiction, but . . ."

Orion passed on the message, then snapped his phone shut. "The ambulance and Casey are on their way. So are Edgartown police and the state police."

"I've got to go back to her."

"I'll let Trip know what's going on, and be right with you. Where is she?"

"Lying on her back in the flower border, pretty well hidden. Behind a large clump of crushed delphiniums, with an empty bottle of Scotch."

"I don't know how you do it, Victoria," said Casey, after the ambulance had taken Dorothy away. "The reporter for the paper was looking for her, but no one else would have thought a thing about her not being around."

"She was drunk," said Victoria.

"The bartenders refused to serve her after she'd had at least five drinks. But you know we found an empty pint of Scotch near her in the flower garden, and another almost-empty pint in her handbag. That much alcohol in her bloodstream, she'd be dead, if you hadn't found her."

When Victoria stopped at the door of Dorothy's hospital room that evening, she had to control her aversion to the wraith on the bed. Dorothy looked like death itself.

She lay on her back, her skin gray, eyes closed, arms by her sides resting on the light blanket that covered her up to her waist. Clear oxygen tubes led to her swollen and bruised nose. Her black eyes had turned a hideous yellowish green. An IV drip was taped to her right arm, and a plastic identification tag was snapped around her left wrist. The hospital gown, which looked like some man's underwear, completed the dreary picture of the once glamorous Dorothy.

Victoria shuddered.

"Auntie Vic, are you okay?"

Victoria spun around, almost losing her balance. Her grandniece, Hope, head nurse at the hospital, steadied her.

"Whoa, Auntie Vic. Take it easy. She'll recover." Hope kept her arm around Victoria's shoulder. "Friend of yours?"

Victoria shook her head, unable to speak.

"Whatever. I'll assume you're the person responsible for her now. Privacy rules, you know. Come on into her room and sit down. You look as if you need to."

Victoria followed this cherished strong grandniece into the room and sat in the chair by the window at the foot of Dorothy's bed feeling unaccustomedly helpless.

"Acute alcohol poisoning, as I guess you suspected."

Victoria was vaguely aware of the bird feeder hanging outside the window, full of tiny chattering sparrows, and the rose garden in full blowzy bloom beyond.

"We pumped out her stomach, tested her blood alcohol level— almost point seven, incredibly high—gave her a shot of vitamin B, and put her on a dextrose drip."

Dorothy groaned. Victoria started to get up.

"Sit still, Auntie Vic. She'll be okay. She'll feel pretty rotten for a while, but if she hasn't abused her body too much in the past, she'll recover."

Dorothy mumbled, "I can't do it. I can't do it."

Hope looked quizzically at Victoria. "Know what she's talking about?"

"Yes," said Victoria. "I'm afraid I do."

Early the next morning, three of the organizers of the auction met with Maria Rosa, winner of the Ditch Witch item, at Maria Rosa's second-floor suite at the Harbor View. Her suite overlooked Edgartown Harbor and the lighthouse. Last night, after the auction, she and Bill Williams had again walked down the sandy path, hand in hand, and she was still caught up in the magic of the evening, in fact, of the entire day.

She turned politely to the man sitting to her right, who introduced himself as president of the local bank, and the two women with him as treasurer of the auction and a columnist with the local newspaper.

The bank president wore a blue blazer and white duck trousers, had snow white hair, and was healthily tanned.

"Thank you for your extraordinary contribution to the auction," he began.

Maria Rosa nodded. "It was my pleasure." And it was, too, she thought. A pleasure.

He looked down at his papers. "Unfortunately, the woman offering the item, the ride on the Ditch Witch drill rig, is in the hospital. She's expected to be there for several days."

Maria Rosa put her hand to her throat and stroked the emerald necklace. "I'm so sorry. Was it a heart attack?"

"The hospital isn't releasing information, naturally. We assume her collapse was brought on by stress."

Maria Rosa looked out across the harbor to Chappaquiddick, enticingly green in the morning light. Sailboats were leaving the harbor, perhaps for the day, perhaps bound for faraway places.

"The committee felt it was only right to credit your account with the money you so graciously donated."

The treasurer and newspaper columnist nodded.

Maria Rosa stood. "I don't need to ride the Witch. Keep the money."

"My dear Mrs. Vulpone!"

Maria Rosa smiled. "But I accept the luncheon. I've already invited a group of fifty."

"Friends from New York?" asked the columnist.

"Not at all," said Maria Rosa. "Fifty patients from your nursing home."

"Windemere?" asked the treasurer. "Walkers and wheelchairs?"

"Certainly," said Maria Rosa. "Those things can be managed."

CHAPTER 39

On Monday, Primo drove Victoria home from the hospital, where she'd visited Dorothy. "How's she doing?" He glanced in the rearview mirror.

"Physically, she's recovering, but I think she's having some mental problems. I don't feel sorry for her." Victoria paused. "I suppose I should, even though she brought this on herself." She met his eyes in the mirror. "I need to talk to you and Umberto. The girls, too."

"I'll pick them up. The girls are shopping and Umberto's at the beach."

He dropped her off and went to fetch the others. She was still standing at the top of the steps when Sean, the beekeeper, arrived.

"Our friend Sandy has information for you, Mrs. Trumbull." He turned back to the truck. "Out, kid."

The eight-year-old slid out of the passenger seat and pushed his sandy-red hair out of his eyes. He scuffed toward Victoria, a plume of dust rising behind him.

"Pick up your feet," said Sean.

They sat in the cookroom, the boy's large eyes watching her. His freckles stood out like green dots on his sunburned face. His sneakered feet swung nervously.

"What sort of news do you have, Sandy?"

"Nothin' much."

"Ma'am," said Sean.

"Yes, ma'am. You asked if anyone seen that big fat man from New York on the Island, and I seen, saw him."

"You recognized him from my description?"

"Well," Sandy swung his feet, "he's not tall, like you. He wears sunglasses most of the times I seen him . . ."

"Most of the times? How often have you seen the man?"

"Well, I hang out at the airport. Sometimes one of the pilots gives me a ride in a plane, ma'am." He glanced at Sean. "I seen him five or six times at Cape Air."

"Are you sure this is the man I'm talking about?"

"I guess. He's pretty fat and he has kind of a yellow face and he wears a belt with a green buckle shaped like a dollar sign." He drew the shape of an S in the air. "He's got a belly so you can't always see the buckle."

"Did he notice you?"

"No, ma'am. Nobody sees me if I don't want."

"Go on," said Victoria.

"He looks like a hopping toad. Big thick lips and when he takes his glasses off, his eyes stick out like a toad."

"Did you ever hear his name? Did he give it to the person at the counter?"

"Sometimes he says Bruce, sometimes something else."

"Could you hear any last name?"

"Volcano?"

"That's close enough," said Victoria. "What sort of luggage did he have?"

"Luggage?"

"Suitcase or briefcase or packages."

"Well, sometimes when he comes here, he didn't, doesn't . . . ?"

"That's all right, I won't correct your grammar. Just tell me what you remember."

"Well, coming here he doesn't have nothin' with him. Maybe a briefcase. But when he leaves, he almost always has a package, a Cronig's bag, you know?"

Victoria nodded.

"Tied with string, like it's going UPS."

"When did you first see this man?"

Sandy scratched his head. "Well, school let out in June and before then I only went to the airport weekends, and only when it was warm and I'd helped my dad planting."

"Do you recall what flowers were in bloom then?"

"Your lilacs."

"May," said Victoria. "Excellent, Sandy. Did someone pick him up at the airport?"

"Mostly an old lady with dyed orange hair."

Victoria smiled at the vivid description of the false Dorothy Roche. "What about the past two or three weeks? Did the man carry packages away as usual?"

Sandy kicked his feet "I don't know. Maybe."

Victoria heard the Ferrari drive up. Sandy looked out the window and his eyes widened. "I seen that car here before. That guy knows you?"

"Yes, he does. Would you like a ride in that car?"

"You mean it? You mean it?" Sandy sprang out of his chair. "Honest?"

"We'll have to ask him," said Victoria. "But when he hears what you've told me, I think it's quite likely."

Sean, who'd been leaning against the door frame, said, "When you get through joyriding, kid, you got a job to do. Getting those frames out of the hives."

Fifteen minutes later, Primo returned with a deliriously happy Sandy, who rushed off to Sean and the bees. Orion showed up a few minutes later. Victoria, Orion, the two Vulpone sons, Ginny, and her actress sister crowded around the cookroom table. Umberto held Ginny's hand under the table, presumably so no one would notice.

Victoria said, "I should tell you, Ginny, the police aren't pleased with the way we collected our information."

"You didn't tell them that I . . . ?"

"No, of course not. I couched our information in terms of educated guesses on my part. I simply wanted you to know you're not likely to get the credit you deserve."

"Thank goodness!"

"The police aren't stupid. They know that you, by some means, have made it possible to narrow down the identity of Angelo's killer. Trapping him is another matter and one the police would never condone."

Orion folded his arms across his chest.

"With what Sandy told me, we may be able to tease loose some of the strands of this mess."

"You know the killer?" asked Ginny.

Dorothy, the actress, brushed her hair away from her forehead. The others looked at Victoria.

"Primo was able to question your Uncle Basilio's mistress. She calls herself Dorothy Roche."

"Me?!" said the true Dorothy.

"She used your name so Uncle Basilio could charge her expenses to the television studio," said Primo.

"That's outrageous!" said the actress.

"That's only the beginning," said Victoria. "Your uncle and his mistress are involved in drug trafficking."

"I should have guessed," said Primo. "That's where his money comes from."

"Sandy, the beekeeper's apprentice, gave me information that seems to confirm it."

Primo nodded. "Sounds like the mob."

"Your uncle may have been scouting for a pickup and transfer place for drugs. When your father told him he planned to invest in an Island-wide project, Basilio realized that would be a good cover."

"Sure," said Umberto, releasing Ginny's hand and gesturing. "That makes sense."

"He could make numerous trips to the Island, picking up deliveries that arrive by private boats," said Victoria.

Orion leaned forward and set his elbows on the table. "He and the false Dorothy needed a courier. Tris Waverley?"

Victoria nodded. "That seems likely. They hired him to spy on you, but really to pick up and deliver drugs."

"Did Uncle Basilio kill our father?" asked Umberto. "I know he hated him."

"Your father's interest in the fiber-optics project gave him an excuse to visit the Island," said Victoria.

Primo and Umberto glanced at each other. "Perhaps we should mention . . . ?" said Umberto.

Primo nodded. "Mrs. Trumbull and Mr. Nanopoulos. We've been going through our father's papers. He had decided, a week before he died, that he would not invest in Universal Fiber Optics."

There was silence around the table. Victoria heard crows cawing in the distance, a signal of some kind. Nearby, another crow responded.

"Who knew about that?" asked Victoria, breaking the silence.

"We have no way of knowing," said Primo.

Victoria traced the pattern in the checked tablecloth with her thumbnail.

"So Uncle Basilio might have killed him," said Primo.

"Or the false Dorothy Roche. Or Roger Paulson, or Finney Solomon," said Victoria.

"How does that woman figure in this, Mrs. Trumbull?" asked the real Dorothy.

"We knew her only as Dorothy Roche until we learned about you, then we called her the false Dorothy Roche. Her real name is Nora Rochester. This is what I think happened." Victoria sat back in her chair, her elbows on the chair arms, her hands clasped on the table. "Nora Rochester was Angelo's mistress."

Umberto grunted.

"Your mother learned about the liaison and gave your father an ultimatum to drop the other woman, or else."

Primo sighed. "I suspected something like that. Our father was not a saint, but he expected us to be."

"Your uncle, to thumb his nose at your father, set her up as his own mistress. The mob had approached him about the drug business, but needed certain conditions met. One was that he have a trustworthy partner."

"Trustworthy!" said the real Dorothy Roche.

"I suppose since she'd been our father's mistress, the mob had already vetted her," said Primo.

"Most likely," said Victoria. "Then when your father decided to invest in the project on Martha's Vineyard, your uncle realized this was the perfect opportunity for a drug trafficking scheme."

Orion leaned forward. "With Basilio's TV expense account, Dorothy—the false, that is—rented a house in Edgartown with all the trappings, then hired Tris Waverley, a mediocre electronics technician, to spy on me, but actually as a drug courier. That spy business seemed much too obvious, as though she wanted me to know about it."

Victoria said, "It fits together, doesn't it. Basilio wanted her to show interest in the project while she was monitoring Tris Waverley. But she knew the whole setup was likely to fall apart, and thought she could make more money by taking over Orion's company, using Basilio's money."

Ginny laughed. "What a lot of double-crossing."

Primo shuddered. "Nobody double-crosses my family."

Orion said, "I suppose Tris Waverley got cold feet about the drug business and Basilio killed him."

"Or greedy," said Umberto.

"I'm not sure Basilio ever had any contact with Tris," said Victoria.

"Then who killed our father?" asked Primo.

"I'm not sure," said Victoria. "We need to set a trap, and the police are not going to be pleased."

CHAPTER 40

Victoria wanted to tell Casey what her Edgartown Road Irregulars had discussed. She hiked the quarter-mile to the police station, not waiting for her chauffeur. She'd have to wean herself away from the luxury of summoning a car and driver now that the killer was about to be nabbed.

As much as she enjoyed the Bentley, she'd missed the feel of the tarred road and earthen path beneath her feet and the smells and sounds the car had insulated her from.

She reached the police station out of breath, spoiled by that car, scattered crusts for the ducks and geese, folded the paper bag, and climbed the steps.

Casey greeted her warmly. "How's it going, Victoria?"

Victoria plopped into her usual chair and fanned herself with her folded-up paper bag.

Casey picked up her stone paperweight and toyed with it while she listened to Victoria's latest thinking on the murders.

Victoria finished by saying, "I need your help."

Casey sat back. "Have you decided who the killer is?"

"I intend to set a trap."

"Don't even think about it, Victoria. You've narrowed down our list of suspects. The state police will do the rest, legally."

Victoria leaned her hands on her stick. "If you don't wish to get involved, I'll go ahead anyway."

"You're supposed to be a police deputy, Victoria."

"I'm also a citizen with rights."

Casey flung down her stone.

Victoria looked at her. "Will you help me?"

"Lord help *me!*" said Casey, looking up at the ceiling.

"Thank you," said Victoria.

Victoria's plan was a book launch. She gathered her four young friends around her to discuss the logistics. Her latest poetry book was due out in a month and she had the advance reading copies in hand. The invitation list included an assortment of poets and writers, state police in plainclothes, Orion, Sean the beekeeper, Aunt Maria Rosa and her new friend, Basilio, Dorothy the false, Finney Solomon, and Roger Paulson.

"We need to act quickly," said Victoria. "What about the day after tomorrow?"

Casey arrived first. "Smalley parked out of sight down New Lane and brought three troopers with him, all in plainclothes. I don't need to tell you, Victoria, he's not happy about this. He's bending all kinds of rules and is justifying it on the basis of my telling him that's the way we do things on this Island."

"If nothing else, it's a good practice session," said Victoria. "Where are they?"

"One's in the kitchen playing chef's assistant and monitoring the two outside doors, a second is trimming the bushes around the front door, monitoring that. The third is upstairs with electronic eavesdropping equipment—you signed all the papers, didn't you?"

"Of course."

Doc Yablonsky arrived. Then the poets. Maria Rosa swept in wearing a pale blue linen sheath and her emerald necklace followed by her tall new friend, Bill Williams.

The doc strode over to them and held out his hand to Williams. "Bill Yablonsky, here. I'm a great fan of your broadcasts."

"The poet? G. William Yablonsky?" said Bill Williams. "My god, I love your work."

Finney Solomon arrived and glanced around furtively. Orion was in the library, opening wine. Finney recognized Maria Rosa and her emerald necklace from the Outstretched Palm auction and introduced himself to her.

Maria Rosa smiled.

Finney glanced around again and said, "I'm with the company that owns the drill rig. I have a prospectus here." He reached into an inside pocket. "Since you were interested in the auction item, you might like to invest in the company." He held out the prospectus. "I'm chief financial officer. Mentored by none other than the great Angelo Vulpone."

Maria Rosa looked down at her formfitting dress. "Why don't you mail it to me. I'm Maria Rosa Vulpone, Angelo's sister-in- . . ."

At the mention of her name, Finney gulped, withdrew the outstretched prospectus, and looked over his shoulder. Orion stood behind him, grinning.

"Excuse me," Finney mumbled. "I see someone I must talk to." And he darted away.

"What an odd man," Maria Rosa said to Orion.

Roger Paulson came with a huge bunch of wildflowers. Sean, with a quart jar of honey. Basilio arrived and pointedly ignored his wife and her escort. The reporter and photographer from the *Island Enquirer* showed up. Victoria's book launch was an occasion no one wanted to miss.

Primo carried a tray of filled wineglasses out of the library, doing a double take when he recognized his aunt. He set the tray down and kissed her on both cheeks.

"You look fantastic! *Bellissima!*"

Maria Rosa laughed a beautiful, silvery laugh. "This is my friend, Bill Williams."

"The Bill Williams!" said Primo, glancing from his aunt to the man next to her. "Wow!"

Basilio looked over briefly, grunted, and seated himself near the food.

The reporter moved around asking innocuous questions. The photographer snapped away, unnoticed.

The false Dorothy Roche sidled in through the kitchen door.

The green around her eyes had faded to yellow, giving her a jaundiced look. She wore a sundress and a straw hat with pink and green silk flowers that matched her dress. She found Victoria. "Darling, thank you so much for inviting me."

"Of course," said Victoria.

At that point, Dorothy the true, star of Basilio's vampire films, came through the front door. The air around the actress seemed to shimmer. Her long, blue-black, silky hair fell almost to her waist. Her face was pure ivory. Her eyes, rich almonds. Her simple black dress emphasized the figure that triggered dozens of fan letters each week.

Basilio choked on the ham-and-cheese biscuit he'd stuffed into his mouth a moment before. Bill Williams strode over and slapped him on the back until Basilio coughed up the biscuit crumbs.

Victoria introduced the actress.

Dorothy the false put her hands up to her throat where she wore a chunky strand of pink, green, and blue shells in place of the sapphire necklace.

Primo passed through the gathering filling glasses for the third or fourth time, Victoria had lost count.

Orion reappeared in the dining room.

Dorothy the false said, "Darling! I hope you've forgiven me?"

Orion put an arm around her shoulder. "I think this is a good time to congratulate Victoria on the publication of her new book." He held up his glass.

"Hear, hear!" said Doc Yablonsky. "Speech, Victoria."

Victoria stepped forward, the crowd moved back. Orion brought out a chair from the library for her.

Most of the group found seats, some stood. Basilio reached for another biscuit.

"I've written a prose poem for this occasion," Victoria said. "I prefer formal poetry, the kind with meter and rhyme, but this seemed appropriate." She rustled a sheaf of pages, handwritten in her loopy backhand, and looked up. "I'm afraid I've got the pages out of order."

A few smiles.

"Here we are." She read in her deep, clear voice. The poem was about bees and the magical rites of a beekeeper and the beekeeper's young apprentice. It told how the apprentice played a near lethal trick with bees, and spoke of his attempt to make amends. Truth was woven into fantasy. The apprentice saw a winged fiend carrying poison away from the Island, witnessed the slaying of the fiend's disciple, whose body was left in a carriage along with the bones of other creatures to be eaten by vultures.

Victoria read on.

Doc Yablonsky stood transfixed. Bill Williams nodded in appreciation. Casey and Orion watched the group.

At the mention of the winged fiend, Basilio glanced at the false Dorothy, who was examining her nails. Further into the poem, Basilio looked at his watch and stood.

He interrupted the smooth flow of Victoria's story. "Sorry to interrupt, folks. I've got a previous engagement. Nice to have met you all."

Victoria held her finger at the place where she'd stopped reading.

Dorothy the false also stood. "You're not leaving me like this."

The assemblage looked from Basilio to the false Dorothy and back, eyes watching a tennis match.

"What in hell you talking about?" Basilio bunched up his fists.

The group, standing and sitting, was still, not a movement, not a sound, not a heartbeat, not a breath.

"You'd hit me, wouldn't you?" She pointed at his fists. "You killer!"

"Shut up!"

"Jealous of your brother, weren't you?"

Someone cleared his throat.

"What in hell you talking about, bitch?"

Dorothy's hat had slipped down on her forehead. She pushed it back, exposing a tuft of metallic red hair, damp with sweat. "You're not half the man your brother was."

"Bitch! Bitch!" Basilio reached across the table, knocking over the flowers Roger Paulson had brought. No one moved and the water ran across the table and dripped onto the floor. He grabbed her shell necklace and yanked her toward him partway across the table. "That spy of yours. Found out too much? He want more money?"

"Let go of me!" she screamed. "You're choking me."

He yanked harder and the necklace broke, scattering shells over the table and floor. She fell backward and Bill Williams caught her.

From where she sat, Victoria could see no movement except for eyes. The group was carved out of tree trunks.

"You think you're such hot shit, you stupid bitch. Thought you could set yourself up in my brother's company."

"Your brother's company? That wasn't your brother's company. He never put a cent into it."

Basilio stopped suddenly. "I see it all now. You hated him, didn't you? Threw you over, hey?"

"Don't spin that on me."

The group moved slightly, one organism, as the battle between Basilio and the false Dorothy shifted.

Victoria, eyes half-closed, watched and waited. The half of her poem she hadn't yet read was the part she'd thought would provoke some reaction. She hadn't expected this, and was not sure this battle between Basilio and the false Dorothy was going to unveil the killer. The two combatants had cooled down somewhat.

"You wouldn't have the guts to kill my brother." Basilio's eyes moved over the group, touched on Finney and stopped. Touched on Roger Paulson and stopped. Went back to the false Dorothy.

Roger Paulson didn't move. He stared back at Basilio, his eyes ice blue.

"I know about Waverley," Basilio shouted suddenly, and Dorothy the false flinched. "Thought you were spying on that Orion character? Who did you think was spying on you?"

"You couldn't," she said softly, hands at her throat.

"Oh, no? Who rented that house for you? Who got that maid and that chauffeur for you, hey? Whose car you using, hey? You think I don't know every goddamned move you made over the past two, three months?"

"No," said Dorothy.

"Don't you think the cops would like to see the proof I got?"

"You can't have," she said again. "I was meeting with Finney." She looked about wildly. Finney was studying the floor, arms crossed.

"Think so, hey? Look at him. Thought he was a rich boy, hey? Thought he'd be the golden touch so you could double-cross me, hey?" Basilio jerked his head at Finney, who was still looking at the floor. "The guy's a loser. Lives in a walk-up in Union City over a strip joint. Owes money on four credit cards he can't pay off. Got a record for small-time stuff. Beating up girls. Can't even do crime right. That your financial advisor?"

"He was Angelo's friend."

Basilio barked a nasty laugh. "Friend of Angelo's? You think my brother would be a friend of that? My brother's next move was to get the guy terminated, only the guy wasn't worth the trouble."

Finney's face went from dead white to red and back to dead white again.

Someone coughed.

The guinea fowl in the west pasture called their metallic cries. Basilio and the false Dorothy seemed to have forgotten that a dozen people watched them, and the dozen people were frozen in place.

Dorothy's voice was so soft Victoria could barely make out the words. "Finney killed your brother."

"Finney? Hasn't got the nerve."

"He knew Angelo was on to him."

Basilio laughed. "There's the guy who's hated my brother for thirty years." Paulson was leaning against the door frame. "My brother screwed him royally. Tried to break him and couldn't. Angelo was a louse, and I salute the guy who rid the world of him."

Paulson said clearly, "No love lost between us." He hadn't moved from the door frame.

"You killed him," said Basilio.

"You accusing me?"

"I'm asking," said Basilio.

"Better not accuse me, Vulpone. That's libel and I've got more lawyers than you do."

Paulson pushed himself away from the door frame and stood up straight. "If you'll excuse me, it's getting stuffy in here." He nodded to Victoria. "Sorry I didn't get to hear the rest of your poem, Mrs. Trumbull. I hope to read it at some future time."

Victoria folded up her pages. Smalley's men closed in. Smalley said to the false Dorothy, "We'd like you to come to the barracks and make a statement, if you would."

"Ask him, too," Dorothy pointed at Basilio. "And him." She pointed at Finney. "And that Paulson person."

"Yes, ma'am. We'll talk to you and Mr. Vulpone first."

CHAPTER 41

After the state police left with Dorothy the false and Basilio, Victoria remained seated. Conversation slowly picked up again, mostly about the shouting match between Basilio and the false Dorothy.

Casey knelt down next to Victoria. "You okay?"

"No," said Victoria. "Something went terribly wrong. I got only halfway through my poem before they started shouting at each other. Had they waited, things might have turned out differently."

"Basilio was telling the state guys on the way out that he'd put a tracking device on her car and bugging devices in her house. Nice guy. When the drug enforcement guys get through with him, I hate to think what his life wil be like." Casey shuddered.

"And Roger Paulson?" asked Victoria.

"He was waiting outside for the state police." Casey got up from the floor and moved a chair next to Victoria. "I gotta sit."

"He didn't admit anything, either," said Victoria.

"Too smart to. As he said, he's got lawyers."

"Something's not right," said Victoria.

There was a knock on the front door. Casey glanced at Victoria. "Are you expecting anyone else?"

"No one." Victoria was too preoccupied with puzzling out what went wrong to care about company.

Someone knocked a second time. "I'll get it," said Casey, heading for the door.

Two men stood on the wide front step. Both wore wraparound sunglasses, dark suits, white shirts, and ties, and, except for a difference in height, could have been an artifact of double vision.

Definitely not Islanders, thought Casey. Missionaries, perhaps. Mormons or Jehovah's Witnesses?

"We're looking for a Finney Solomon," said the shorter of the two men.

The mob, thought Casey. Come to eliminate Finney Solomon. Victoria was right. The mob would kill openly, gun down the victim in front of friends and family.

"Please tell me who you are," said Casey.

Both produced black leather folders from inside jacket pockets and flipped them open.

"Oh," said Casey, examining their credentials. She suddenly felt uncomfortable out of uniform. "I'm the West Tisbury police chief. How can I help?"

"Solomon here?" asked the taller of the two.

"I believe he still is. What's he done?"

The shorter man lifted his glasses to his forehead. "Like to see your ID, ma'am."

"I don't have it with me," said Casey.

"Right. Where is he?"

Victoria had arisen from her chair. "Can I help you?" She studied the suits and ties. "Thank you for coming, but I'm active in my own church."

"Feebs," said Casey, straightening her skirt. "Federal agents. FBI."

"We're looking for Finney Solomon," the shorter man repeated, again producing his leather folder.

"Ah," said Victoria. "I believe he's in the library."

"Know what he looks like?" asked Casey, feeling disrespected.

"We do," said the shorter man. "Excuse me." He elbowed his way past two poets, who were blocking the door.

Finney looked up from the glass of wine he was pouring.

"Finney Solomon?" asked the shorter man.

Both flipped open their folders and the gold badges shone in the afternoon light.

Finney glanced around. Chatting poets blocked his way out in both directions.

"We have a warrant for your arrest."

"Who, me?" said Finney. "What for?"

The taller man answered. "Credit fraud."

The next morning, Victoria called Roger Paulson and came right to the point. "I'd like to talk to you, Mr. Paulson. We didn't get much of a chance yesterday."

"Roger's the name."

"Can you come to my house right now?"

"Be a pleasure." He laughed. "But it'll take me almost an hour to get there from Chappy, can you wait?"

"I'll make lunch."

In less than an hour, Victoria saw his car drive up. They went into the cookroom and Victoria sat with her back to the window.

"You know a great deal more than you're willing to say, don't you?" Victoria said.

"True."

"My guess is that you know who the killer is, and it's not you."

"Possibly."

"Were you at the ball field the night Angelo was killed?"

"Maybe."

"Why don't you tell me about it?"

"So you can write another poem?"

Victoria smiled. "It's already been written. The part you didn't hear." She handed a copy of the poem to him.

He paged through it. "Right on top of things, aren't you, Mrs. Trumbull."

"Victoria."

"I assume you're not wired?"

"I have Wi-Fi," said Victoria.

"That's okay, then." He sat back and neither of them spoke for a long time. Finally, he continued. "I called Angelo months ago, as soon as I heard about Orion Nanopoulos and his fiber-optics cable. I told Angelo I was ready to make peace. Bury the hatchet. Water over the dam. I'm as rich as I want to be, I told him, live where I want to live, and have a business I'm proud of. Even said I'd let the wife go." Paulson stopped there and glanced out the window behind Victoria. The village was almost hidden by trees. "I told him about the project, and suggested we could team up again."

"Wasn't he skeptical?"

"Certainly he was. But he was a greedy, unscrupulous man. He checked out Nanopoulos and his prospectus, and decided it was, as he said, a gold mine."

"He was willing to work with you?"

Paulson laughed. "Does a leopard change its spots?"

"Did you plan to kill him?"

"You're getting ahead of my story, Victoria, but yes. I planned to kill him. I'd waited thirty years for the right time and place."

The guinea fowl chucked and clattered in the drive. Crows called and answered. Victoria took a deep breath.

Paulson went on. "He saw this as an opportunity to kill me, too. I'd been a thorn festering in his flesh for every one of those thirty years. He saw this as the chance to lure me to a remote spot and . . ." He slashed his hand through the air. "I knew Nanopoulos was laying cable in the trench. I called Angelo, suggested he charter a plane; I'd pick him up at general aviation, and we could have supper together. Check the place out after."

"Wasn't he suspicious?"

"Of course he was. But this was what he'd been waiting for. Remote is what we both wanted. I trusted him as much as he trusted me. Zilch. Zero. I knew he'd have backup near at hand, and he knew I would, too."

Victoria ran her hand through her hair. "A duel. An old time shoot-out. And your seconds?"

"Two of my dealers from western Mass. Armed."

"Did they know you planned to kill Angelo?"

"Yes."

"And you trusted them?"

"Yes. Absolutely. On the other hand, he was ruthless, and couldn't trust anyone but his two sons."

"And Angelo's backup?" She didn't want to ask, but did. "His sons?"

"Good god, no. Not his precious sons. They were brought up to be law-abiding, decent human beings."

"Their mother's influence?"

"Yes and no. Angelo's family was sacred to him."

"I'm not sure I understand how things worked out. You met Angelo at the airport?"

"I went to the airport, made sure I was plenty early. He was already there in the general aviation waiting room. Said his plane was early. I found out later someone met him earlier, drove him to the ball field, where he spoke to the town guy, then returned him to the airport. One of his backup men, I reckon."

"And his other backup people?"

"Strictly pros. Never saw them, he never saw mine."

"Didn't you check for weapons?"

"Hardly. I assumed he was carrying. He probably assumed the same."

"Go on."

"We left the airport, had dinner in Vineyard Haven, then drove to the ball field. There was enough light to see where we were going and it was beginning to rain, which suited us both. My guys were lying on their bellies, rifles aimed at Angelo. His? I don't know. We reached the end of the trench. Raining hard. You could cut the tension. Who was going to move first, and what would that first move be. You're right, it was like *High Noon*."

Victoria shivered.

"Suddenly, a woman screamed. Startled the hell out of us both. Angelo turned. I heard a shot. He fell. I cleaned out his pockets, rolled him into the trench, and left."

"And the person who shot him? Was it the woman?"

"Never saw her. In the time it took me to roll Angelo into the ditch, she vanished."

"Could you identify her by her scream?"

"I doubt it."

"Could it have been the false Dorothy Roche?"

"Possibly."

"She knew Angelo, didn't she?"

"She was his mistress for a couple of years. He promised to support her for life. When his wife threatened to leave and take the boys, he ditched her with nothing."

"And you're covering for her."

"I'd have pulled the trigger if she hadn't. I've got legal staff to protect me. She's got nothing."

"She may be facing another murder charge. Basilio tracked her car from Tris Waverley's place to where he was killed that day. She probably told Tris she wanted him to see the Ditch Witch, then suggested he sit in the old truck and she'd take a picture of him for his sister, a shot over his shoulder showing the dead skunk. She got behind him. A twist of a scarf around his throat."

"Stupid of her. She'd never have been convicted of Angelo's murder. I felt sorry for her. She was powerless against Angelo and his brother, and had been screwed by both of them." Paulson stopped abruptly. "I wonder if Basilio was tracking her that far back."

"That would help clear you. What happened to her gun?"

"We live on a small Island in the middle of a large ocean, Victoria. A simple matter to rid oneself of a gun."

"I suppose Tris Waverley knew too much. She'd killed once. A second killing was easier."

CHAPTER 42

"Orion, were you here when the FBI agents came for Finney Solomon on the day of my book launch?" asked Victoria.

"FBI agents," repeated Orion with a pleasant smile. He lifted his tea bag out of his mug and dropped it into the compost bucket. "Interesting."

He moved away from the kitchen sink. Victoria rinsed the breakfast dishes and began to load the dishwasher. "You had something to do with the appearance of the FBI, didn't you?"

"*Moi?*" said Orion, laying his hand on his chest.

"After shaming him in front of people he was trying to impress and ordering the FBI to haul him away in chains . . ."

"Ordering the FBI?" said Orion. "In chains!"

"Metaphorically speaking. I believe our young Mozart of money may have gotten the message."

Victoria loaded the last dish and was about to start the dishwasher when Primo and Umberto showed up.

"We'd like to talk to Mr. Nanopoulos," said Primo.

"You're welcome to talk in the library," said Victoria. "I need to work on my column."

"We'd like you to hear this, too, Mrs. Trumbull," said Primo. "Your kitchen is a fine place to do business."

"An excellent place," said Umberto.

Victoria dried her hands and hung the towel on the wooden rack, then sat at the table. The three joined her.

Umberto gestured with his hands, palms up toward his brother, indicating that Primo should speak.

"As you know, our father—bless him . . ."

"Bless him," echoed Umberto, crossing himself.

Primo continued, ". . . was an astute businessman."

Orion folded his arms.

"As you know, our father originally planned to invest eight million in your project, Mr. Nanopoulos, then changed his mind for some reason and decided not to invest."

Sean's red truck turned into the pasture. The passenger door opened and Sandy bounced out holding the bee smoker. Victoria folded her hands in her lap.

"Umberto and I are executors of our father's estate, and we intended to carry out his wishes."

"We had every intention of doing so," said Umberto.

Orion stirred his tea, studying the eddies and swirls, watching the rising steam.

"However." Primo held up a hand. "However, we've studied your operation and find that we don't agree with our father's last decision."

Far away in the west pasture, Sean's white suit billowed in the wind.

"We have some paperwork here," said Umberto, opening his attaché case and shuffling through various pages until he found three paper-clipped documents. "If you'd sign all three, Primo and I will also sign, and if you, Mrs. Trumbull, would witness our signatures?"

Victoria felt mildly disappointed. Any investment would help, but the eight million had been only a third of what Orion needed, and now it looked as though Orion wouldn't get even that much. She thought how her perspective had changed. Eight million dollars. A fortune. And here she was, thinking eight million wasn't enough.

Orion riffled through the papers. He sat back and tossed his pen onto the table. He looked up, first at Umberto, then Primo. He looked down at the papers again.

Victoria knew this was no time to ask questions. In the distance she could see smoke rising near the beehives.

"You're serious," said Orion.

"Yes, sir," said Primo.

"You're not asking for a share in the company?"

"We have no experience in running a project like yours. Our father trained us to delegate and he had great confidence in you."

"Twenty-four million," murmured Orion. "The entire projected cost."

"You can see," said Umberto, pointing to a section in the document, "the money is paid out only as you complete each goal that's been set out."

"I don't know what to say," said Orion.

"We believe this is mutually beneficial," said Primo. "Our own research confirms our father's original opinion. However, we believe he was overly cautious in the beginning, and mistaken in the end."

Victoria got up from the table. "This calls for a fresh cup of tea."